DUSK CORNERS

A LOGAN AND SCARLETT THRILLER

DAN PADAVONA

GET A FREE BOOK!

I'm a pretty nice guy once you look past the grisly images in my head. Most of all, I love connecting with awesome readers like you.

Join my VIP Reader Group and get a FREE serial killer thriller for your Kindle.

Get My Free Book

www.danpadavona.com/thriller-readers-vip-group/

1

Sheila lowered the window in Brady's Ford Focus, because she'd rather listen to the wind than risk another argument. He eased the Focus around something dead in the middle of the desolate Texas road and swung the car out of the oncoming lane. Not that he needed to hurry. There wasn't another car in sight for as far as Sheila could see.

They were traveling from Denver to Roswell after stopping in Lubbock, where Brady had wanted to visit a football teammate from high school. These days, the friend played linebacker at Texas Tech. The problem was, the kid banged up his leg during practice and was at the hospital when Brady drove into town. Since the failed get-together, Brady had been sullen, and Sheila wondered if he even cared that she accompanied him. After Lubbock, they planned to stay at a Hampton Inn in Roswell and attend a music festival outside the city. Like everything touristy in Roswell, the festival employed an alien theme, with the stage shaped into a humongous, crashed spaceship.

Ten miles south of Lubbock, Brady dodged a May hailstorm and exited the highway. According to the map, this new road,

Highway 6, would take them to the New Mexico border. Now Sheila wondered. The map claimed a town called Joliet existed a few miles ahead, but there was no town, only pancake-flat clay and meadow, and the occasional pumpjack, slamming the earth in search of oil. No farmers riding tractors, no travelers to prove humanity existed southwest of Lubbock. Only the occasional festering roadkill suggested vehicles, probably eighteen-wheelers, motored down Highway 6. Now that Sheila thought about it, she hadn't noticed a road sign since they passed through a sleepy town called Dusk Corners twenty miles back.

"Where are we?"

"West Texas," he said, peering at her as though she were a simpleton. Though Brady hadn't played football since high school, he still possessed an athletic physique—mountainous shoulders, rock-hard biceps, tree trunks for legs. "This road leads to New Mexico. Better than dodging semis on the interstate, don't you agree?"

"Are you sure this is the highway? Where's Joliet? Where are the highway markers?"

"Sheila, we've been on the same road since we passed through that ghost town. Duskville?"

"Dusk Corners."

"Whatever."

"Are you sure six didn't branch off? Remember the fork in the road after Dusk Corners? I'm just saying, maybe we should stop and ask for directions."

He ground his teeth and stared through the windshield. "The sun is dead ahead. That means we're traveling west. And what's west of Texas? New Mexico. Unless all those U.S. maps I memorized back in grade school were fabrications, we'll drive straight into New Mexico, even if we're blindfolded. Check your phone if you're so worried."

Little good that would do. Sheila hadn't noticed a single bar on her phone since Lubbock faded from the mirror.

"Let me concentrate on the road. You're making me nervous." He flipped on the stereo and boomed a heavy metal song that gave her a headache. "And close your window. It's a hundred degrees outside. All you're doing is letting the bugs in."

As if to emphasize Brady's point, some furry, winged insect the size of a golf ball slammed against the hood and splattered guts across the windshield. A trickle of cleaning solution spit across the glass as Brady ran the wipers. She'd warned him to check the fluids. He never listened. Brady only cared about getting from point A to point B in the quickest time possible.

Sheila raised the window, then twisted the volume knob and lowered the music to humane levels. He glared ice picks into her. If Brady reached for the knob and cranked the music again, she'd give him a piece of her mind.

Closing the window and turning the music down trapped her in quietude with Brady, and neither seemed in the mood for talking. Her stomach flip-flopped, and she touched her belly. This was the third time this week her stomach had soured. It seemed especially bad in the morning. She stamped down the voice in her head, reminding her she hadn't gotten her period. Which wasn't unusual. Sometimes it arrived a week late. But she'd slept with Brady several times over the last month, and though he'd used protection, she accepted birth control wasn't foolproof.

The stomach upset was nothing to worry over. Indigestion or a spring flu going around. Sheila and Brady attended a college party Friday night, and there had been a boy handing out drinks and displaying cold symptoms.

She watched Brady from the corner of her eye. His hands formed a death grip on the steering wheel. She was being too hard on him. Knowing Brady, he was just as nervous as Sheila. More so because he held the macho, Neanderthal belief that it was the man's duty to protect his woman. How would he protect her when he didn't even know where he was?

Beneath the screeching guitars, Sheila discerned a ticking sound, as if someone had glued a time bomb to the engine block. She'd first heard the sound at a red light in Lubbock. She'd written it off after the ticking stopped. It was back again and persistent this time. She knew a little about cars from watching her father tinker in the garage years ago. A ticking sound might indicate dirty fuel injectors or low oil pressure. Or the engine was overheating. She eyed the needle on the oil gauge, which sat in the normal range. The car interior was so damn hot. At least with the window down, the wind tunneled through the vehicle and blew the sweat off her face. Now she spied the maxed out air conditioner and wondered why the vents pumped heat into the vehicle.

She opened her mouth to suggest there was a problem and stopped, not wanting to fight again. They were lost and exhausted. Arguing wouldn't solve anything. Brady's T-shirt became a sopping rag, clinging to his flesh. Long sweat stains dripped from his armpits.

The ticking grew louder. Sheila pictured a gremlin-like creature with a tiny hammer banging the engine beneath the hood.

"Did you take the car into the garage like I asked?"

He shifted his jaw in answer. No, he hadn't. Great. He was driving a failing car through the middle of nowhere in the Texas heat. If they broke down without cell coverage, they were in trouble. Hell, they might die out here.

"Brady? You seriously didn't take the car in—"

"Will you shut up and let me think?"

"It's a seven-hundred-mile trip. What did you expect to happen?"

"I had exams all week. When the heck was I supposed to bring the car in?"

"You had time to drink with Paul and go to that party. You had time to—"

"Shut up! Shut up!"

He pounded the dash and made her jump. She'd never seen him like this before. Sheila shifted in her seat and turned to stare through the side window. He silenced the music.

"Hey, I'm sorry. I didn't mean to yell."

She sniffled and wiped her eyes with her shirt collar.

"Sheila, I'm sorry. I screwed up, I admit it. But we have two hours of driving ahead of us, and it's nerve-wracking not seeing anyone around."

Brady placed a hand on her bare knee and gave it a gentle squeeze. He kept it there until she looked over at him. Brady wore a sheepish grin that made him appear childlike. She didn't want to forgive him. He'd screwed up, big time, and they were in a world of hurt if the Focus died.

"It's not too late to turn around," she said, fanning her face. "We passed through town twenty minutes ago."

Brady chewed his lip. "Twenty minutes to Dusk Corners, or ninety if we drive straight through. It's not that much farther to Roswell."

"Is it worth the risk?"

"Did you notice a garage in town? All I saw was a bar and a hotel. What if we drive all the way back to town and they don't have a mechanic? Then we'll really be in trouble. You want to dodge storms and go back to Lubbock? Better to keep going, I say."

She wondered if Brady had a point, or if he was whistling past the proverbial graveyard. The ticking sound had stopped while they considered their options. Sheila leaned across the seat and examined the gauges, unsure of what she expected to find. None of the indicators issued alarms.

"Besides," he said. "How do you suppose the locals would treat us? Two university students from Denver. That wouldn't go over well in Dusk Corners."

"That's prejudiced. Everywhere you go, people are people."

"So you'd feel comfortable walking into that saloon without me around?"

An indecisive argument moved through Sheila's chest and latched onto her breastbone. It was easy to act enlightened, as though the world would treat her as she'd learned to treat it through her liberal arts coursework. See the positive in everyone, and they'll treat you with kindness. A sort of reverse-ostrich effect. Could she stroll into a sleepy cowboy town like Dusk Corners? Or walk through a slum?

He shut off the air conditioner. "You know what? Lower your window. Might be good to get some air in the car."

"What about the bugs?"

"No worries. What harm can a bug do? When we get to Roswell, I'll have a mechanic check the car over, just to be sure. It's been forever since anyone serviced the AC. Then again, I never drove through one-hundred-degree heat before. The ride back to school will be a lot more comfortable, I promise."

He set his hand on her knee again, and this time it stayed there. Her face flushed when his hand inched between her sweaty thighs.

She touched his wrist, wishing they were in the hotel room with the door bolted and the curtains drawn. Her stomach no longer protested, the engine behaved, and the blowtorch sun tracking toward the western horizon no longer seemed intent on melting them.

He drove with one hand, the other resting between her legs.

Sheila forgot that she'd been angry with him five minutes ago, that his carelessness had placed her in this bind. She struggled to ignore the instrument panel, but her eyes kept drifting back to the lights. And wasn't the temperature gauge higher than it had been?

As they passed a farm with a red barn, Brady's car made a high-pitched whining noise. They met each other's gazes until the sound stopped. Neither spoke. There was something seriously wrong with the car, and the nearest mechanic was nowhere in sight.

Sheila peeked in the mirror and saw a shimmering light flying at them, like a meteor shooting up the road. It was a truck, a big one. She twisted the mirror for a better view, drawing a curious glance from Brady. He checked the side mirror and rubbed his scalp. The truck was closer now, a black Dodge Ram 3500 rumbling on oversize tires. The dusty sheen made it appear as if the truck had crawled out of the earth.

Sheila peeked at the speedometer. They were doing seventy-five, and the truck grew closer by the second. Brady had always had a lead foot. A state trooper had caught him speeding at twenty mph over the limit outside Denver last autumn. Still, Brady eased toward the shoulder, so the driver had room to pass. Whoever this maniac was, Brady wasn't about to slow him down.

The truck didn't swerve into the other lane. It lurched forward like a hungry beast, its weed-and-grass-choked grille reminiscent of alligator jaws.

"What's this guy doing?" Brady asked himself.

Sheila turned to look, and the driver punched the gas and pushed the truck up to their bumper. The sun made it impossible to see beyond the gritty windshield, but Sheila caught the impression of two men in the truck. The driver leaned over the wheel and glared at the tiny Ford Focus. Sitting in the passenger seat was an impossibly large man, so huge Sheila figured it was a trick of the light. The passenger filled the cab, with his head brushing the ceiling.

"Move over," Sheila said, swinging her head around again when the truck's motor growled.

"I'm on the shoulder. I can't go any—"

The grille clipped the Focus. Tires screeched as the vast, empty plains spun past the windshield like a lunatic amusement park ride. Sheila grabbed the door handle. The back end of the car whipped off the road and collided with something solid in the ditch. Sheila shot forward. The seatbelt yanked her back before her head could strike the dashboard.

The car made a high-pitched whine, the sound of an injured animal dying. Sheila thought the collision had knocked Brady unconscious, but his eyes blinked in shock and disbelief. The crazy driver had run right into them.

The doors opened on the Ram as Brady shook the fog out of his brain. His mouth fell open as he stared into the mirror.

"Sheila, get out of the car."

"What?"

"Run!"

Sheila didn't register his words until a humongous shadow filled the rear windshield. She threw the door open and stumbled on sea legs onto the shoulder. A hand grabbed her arm. She yelped, not realizing it was Brady. He tugged her forward, urging her to run as footsteps crashed behind them. She was too slow. Brady was faster than Sheila and could have outrun their attackers. Instead, he threw himself between Sheila and the two men.

"Run until you find help, Sheila! I'll catch up to you."

"What are you doing? Come with me!"

She turned back, intent on dragging him away from the

thugs. Brady set his shoulders and cocked a fist. The driver converged on Brady first. Brady clipped the man's jaw and knocked him sideways. He raised his fist again and stopped. The monster staggered up to Brady, standing almost a foot taller than the ex–football player. He was more mountain than man.

Brady slammed a punch against the man's face, to no effect.

"Run, Sheila! I can't—"

Brady's warning cut off when the monster lifted him and swung him like a rag doll. Brady's legs kicked uselessly as the man constricted his arms in a bear hug. Sheila screamed and ran faster. Behind her came a cracking sound, like someone crunching a boot down on eggshells. Brady issued an inhuman screech.

Sheila ran blindly down the road, her vision blurred by tears. She heard them coming now, though she dared not turn back. If she did, she'd see the monster from the passenger seat roaring toward her like a runaway freight train, the man's eyes red with bloodlust.

A hand snagged her hair and ripped her backward. The driver threw her face-down to the macadam. Air rushed from her lungs, and something snapped in her ribcage. Blood poured from her mouth as she hacked and coughed. Sheila twisted onto her back and scrambled up to her elbows. The man grinned and tore her shirt open. His hand covered her mouth and shoved down, slamming her head against the blacktop. As she squealed and thrashed, he ripped the bra off her chest and snaked a slimy tongue into her ear. He meant to rape her.

But it was the monster standing over the rapist's shoulder that froze Sheila's heart. Blocking out the sun, the beast pulled a knife from his pants pocket.

Sheila's eyes rolled back. This couldn't be happening. It was just a horrible nightmare she'd awaken from.

The monster dragged the rapist off Sheila and plunged the

blade into her chest. The pain was real and unforgiving. Blood spurt and speckled the murderer's face.

Then there were only the cicadas chittering along the roadside as full darkness enveloped Sheila.

2

Logan Wolf stopped his Jeep Wrangler behind a minivan outside Clem's Diner. He'd stolen the Jeep in Nebraska, filched a license plate off another vehicle near a shopping mall, and fixed the new plate onto the Jeep. His picture was a permanent fixture on the FBI Most Wanted list and had been since 2013, after Don Weber from CIRG, the Critical Incident Response Group, framed Wolf for murder. Once the Behavioral Analysis Unit's most-respected profiler, Wolf had been a lock for the deputy director position until he returned to his Virginia home and found his wife, Renee, murdered in the kitchen, her throat slashed and a sack dragged over her head.

Now he climbed out of the stolen Jeep and scanned the parking lot. A gray-haired man with a walker inched toward the diner doors, led by a stooped-over woman. No cops, no vehicles with tinted windows concealing federal agents. Wolf pushed his sunglasses up and rubbed the fatigue out of his eyes. He couldn't recall the last time he'd eaten. Two or three days ago, he assumed. Inside his wallet, he found a little over six-hundred dollars, plenty enough to pay for food, but a paltry sum, if he purchased a hotel room.

After Don Weber won the deputy director position and named Wolf the nation's most-wanted fugitive, Wolf had spent the better part of a decade searching for Renee's murderer. Weber was a power-hungry politician, not a serial killer. It was obvious Weber had hired someone to do his dirty work. Hiding from the FBI, Wolf's grasp of reality became tenuous, as he tracked active serial killers, determined to catch the man who'd butchered Renee. After his search failed, he took the law into his own hands, murdering serial killers and mimicking the method Renee's murderer used. Wolf knew he'd eventually attract the killer's attention, which he did last year, when he caught the murderer and ended his life and rescued two BAU profilers—Scarlett Bell and her partner, Neil Gardy—while they hunted the killer. Agent Bell promised to clear Wolf's name. But it would never be safe for Wolf to return home. Not without Renee, not when there were too many active serial killers for the FBI to track.

Wolf stretched his back and stuffed the wallet into his pocket. While he crossed the parking lot, his eyes swiveled beneath the dark lenses of his sunglasses, searching for unseen threats. He was almost to the door when he spied a red Volkswagen Jetta with the hood raised. A girl no older than twenty leaned over the engine. She wore a confused grimace as she poked and prodded. Greasy food scents wafted out of the diner, making Wolf's mouth water. He sighed and angled toward the Jetta.

"Rather enterprising of you, fixing your own vehicle."

The girl lifted her head in alarm. Her eyebrows and short-cut hair were preternaturally black, an obvious dye job. The eyeshadow and lipstick matched her hair. The girl's cutoff jean shorts displayed shapely legs, and despite the heat, she wore a gray hooded sweatshirt with UCLA printed across the front.

She clutched a wrench in one hand and appeared ready to

use it, though it was clear she didn't know what she was looking at beneath the hood.

"It won't start," the girl said, eyeing Wolf.

He stopped a few paces away, not wanting to threaten the girl.

"Pardon my tiresome inquiries, but the car drove okay until you arrived?"

"The engine sputtered on the highway, so I pulled into the parking lot and stopped. Big mistake. As soon as I tested the engine . . ." The girl lifted her palms to finish the sentence. "Do you know anything about cars?"

"Engine repair is not my expertise. I can give you a ride to a mechanic, if that helps."

She narrowed her eyes. "Are you a police officer or something? You look like a cop."

"No, I'm not an officer of the law, thankfully."

She stared, unconvinced. "The closest mechanic is two towns away. I checked. There's nothing in this town. Besides the diner, all I noticed was a convenience store and a vintage movie theater with boarded-up windows."

"You're not from these parts?"

"I'm traveling. Well, I was until my car up and quit. You?"

"Driving south." He glanced at the diner. "I'm about to go inside for a bite to eat. Looks like you're having an unfortunate day. How about I buy you lunch? Then we can discuss what you want to do about your car."

"I'm not a charity case."

"I never said you were." The sea-green swimming in her eyes demanded his attention, reminding him of Renee. He swallowed. "I'm hungry, dear girl. Are you coming or not?"

She tapped the wrench against her palm three times and sighed. Lifting herself up on tiptoe, she closed the hood and tossed the tool on the car seat.

"I'm Sara, by the way."

"Logan," he said, unconcerned he'd told her his first name. The world held enough Logans, and using his real name prevented his life from becoming too complicated. Better to minimize the lies and keep them straight. Besides, he spotted something trustworthy in Sara, something that made him want to share a meal with this girl and engage in genuine conversation, a rarity for a man on the run. Perhaps it would help him feel human for a few minutes.

For the past month, he'd used a fake ID, which claimed his name was Don Weber. The Don Weber Wolf knew was serving twenty years in federal prison, but there were a lot of Don Webers in the U.S.

"Okay, Logan. I could go for a BLT."

"Does this diner serve good BLTs?"

"Don't all diners?"

"Then it's settled. Follow me."

A skinny man, wearing a dingy shirt and pants with worn cuffs, leaned against a mailbox, with his eyes closed and a coffee can resting between two dusty palms. The can read *Desert Storm Veteran, Praise God*. Sara bent to listen and nodded back to Wolf after she confirmed the man was breathing. She reached into her pocket and pulled out a ten-dollar bill, then slid the money into the can without waking the man. Wolf followed suit and donated another ten.

Wolf led Sara into the diner, not removing his sunglasses until he stepped into the lobby and studied the faces at the tables. The bearded server brought them water and bread while they pored over their menus. As promised, Sara settled on the BLT, while Logan shifted his attention between the sandwich options and the grizzled, overweight man behind the counter, eyeing him.

"That's right," Sara said, speaking into her phone. "It's a red

Volkswagen Jetta with California plates. I'm at Clem's Diner on Route 11."

Sara set the phone down and shook her head. "I have a bad feeling about this. I put thirty-thousand miles on the Jetta last year."

Wolf sipped his water. "Thirty-thousand. That's a lot of driving."

"I don't stay in one place for very long."

"Are you in sales?"

She chuckled. "God, no. And shoot me if I ever become a salesperson. In my mother's words, I'm still finding my path. Which is to say I don't have a steady job, and I don't attend college, if you're wondering why someone my age isn't studying for final exams."

"I don't pry."

"I'll find my calling at some point. Right now, I'm enjoying life and catching up with friends, experiencing places I'll never see once I'm tied down and working a dead-end job." She wiped the condensation off the glass and dabbed it against her cheeks. He didn't blame her. The inside of the diner had to be eighty degrees. "What about you, Logan? You sure you aren't a cop?"

Wolf didn't answer. He focused on the man behind the counter, who lifted a phone as he glared at Wolf and Sara. Perhaps this guy recognized Wolf's face from a wanted poster.

As Sara talked about her travels, Wolf slid his hand into his pocket and clutched his fingers around the hilt of a serrated hunting knife. The man behind the counter hung up the phone and argued with a server.

Then the room vanished, and a shadowed kitchen stood in its place. Mottled moonlight filtered through the curtains and drew confusing shapes across the tiled floor. Renee's leg poked out from behind the table. Her blood appeared black in the moonlight as police sirens shrilled in the distance.

". . . so I left California and spent a few months in the Rockies before I settled in West Texas. The cost of living is cheap, it's easy to find temporary work, and . . . hey, did you hear anything I said?"

Sara's voice pulled Wolf out of his thoughts.

"I'm listening. You live in West Texas, and you work temp jobs to make ends meet."

The server set their lunches in front of them.

"You already listen better than my parents. Thank you." Sara bit into the BLT and closed her eyes. "Oh, that's good. It helps when you're starving." She drank her water. "The dude from the garage will be here in fifteen minutes. But he can't work on my car until tomorrow morning."

"I can drive you to your apartment. Do you live nearby?"

"Just outside of Lubbock. That's a long drive. I don't want to put you out."

"Not at all. It's only an hour, and I'm headed in that direction."

She cocked a skeptical eyebrow. "That's rather convenient. Where are you traveling, Logan?"

"A quaint, old west town off the Caprock. You haven't heard of it."

"Try me."

"It's unimportant."

"Fine. You don't have to tell me. You're probably an international spy or something."

Wolf chewed his chicken sandwich. It tasted dry, and he wished he'd chosen the BLT. "What makes you think I'm a spy?"

"The way you study the room, like you're sniffing out a threat." She pointed a finger at him. "You might not be a cop, but you're in law enforcement. Give me a few minutes and I'll figure it out."

A tow truck rumbled into the parking lot.

"Your mechanic arrived, Sara," Wolf said, thankful for the distraction.

Sara swung her head around. "Oh, snap." She wiped her face with her napkin. "I'll be right back. Don't eat my BLT."

Wolf followed her out the door with his eyes. A part of him wanted to accompany Sara and ensure the guy didn't railroad her, except she seemed capable of handling an unscrupulous mechanic. Wolf picked at the chicken sandwich as the lunch crowd cleared out. The police never showed up, so Wolf assumed the counter man's conversation had nothing to do with him.

The mechanic towed Sara's car away. She sulked into the diner with slumped shoulders and slid into the booth across the table from Wolf.

"Bet you five bucks that's the last time I drive my car," she said, ignoring her half-eaten sandwich.

"Bad news?"

"I'll find out soon. The odometer ticked over 170,000 last month. Even if the guy fixes the Jetta, how much longer will it last?"

"Keep the faith. When will he give you an answer?"

"He claims tomorrow afternoon, but you know how these things go. He'll fix one part, then discover five more issues."

After lunch, Sara climbed into the Jeep Wrangler and buckled the seatbelt. Wolf turned the key and scratched his chin before pulling out.

"What?"

"It's nothing," he said.

She'd strapped herself into a stolen vehicle and accepted a ride from a serial killer wanted by the FBI.

As he drove toward Lubbock, she stared at the pancake-flat landscape, which stretched to the ends of the earth.

"If my mother could see me now," she said, shaking her

head. "Accepting rides from strangers. You're not a psycho, right?"

He wiped the back of his hand across his mouth and turned up the air conditioner. "Not usually."

"Good, because terrible things always happen to people who hitch rides in horror movies." She lifted her chin at a distant farmhouse. "You ever see *The Texas Chainsaw Massacre*, Logan?"

"Live theater is more to my liking."

"I love scary movies. They're like riding a roller coaster, don't you agree?"

He shrugged. "Real life is a lot more terrifying than any movie. I don't see the point."

"You've heard of the Devil's Rock, right? That's where you're heading."

Wolf's pulse kicked into a higher gear. The media referred to the Caprock as the Devil's Rock, after a decade of unsolved, gruesome murders.

"Can't say that I have."

"You're not from around here, are you?"

"Never visited."

"Please be careful. You seem like a nice guy, buying me lunch and driving me home. I don't want anything to happen to you." She waved a hand through the air. "Don't get me wrong. The people here are down to earth. After they meet you, they'll treat you like family. But there are dangerous places you shouldn't visit. What's your business on the Caprock?"

He turned on his blinker and coasted down the exit ramp. "You ask a lot of questions."

"So you won't tell me? You really are an international spy."

"Just a little hunting."

Five miles east of Lubbock, Sara directed Wolf through a suburban neighborhood.

"That's my place," she said, pointing toward a microscopic efficiency apartment over a used furniture store.

He stopped along the curb and idled as vehicles raced past. She grabbed her bag and slung the strap over her shoulder.

"Change your plans, Logan," she said, one hand resting on the door handle. "If you want to hunt and fish, I can name you a million scenic places between California and Colorado."

"Don't worry about me."

"Texas isn't a joke. Between the rattlesnakes and the mountain lions, you won't survive the week without a local guiding you. Everything bites and stings in West Texas. Heck, I read about a whitetail deer attacking a hunter a few years back. The dang thing impaled its antlers through his face."

"I'll keep it in mind."

Sara stepped out of the Jeep and paused in the doorway. "At least give me your phone number so I know where to send the search party."

"I don't own a phone."

She rolled her eyes. "Great. Then I'll read about you in the obituaries."

3

The metallic-green road sign welcomed travelers to Pronghorn County. The sign displayed the Texas flag and an admonition to drive safely or go home. Ten miles down Highway 6, a sleepy town called Dusk Corners sprang from the earth like a forgotten cemetery.

As Wolf drove into town, he half-expected to spy a villain dressed in black hop off his horse and draw a six-shooter. Before finding the town on the map, Wolf had never heard of Dusk Corners. The town nestled on the edge of the Devil's Rock, where he'd track down the murderer butchering unwary travelers. A saloon waited at the edge of town. No restaurants, no constable's office. He hadn't even seen a gas station for several miles.

Wolf spotted the Irvin Hotel, a paint-chipped, dusty gray, old west dinosaur with six pillars supporting a second-story porch overhang. A string of unmanned rocking chairs lined the hotel, moving on their own whenever the wind blew. Only one vehicle, a blue Chevrolet truck, waited in the parking lot as Wolf pulled in. He assumed the truck belonged to the manager.

Inside the hotel, knotty pine lined the walls, and long gouges ran through the hardwood floor. A white-haired man with a horseshoe mustache worked behind the desk. The name on the desk read *Pete Chapman, Proprietor*. Paging through a ledger, Chapman glanced up when Wolf approached. His eyes widened for a moment, then he closed the ledger and set his palms on the desk.

"Credit card machine is down. If you want a room, you'll have to pay cash."

"Not a problem," Wolf said, removing his wallet. He caught the proprietor glaring at the stack of bills. "How much per night, my good man?"

"Hundred-twenty per night, five hundred for the week. How long you plan on stayin'?"

"Four nights, perhaps longer."

"I might be willin' to lower the price to a hundred per night, if you pay up front."

"You have yourself a deal."

"Not so fast," Chapman said, watching Wolf through the tops of his eyes. "I'll want to see some ID. Even with you payin' cash, I need to know who's rentin' my room. You have ID, don't you?"

Wolf pulled a Virginia driver's license in Don Weber's name out of his wallet and handed it to Chapman. The proprietor held the license up to the light, turning it over in his hand, as though searching for a flaw, some inconsistency that would prove the ID was a fake. It was, of course, but Wolf paid top dollar for identifications even an FBI agent wouldn't suspect at first glance.

A brown recluse spider skittered across the desk and disappeared down the side, giving Wolf pause. The brown recluse thrived in hot and dry climates. Venom from the spider rivaled that of a black widow, sometimes causing the skin to rot around the bite wound.

"Come a long way from Virginia," said Chapman, still

holding the driver's license. "What's your business in Dusk Corners?"

"Sight-seeing."

"Few sights to see around these parts, 'less you're headed up to Amarillo or such."

"I enjoy nature. May I have my license back?"

Chapman glanced down at the driver's license as if he'd forgotten about it, and slid it back to Wolf.

"We don't serve breakfast, but there's a diner on Route 7 eight miles east of town. You've got Miller's Pub at the end of the street, in case you need to tie one on. Behave yourself, though. Sheriff Rosario doesn't take kindly to drunks in his county." Chapman scratched his head. "Four nights, eh? I won't argue with a man who wants to give me money. But I'll warn you. You'll be bored stiff by this time tomorrow."

While Chapman retrieved the room key, Wolf reached into his bag and removed a picture of a thick-necked, muscular college student named Brady Endieveri and his girlfriend, Sheila Jarvis. Endieveri draped an arm around his girlfriend's shoulders. Both displayed the glassy-eyed smiles of the inebriated. The large number of students in the background suggested someone took the picture at a party. Endieveri and Jarvis had vanished last week while traveling from Denver to Roswell. A more direct route existed between the two cities, but Endieveri's social media accounts boasted he was stopping at Texas Tech to party with an old high school friend. That was the last anyone had heard from Endieveri and Jarvis. The drive from Lubbock to Roswell would have taken them down Highway 6, possibly through Dusk Corners.

"Do you recognize the students in this picture?" Wolf asked. "They would have come through Dusk Corners last Monday or Tuesday."

Chapman squinted at the photograph and handed it back to

Wolf. "Nope. I would recognize them if they stopped by. We don't get many visitors in town."

Wolf tapped a finger on the picture. "I'm sure they came this way. Are you certain you don't remember them?"

"Positive. These people friends of yours?"

"My niece and her boyfriend, yes. They were on their way to New Mexico and never arrived. I assumed they had car trouble and visited your establishment."

Chapman furrowed his brow. "It doesn't seem to me that you're sight-seein'. You're lookin' for your niece and boyfriend, and that's the sheriff's job. If you can't find them, I suggest you speak with Sheriff Rosario. Should I give you his number?"

"I'd appreciate it," Wolf said, though he wouldn't contact Rosario. The sheriff might recognize Wolf and phone the FBI.

Chapman scribbled the number and pushed the paper across the desk.

Wolf climbed the stairs under Chapman's watchful glare. After he unlocked the door, Wolf stepped into the room and brushed the sweat off his forehead. He found the room clean. Honey-stained wood lined the walls, and a standing wardrobe rested in the corner. A four-poster bed took up most of the floor space, and a wooden desk with a chip on the corner stood against the far wall.

He closed the door and carried his bag to the bed, where he placed it beside the pillow. From the bag, he removed a worn, outdated laptop and opened it on the desk. After the computer rebooted, he shook his head in amazement. The Irvin Hotel had Wi-Fi.

While the computer connected to the internet, Wolf wandered to the window and peeled back the curtain. One road arrowed through Dusk Corners. He spotted Miller's Pub on the corner. Two windows on the second floor above the bar implied an apartment dwelling. Perhaps the bar's owner stayed upstairs.

Wolf wondered why anyone would live in this town. One needed to drive five miles to purchase groceries and twenty miles to find the nearest restaurant.

The road out of town forked in the distance, with Highway 6 continuing to the right. An unmarked road branched off to the left and disappeared into the horizon. Wherever Wolf stared, he found a vast nothingness of flat land and tumbleweeds. He spied a farm on the edge of his vision. The sky seemed larger than life. Great cumulus clouds bubbled mushroom-like through the hazy blue, and a darker strip of gray hinted at coming storms.

Through the upstairs hallway, footsteps shuffled past Wolf's room and stopped outside the door. He removed the hunting knife from his pocket and placed his back against the wall. Without a peephole, he couldn't see who was on the other side of the door.

The person lingered for a long time. Wolf stared at the doorknob, waiting for it to turn, before the footsteps trailed away.

4

A decade of relentless wind and Texas storms had faded the home's yellow paint to a dirty, ashen coloration. A long dead sycamore tree stood as a sentinel in the middle of the yard, its branches worming skyward, gnarled and leafless. The single-story house held an attic accessed by a trap-door, and a dormer window in the attic provided a view of the plains and meadow.

Jacob scratched a festering spider bite on his arm and rounded the house, where a red Ford Focus slept in the back-yard. Flies swarmed inside the car. Even with the windows and doors closed, the insects had found the bodies inside and feasted on the decaying corpses. A festering stench reached his nose, and he took an involuntary step backward. The shadows of the victims' broken bodies slumped in the backseat. The trunk wedged upward where the Ram 3500 had crushed the car from behind, and the rear windshield fissured and shattered in one corner.

He bit the inside of his cheek until warm blood cascaded onto his tongue. His brother, Balor, had murdered the girl before Jacob could have his fun with her. She wasn't the prettiest girl they'd ever captured, but young enough to keep alive for a while. After Balor stabbed the girl, Jacob had snatched his brother by the shirt collar and screamed at him for ruining his plans.

"You have to get them off the road before you kill them. Don't you ever learn?"

Balor stared at him as if Jacob spoke a foreign language. Jacob was the older brother, though nobody would have guessed, given Balor's size. Balor outweighed Jacob by a hundred and fifty pounds.

Jacob kicked at the dust. He was always fixing things after Balor's mistakes. Murdering the boyfriend hadn't caused a problem. After Balor snapped the boy's back like a toothpick, he carried the lifeless corpse to the Ford Focus and stuffed it in the backseat. Then, while Jacob ripped the girl's shirt open, Balor lost control—as he always did—and stabbed the girl. The blood splashed everywhere: across the pavement, onto the weeds bordering the road.

Given enough time, rains would wash the blood away, and bugs would take care of the rest. But Jacob didn't have time. Eighteen-wheelers traveled the road. Someone was bound to notice the macabre splatter of red across the blacktop. Without a choice, Jacob retrieved a jug of cleaning solution and a handful of rags from the truck. In the searing heat, he scrubbed the blacktop until his hands blistered, while Balor loomed over his shoulder without a hint of understanding on his face.

"You see what you put me through?" Jacob yelled back at Balor. "If you'd only waited until we got home. What if a patrol car comes along and finds all this blood on the road?"

While Jacob worked, he ground his teeth together, convinced someone would drive past and spot the wrecked car in the ditch. He needed to work fast, no thanks to Balor. Thankfully, nobody drove down the road before Jacob finished. After they threw the girl in the backseat with her boyfriend, Balor drove the Ram back to the house, with Jacob following in the wrecked Focus. The wheels wobbled, making it difficult to keep the car on the road, and he couldn't see past the rear windshield's shattered glass. The engine ticked and banged during the trip. Eventually, the stupid college kids would have broken down, even if Jacob and Balor hadn't caught them after they took the wrong turn and exited Highway 6.

Now Jacob worried over the car. The Focus was invisible from the road, but if someone trespassed on their property, they'd find the car and smell the bodies.

He grabbed a handful of landscape pins and a blue tarp from the shed. Stretching the tarp over the car, he anchored the covering and pushed the pins into the earth with the heel of his boot. Until he found somewhere to dispose of the vehicle, the tarp would suffice.

When he entered the front yard, he saw Balor staring into the distance, swaying on his feet. Jacob loved and protected his brother, but he was ashamed to admit Balor frightened him. The monster killed with his bare hands, and he possessed inhuman strength. Worse yet, Jacob couldn't predict when his brother would snap and turn murderous. The behemoth seemed as unpredictable as the weather, which had acted fitful and ominous all week. Jacob rolled a shiver off his shoulders. Something was on the horizon, something more dangerous than a spring storm. He shook off his paranoia and crossed the yard. Off in the distance, the pumpjacks pounded the earth like hungry dinosaurs chewing flesh.

"What are we gonna do about the car? I covered it with a tarp, but we can't just leave it here. Someone's bound to come looking for those kids, and if they see our house and knock on the door, I don't know what I'll tell them."

Balor didn't speak. Instead, he raised a bear-like arm and pointed west, where a mound set against the sky marked the gravel pit. Three years ago, Jacob had dumped two bodies in the pit.

"Can't," Jacob said. "The sheriff watches the pit now, just in case we come back. How the hell do we get rid of a car?"

Without answering, Balor turned away and lumbered toward the front door. When the long shadow passed over Jacob, he felt as though some unspeakable demon had laid an icy hand on the back of his neck. The door opened and closed. Thunderous footsteps stomped across the downstairs before Balor lowered the trapdoor to the attic and climbed up. Jacob studied the horizon and wondered where they might ditch the Ford Focus, so nobody traced it back to them. His fingerprints were all over the steering wheel and the interior. He hadn't thought to bring gloves. Usually, when they found a new target, they followed the woman until she left the road. Balor had lost control when he spotted the two college students driving through the country so close to the house. He'd demanded Jacob pursue the students, and Jacob wasn't about to argue with a man twice his size—a man who dismembered victims with his bare hands.

Jacob turned around and spied Balor staring at him through the attic's dormer window. Jacob lifted a hand. Balor didn't respond.

An idea struck Jacob. What if they drove the Focus to Amarillo and dumped the car in a shopping plaza parking lot, somewhere busy where the car blended in? No, that wouldn't work. The shattered rear windshield would attract attention, and he didn't trust the car's engine after all that infernal noise it made. Furthermore, Balor would need to drive the Ram and follow Jacob down the highway. Balor knew how to operate the truck, but he didn't own a license, and he wasn't adept at driving. He weaved across the road and panicked in heavy traffic, which they would encounter in Amarillo. Besides, a man of Balor's size drew eyes. People tended to remember a seven-foot monster, with insane eyes glaring out from a bearded face.

Jacob folded his arms and scanned the horizon. There was a grocery store fifteen miles to the east and a highway travel center a half-hour to the south. If the Focus survived a trip to the grocery store, Jacob could dump the car and walk home. The walk might take him four or five hours, but at least he'd rid himself of the car.

Too risky. Better to find another gravel pit or a tree grove so the authorities wouldn't find the car for a long time.

He picked up a stone and hurled it into the meadow. How long would he need to clean up his brother's messes?

5

D espite the fortunate surprise that the Irvin Hotel offered Wi-Fi, the internet proved fickle, the feed slow and prone to stopping altogether while Wolf researched the Devil's Rock murders. An ethernet jack on the wall offered a direct connection to the world wide web, but he didn't carry a cable with him, and he doubted Pete Chapman would loan him one. After Wolf heard the footsteps outside his door, he'd attuned his ears to any movement on the second floor of the hotel. He assumed Chapman, curious why a visitor had chosen Dusk Corners and the Irvin Hotel, wanted to eavesdrop on Wolf.

These days, a growing number of police and sheriff's departments stored case files in the cloud. To protect sensitive data, law enforcement relied on storage providers to encrypt their data and keep it safe. Before Weber framed him, Wolf had been the Behavioral Analysis Unit's top hacker, as well as its most-gifted profiler. Storage encryption proved an easy challenge for Wolf, who accessed serial killer case files from the cloud and downloaded the documents to his personal computer, stealing the data from under law enforcement agencies' noses.

With the Wi-Fi struggling, Wolf accessed a downloaded case file on Riley and Luis Domin, an interracial couple found submerged in a gravel pit twenty-two miles southwest of Dusk Corners. Three years ago, a crane operator working at the pit had spotted a hand bobbing above the muddy water and shut off the rig. After yelling to his foreman, the crane operator staggered down from the machine and stared as a pallid arm surfaced and rested atop the murk like the bleach-white limb of a long dead tree. The Pronghorn County Sheriff's Department responded, and the FBI arrived that evening. Wooden stakes protruded through both victims' torsos. Local police discovered the Domins' car in Midland, an hour's drive away. The autopsy revealed that the murderer had raped Riley Domin multiple times.

Wolf tapped his fingers on the desk. He found it unusual for the murderer to rape Riley Domin, then kill her in such a violent fashion. The murder implied rage and disgust. Yet Riley must have attracted the killer for him to rape the woman. Wolf tried to remember a serial killer who followed a divergent pattern such as this and failed.

According to the documents, Riley and Luis Domin had a three-year-old child named Makai. The boy, who would be six now, lived with his maternal grandparents outside Austin. Wolf leaned back in his chair and folded his arms. Was the murder a hate crime? Wolf actively tracked two white supremacist cells operating between Dallas and the New Mexico border, but he'd linked both cells to terrorist threats, not serial murders. Only one piece from the puzzle fit the white supremacist angle— multiple killers. That might explain one man raping Riley Domin, then another driving a stake through the woman's body to express his anger over her sleeping with a non-white male.

Wolf flicked the dust and grit he'd picked up on the road from the corner of his eye. He wasn't looking for a racist sleeper cell. His unsub was deranged and unpredictable, a serial killer capable of hiding beneath the radar, despite his fits of rage. And the killer must be strong, considering the way he'd butchered the Domin couple.

A mobile phone that had spilled out of Wolf's bag lay on the bed. He considered the phone for a moment. If he contacted Sheriff Rosario, the man Chapman had encouraged Wolf to call, he risked the sheriff asking too many questions. The investigation file listed Rosario as the responding officer. He was the first law enforcement member to view the bodies of Riley and Luis Domin. Wolf wore many faces, adept at posing as a reporter, a private investigator, even an FBI agent. The latter required he carry a fabricated badge. Though Wolf couldn't tell the fake ID from an authentic FBI badge, Rosario would call Quantico and ask why one of their agents was poking his nose around Pronghorn County without an official invitation.

The Wi-Fi connected and allowed Wolf to access a digital map of West Texas. He captured a screen image before the internet flaked out again and marked the gravel pit's location. Next, he noted Highway 6 outside of Dusk Corners, the most likely route Brady Endieveri and Sheila Jarvis traveled on their way to Roswell, New Mexico. He circled a twenty-mile radius that encompassed both points. Additional murders over the last decade hovered close to the radius and formed a rough circle over the land that the media referred to as the Devil's Rock.

"Where are you?" he whispered to the map.

Downstairs, a door opened and slammed shut, rattling the hotel room's window. Wolf paused and listened as someone shuffled across the lobby. He recognized Chapman's voice. The hotel proprietor spoke on the phone, his voice too muffled to discern. Wolf moved to the door and cracked it open. The long, shadowed hallway ended at the stairway. Two additional hotel rooms bordered Wolf's. He assumed they were unoccupied, as he'd heard no one next door.

"He drives a Jeep Wrangler and paid cash," Chapman said from the lobby. "You think I should call the sheriff?" A long pause, then, "Something about the guy seems off, Chet . . . no, he isn't causing trouble, but . . ." A heavy sigh. "Yeah, I'll keep an eye on the guy and call Rosario if he gets out of hand. I don't trust this Don Weber."

The call ended. Chapman walked to the staircase and stopped on the bottom step. Wolf edged the door shut and carefully twisted the bolt.

At the computer, Wolf checked his Virtual Private Network and ensured it functioned. Wolf didn't believe Chapman possessed the skill to hack into a customer's internet account, but he wasn't taking any chances.

It was a terrible idea to stay in Dusk Corners. Here, everyone knew Wolf's business. He saw no alternative besides locating a vacant house in the countryside and breaking in.

Wolf waited until he was sure Chapman wasn't creeping up the stairs before he called up a satellite image of the Devil's Rock. Farm-to-market roads formed square grids for as far as he could see. Interspersed among the occasional country residence were oil rigs and enough open land to hide in plain sight for a long time. He compared the grids with the map and tagged three areas worth investigating. If Wolf was right, his killer lived in one of the three locations he'd noted. The trouble was, he'd need to cover a hundred square miles with no other tool besides his intuition.

Exhausted, he'd begin the search this afternoon after a few hours of sleep. As he lay his head on the musty pillow, the mattress springs crinkled and squeaked beneath his weight. His thoughts returned to Renee and Sara, and why the dark-haired girl he'd driven home reminded him so much of his late wife.

His mind was playing tricks on him again, forming visions of Renee wherever he looked.

When Wolf turned onto his side, stomach pain shot through his midsection and rocketed up his back. For three years, he'd experienced stomach upset, but the searing agony was worse this time. It seemed someone had stabbed him in the gut with a white-hot fireplace poker and twisted the tip through his intestines. He couldn't write the pain off as simple indigestion anymore. Something was wrong with him. He needed a doctor. Except the most-wanted serial killer in the United States couldn't stroll into a gastrointestinal clinic and ask to speak to a specialist. Besides, he expected bad news. No sense worrying over the inevitable. Everyone died, eventually.

The wave crested, and the pain subsided. Wolf drifted into sleep.

And when he dreamed, he dreamed of a bloodstained kitchen under a midnight moon.

6

Pronghorn County occupies an east-to-west rectangular strip of prairie and clay fields southwest of Lubbock, Texas. During springtime, when the wind blows out of Arizona and New Mexico and carries a wall of desert-dry air into the Lone Star State, one can savor scents of bluebonnet and evening primrose. The land flattens and arrows into the distance, as though the gods drove great steamrollers across the plains during earth's formation. The sky becomes the landscape, the great cumulonimbus clouds serving as mountains, the hazy blue an ocean none can reach. Between April and June, the storms that roll over the prairie bring hailstones the size of soft-balls, tornadoes capable of flattening buildings, and flood waters which scour the land and form transient rivers that drown live-stock and anybody unfortunate enough to place himself in harm's way. Yet the prairie welcomes the storms, for an entire summer of dry, fiery heat awaits the land after storm season concludes. The clay fissures and turns dusty, staining the air when the wind lifts it skyward.

Here, the world's problems seem almost fictional. News from the outside arrives via television, like fantasy prose woven between the hours of five and seven p.m. On rare occasions, Pronghorn County receives its fifteen minutes of Andy Warhol fame. In 2016, the Murphy girl won a silver medal in the high hurdles during the summer Olympics. Two years later, the nation awarded the Pinkerton boy a different medal, after he dragged a fallen soldier into a bunker after their unit took heavy mortar fire in Afghanistan.

Sheriff Edward Rosario flicked his hat at a wasp and stared out at the prairie from a truck stop south of Dusk Corners. Big rig trucks rumbled behind him and puffed clouds of black smoke, and gears screeched as the trucks made their way onto the highway entrance ramp. The charred odors of hot dogs and french fries blew through the air vents behind Rosario, stifling the bluebonnet he was so fond of. The sheriff wrinkled his nose and stepped away from the building.

Behind him, the automatic door wheezed opened, and a heavyset man with sunburned shoulders sauntered into the daylight with a 32-ounce fountain drink in his hand.

"Afternoon, Sheriff," the man said.

Rosario glared at the oaf, then turned back to the prairie as the man hurried to his eighteen-wheeler and drove off.

The sheriff chewed a toothpick and squinted into the afternoon sun. Some smart-ass reporter from Los Angeles had phoned Rosario two hours ago, asking for information about two missing college kids named Brady Endieveri and Sheila Jarvis. The reporter wanted a sound bite about Devil's Rock, the West Texas version of the Bermuda Triangle, Bigfoot, and the Loch Ness Monster. If the reporter wanted Rosario to attribute the last decade's unexplained murders to dark magic and alien beings, he had another thing coming. The hack should have called Roswell. Folks got off on that crap in Roswell. Heck, they built their tourism around that nonsense.

"Bunch of *X-Files* bull," Rosario muttered to no one in particular.

He slapped the wasp out of the air and stomped it dead on the pavement. It had been three years since the last Devil's Rock murders, and over that time, reporters had blamed every missing person's report on some mythical killer stalking the darkness.

Not that Rosario didn't take the murders seriously. He'd been there after the crane operator discovered two bodies floating in a gravel pit between Dusk Corners and the New Mexico border. Rosario was the first on the scene six years ago on the night the sheriff's department scooped the Ripa woman's head out of a drainage ditch. He found no signs of a knife attack. It appeared some malevolent god had ripped the head off Ripa's body and tossed it into the weeds. The rest of her corpse lay in the meadow one hundred yards away. Maggots crawled through the corpse, and the animals had devoured scores of flesh off Ripa's naked body. Even with the animals' bite marks, Rosario could see someone had hacked Ripa's body. It appeared as if someone had run the woman through a meat grinder.

Nine murders in ten years. The back roads of West Texas led to dangerous places.

But he didn't believe he was searching for one killer. Let the media spin their stories about a new Jack the Ripper, this one wearing cowboy boots and a ten-gallon hat. Rosario knew the truth. He attributed the murders to multiple killers. Drug lords from Mexico. The wacko militia groups. Jealous ex-lovers driven to murder.

Rosario didn't buy into the profiling techniques the FBI employed to track serial killers. But even a dimwit could see the murders weren't committed by a single killer. The victims crossed racial and ethnic lines. He'd pulled raped women out of the tall grass and dug dismembered men from shallow graves. He'd found stakes driven through the Domin couple in the gravel pit. Every time, a different modus operandi. This wasn't the work of a lone madman. Serial killers didn't fall dormant for three years, and they didn't rape some victims and hack others into ground meat.

His radio squawked inside the cruiser. With a groan, he shuffled to the vehicle and pulled the receiver through the open window.

"Rosario here. Repeat."

"Sheriff, we received a drunk and disorderly complaint at Billy's in Red Valley. We have two deputies ten miles from town. Should I have Martinson respond?"

Rosario spat. "Negative. I'm five minutes from Billy's. I'll handle it."

"Do you require backup?"

"I said I can handle it. Rosario out."

The shocks protested when Rosario dropped into the seat and slammed the door. He fired the engine and turned out of the parking lot, the tires screeching as he increased his speed. A trucker driving an eighteen-wheeler cut across Rosario's path and slammed his brakes when the sheriff wailed his siren.

The sheriff hit the highway at seventy and weaved past travelers, the lights and siren forcing vehicles into the right lane. Rosario pounded his fist against the steering wheel. That damn news reporter meant to ruin everything. What did a leftist environmental watchdog from Los Angeles know about missing kids in Texas? Rosario had spoken with the families. Endieveri and Jarvis were headed to Roswell for some concert. Chances were, they made it to the festival and were strung out in some hotel after a week of marijuana and cocaine abuse. He'd canvassed Highway 6 west of Dusk Corners and found no broken-down cars, no evidence the college kids ran into trouble in his county. To hell with the Devil's Rock.

After the travelers yielded to Rosario, he muttered an expletive and turned off the siren and lights. The cruiser shot down the exit ramp and turned toward Billy's, a bar and grill on the north end of Red Valley. He paused at a red light, then blew through, kicking the gas pedal to make up for lost time.

Rosario spotted Owen Parsons behind Billy's. A half-drank mug in his hand sloshed beer. The sheriff scowled. He should have known it would be Parsons. The fifty-year-old steel worker couldn't stay out of trouble. Twice in the last two years, Rosario had tossed Parsons in jail for public intoxication. Now Parsons staggered along the back wall of the bar and grill, one hand resting against the siding, the other spilling suds down his pant leg.

Rosario stepped out of the cruiser and adjusted his hat. A sylphlike server with brunette hair tied into a bun hurried to meet him in the parking lot.

"I'm the one who called, Sheriff. The bartender cut him off an hour ago, but somebody bought him another drink."

"Parsons causing you trouble, ma'am?"

"He got into an argument with another patron. I worried it might turn physical, so I phoned your department. He's not a bad guy, Sheriff. Owen is just drunk and needs to sleep it off. And someone needs to drive him home. He'll kill somebody if he gets behind the wheel."

"Go back into Billy's and keep everyone inside while I speak with him. I'll make sure he makes it home."

"Thank you, Sheriff. That's very kind of you."

The sheriff tipped his hat and studied the server's hips until she disappeared behind the door.

"Not a bad guy, my ass."

Rosario clenched his jaw. Owen Parsons abused his wife, Debra. The woman worked the counter at the Red Valley Convenience Mart, and Rosario had spotted her with black eyes and arm bruises on multiple occasions. He would have dragged Parsons to jail for spousal abuse, except the woman denied that her husband beat her and refused to press charges. Rosario knew about wife beaters. His father had been a lowlife drunk who slapped his wife around after nights out with the boys. Rosario grew up under the suffocating quilt of fear, always wondering when his father would burst through the door, stinking of booze and sweat, ranting over work and how he'd take it out on the woman who'd turned his life into a living hell.

His father passed two years before Rosario's fortieth birthday. Cirrhosis of the liver—how appropriate. During the burial ceremony, the priest spoke of Sal Rosario as though he'd been a benevolent husband and a pillar of the community. Edward Rosario walked away, leaving his mother to cry beside Sal Rosario's casket. He refused to dignify the man who'd torn his life apart.

Owen Parsons wavered and caught himself against the wall behind Billy's. He raised unfocused eyes and lifted a hand.

"Howdy, Sheriff," Parsons slurred, barely able to keep his balance.

Rosario glanced over his shoulder. No looky-loos. Inside the bar and grill, music thumped and glassware clinked.

"Had one too many again, Owen?"

Parsons grinned uncertainly.

"What did you plan on doing next? You weren't considering getting behind the wheel and driving home, were you?"

"No, of course not. I just . . . need an hour before I . . . before I . . ."

Rosario walked up to Parsons. The sheriff stood half a head taller than the drunk. Twisting his mouth, Rosario dropped a hand on Parson's shoulder and pinned him against the wall.

"And after you drove home, then what? Slap the woman around? Blame her for your shortcomings, Owen?"

Parsons crossed his eyes and shook his head. "Never. Who told you I hit my wife? Give me a name, Sheriff, and I'll set that man straight."

The sheriff cocked his head around the corner and assessed the empty parking lot. "You know what your problem is? You're a bully. A no-good wife beater and a worthless alcoholic."

"You got it all wrong. It was a long day. No law against blowing off steam after work."

"Don't tell me about the law. I am the law."

Rosario buried his fist into the drunk's belly. Wide-eyed, Parsons doubled over and vomited beer on the blacktop. Spittle dribbled over Rosario's shoe. As Parsons stumbled along the wall and gasped for breath, Rosario calmly slung the muck off his shoe and sauntered over to Parsons. Another check to ensure nobody watched. Then the sheriff punched Parsons in the chest. A feint moan escaped the drunk's throat as he dropped to one knee. Rosario swung his knee into the man's temple. The drunk's neck snapped backward, and he fell to his back, eyes closed, his breath irregular as he panted beneath the Texas sun.

The sheriff stared down at Parsons, knowing there would be questions if the drunk sobered up and claimed Rosario had attacked him without provocation. He kicked Parsons in the stomach. The drunk curled into a fetal position and wept. Blood streamed from the injured man's nostrils. Rosario kicked him again, harder this time. Then again and again, until Parsons rolled onto his opposite side and turned away.

Rosario knelt over Parsons and pulled him up by his shirt collar. The drunk's neck lolled. Rosario grasped the man's head and forced Parsons to meet his eyes.

"Remember that old game show, Owen? *Let's Make a Deal*? We won't mention this altercation to anybody. If you claim I attacked you, I'll say you came at me in a drunken rage and swung first."

"That's a lie."

"Who do you figure a jury will believe? The Pronghorn County Sheriff with an impeccable record, or the town drunk who beats his wife?"

"I never attacked you."

"Oh, I think you did, Owen. That's why I fought back. Self-defense, you understand?" Rosario pulled Parsons's face closer to his. "If you ever hit Debra again, I'll find you. Then I'll dig a hole and bury you in the desert, so you never hurt another woman. Do we have an understanding?"

Parsons spat blood on Rosario's face. The sheriff wiped the spittle away and lifted a fist.

After the next blow, Parsons's eyes rolled around like marbles.

"Owen Parsons, you're under arrest for attacking an officer of the law."

Rosario hauled the drunk into his arms and carried him to the cruiser.

7

"I wish you'd stop," Renee said.

Wolf curled on the bed and ripped the covers over his body, shivering despite the afternoon heat. In his dream, he replayed dinner at Valentino's, Renee's favorite Italian restaurant near their Virginia home. They shared a table for two in the corner, separated from the after-work crowd. Were it not for the candlelight, the shadows would have swallowed Renee's face.

He didn't respond, and she set down her wine and leaned forward, with her forearms on the table.

"You sleep four hours per night, if you're lucky, and you toss and turn and mutter in your sleep. You say things I don't want to hear, Logan."

He ran a hand through his hair. "The BAU scheduled me for a lot of overtime last month. It won't last forever. Just until—"

"Until what? Until they drain every drop of blood from your body? Even when you're home, you're not truly there. You're always thinking about the case, figuring out how you'll catch the next target."

"Three violent criminals captured in the last four weeks. We're doing important work."

"I'm proud of you, Logan, but I won't sit back and watch your job kill you."

He sipped his wine. "Isn't that a trifle melodramatic?"

"Look in the mirror. You've lost weight, and your hair is thinning."

"Losing hair is inevitable at my age, and I assumed you'd want me to drop a few pounds."

"Be serious. The things you say in your sleep . . . Logan, you scare me sometimes."

He glanced across the restaurant, concerned someone overheard. "I'm due for a promotion next year, and once the deputy director position opens, I'll be the leading candidate."

"It's not worth it. Last year, you only had nine weekends off. I never see you. When you're on the road, you can't even tell me where you are. Do you ever consider what it's like for me, worrying you won't come home?"

Logan touched her wrist. "There's no reason to worry."

"Isn't there? You track the most dangerous criminals in the United States. I don't know what I'd do if I lost you."

"You won't. I'm careful, and I always travel with a partner."

"Not always. Don't lie to me."

He sat back and stared at the table.

"We don't need the money, Logan. You don't even need to work, considering the inheritance your father left you."

"It's not about the money. These monsters we track . . . there's no rehabilitating them. We have to take them off the street before they hurt others."

Renee shook her head and studied her wine. "You don't have to do this anymore. If you want to help people, become a police officer. Or a social worker. Anything but a BAU profiler."

"Then support my decision. Once I win the deputy director

position, I won't work in the field anymore. I'll manage the agents."

She lifted her head. The hope lighting her eyes made Wolf's heart clench.

"Is that true?" she asked. "You won't be a field agent?"

"Not anymore. I can't promise I'll be home every weekend. The promotion would entail long hours, and society produces a never-ending supply of killers. But this is the right decision. Nobody knows what our department needs more than me. I can usher the BAU into a new era and instill new methods for identifying potential killers *before* they strike. Please be patient. It won't be much longer."

She gave him an unconvinced smile. His hand met hers, and they interlocked their fingers as conversation droned around them.

Then the restaurant vanished. Wolf stood in his darkened living room. Renee worked inside the kitchen, pots banging together, the utensil drawer sliding open. Trapped in the throes of a senseless nightmare, he wondered why she hadn't turned the lights on, wondered if the power would work if he flicked the wall switch.

A pounding on the door brought his head around. Beyond the front door window, a shadow loomed. An insane thought crept into his mind: if he opened the door, he'd invite death into his home.

The noise from the kitchen stopped.

"Renee? Where are you?"

No reply.

The crazed pounding started again, rattling the door, threatening to smash it off its hinges.

∼

WOLF BOLTED AWAKE. Sweat matted black hair against his forehead. He rolled out of bed and knelt on the floor, as the fading daylight seeped into the room and ignited airborne dust motes.

At the desk, Wolf fell into his chair and scrubbed a hand down his face. The dreams were always different, though inevitably, he'd lose Renee before he awakened. In actuality, Wolf had returned home from a long investigation on that fateful July night in 2013 when he found his wife dead in the kitchen. There hadn't been a stranger knocking on his door and demanding entry. Why the nightmares twisted reality, he didn't understand. Perhaps someone had pounded on the door while Renee was alone in the house. He doubted it. His wife's killer was a silent wraith who'd murdered dozens before Wolf tracked him down.

He opened his wallet and paused when he noticed the receipt from the diner. Wolf swore he'd tossed the paper in the trash on his way out the door, yet here it lay, the bottom crinkled and the tip amount smudged from riding around in his pocket.

He thought of Sara and pondered again why she reminded him of Renee. They didn't look alike, and Sara was several years younger than Renee had been when Wolf first met her. But an undefinable inquisitiveness lit Sara's eyes, just as it had Renee's. Both held the ability to see through Wolf's bull and spot hidden traps before he stumbled into them.

Sara worried Wolf wasn't cut out to handle the hazards of West Texas. She'd wanted his number, and he'd claimed he didn't own a phone, though Wolf always kept a handful of burners. The prepaid phones allowed him to contact Agent Scarlett Bell with the Behavioral Analysis Unit. Bell filled in hidden details about active serial killers, each time swearing she'd never help him again. Yet she always did. Because deep down, Scarlett realized Wolf did necessary work. He took out threats the FBI couldn't eliminate, stopped mass murderers before they killed again. But she wasn't his only FBI contact. Others remained loyal to him, but it was better that Scarlett didn't know their names, even though a few worked side-by-side with her at the BAU. Wolf didn't care that he'd dirtied Bell's hands. A secret darkness existed inside Scarlett Bell. Were Scarlett in his position, she'd do the same. And a part of her knew it was true, even though she wouldn't admit it.

Sudden nausea crashed through Wolf's chest. He stumbled into the bathroom and leaned over the toilet, dry-heaving until every muscle in his upper body screamed.

Wolf slumped against the bathtub and gritted his teeth until the sickness passed. With a moan, he pulled himself up at the sink and splashed water against his face. The face in the mirror belonged to something out of a drive-in horror movie. He dumped his bag on the bed and located the bottle of omeprazole, ignored the instructions to limit himself to one pill per day, and dry-swallowed two. Wolf tossed the bottle aside. Only one pill remained. He needed a refill, and he wouldn't find a pharmacy anywhere near Dusk Corners.

One hand on the sill, Wolf rested against the window and stared down at the town. No vehicles moved down the road, as if everyone in town had been abducted while he napped.

Renee's final admonition played in his head.

You need to stop, Logan. Quit before the job destroys what's left of you.

"You'll finally get your wish. I won't be at this much longer."

8

S ara Mallory used her phone to check her account balance. The synthesized robotic voice read the numbers back. She blew out a breath and fell into a chair beside the kitchen table.

The mechanic had promised to fix Sara's car by midday tomorrow. But at what cost? She barely had enough money for groceries, and the rent was due in three weeks. Outside the apartment window, the sky darkened. The wind picked up, tossing a loose paper bag across the sidewalk as distant lightning flickered. She turned on the television and read the warnings as they scrolled along the bottom of the screen. A tornado watch was in effect until midnight. Last year, the statement would have sent her screaming back to California, where the sun shone daily and nobody who lived there even knew what a hailstone was. Now she switched the channel to the local news. The weather reporter stood in front of a radar screen. It was a typical May afternoon in tornado alley.

Sara's stomach rumbled, reminding her she hadn't eaten since the strange man with black hair and even darker eyes had bought her food at the diner. Logan, he'd claimed his name was.

She believed him, but sensed he withheld secrets she didn't wish to unearth. He seemed nice enough. Logan drove her home and never invited himself inside. He didn't make a pass at Sara, let alone attack her on a desolate road outside Lubbock and leave her in a ditch. She wanted to call Logan and thank him for driving her home. Who in the twenty-first century didn't own a mobile phone?

A crazy idea entered her head. Logan seemed without direction, a wanderer like Sara. Nothing tied Sara to West Texas, and she wasn't sure why she stayed when the entire world lay open to her. If they traveled together and pooled their resources . . .

Dumb idea. She'd concocted a fantasy companionship based on a few hours of small talk.

The phone shrilled on the table. *MOM* displayed on the screen.

"Not now," she said, tapping her fingers on the table.

One ring before the call kicked over to voicemail, Sara ground her teeth and answered.

"Sara, Sara? Can you hear me?"

Lightning drew a white sheet over the window.

"Hi, Mom. Yes, I'm right here."

"I worried because we haven't spoken to you in over a month."

That wasn't true. Mom had called two weeks ago, but Sara wasn't about to argue. Coyness became a learned reflex when dealing with a parent who turned passive aggressiveness into an art form.

"Sorry. I've been busy."

"Aren't you working?"

"Of course I am. I told you weeks ago I got a job in Texas. I'm off today."

"Texas," Mom said, gagging on the word. "What on earth do you hope to find in Texas?"

"It's just a place to live until I save up money."

"And travel to the next hole in the wall. You graduated fifth in your class, Sara. Every university in California wanted you, and you had your choice of—"

"Scholarships. We've discussed this too many times. I wasn't ready for college yet."

"You should be preparing for graduation by now."

Sara dropped her face into her hand and breathed until she bit back a cuss. She'd grown sick of the constant debates, the condescending tone Mom always used when she spoke about college.

"There isn't a reason for me to go to school. I haven't decided what I want to do with my life."

"You planned to be a doctor. Don't you remember?"

"Mom, I was ten."

"You used to play with the stethoscope we bought you, checking the cat's heart rate every ten seconds. A heart surgeon. That's what you wanted to be."

As if people planned their lives at ten years old.

"I haven't wanted to be a doctor since I was a teenager."

Mom tsked. "Because you started hanging around with the wrong crowd. You were such a kind and beautiful little girl before you became friends with those punk kids and dyed your hair."

"Every teenager acts out. Besides, I like my hair black."

"Ugh. And that black makeup. Hideous. Do you want to look like a creature or a lady? No employer will hire some vampire girl." Mom paused. "Corbin called and asked about you."

Sara drew in a breath. After high school graduation, Mom had arranged a date between Sara and Corbin Berriman, a boy two years older than Sara, and a junior at UCLA. Sara knew Corbin's mother through common philanthropic activities.

Corbin had seemed the perfect gentleman. Sara and Corbin

ate dinner on Manhattan Beach on their first date, then danced in Hollywood until the club shut down for the night. After two months of courtship and the best sex Sara had ever experienced, Corbin invited Sara to live with him in his off-campus apartment in Los Angeles.

"No obligations," he'd said, flashing his million-dollar smile. "Why work to pay rent, when you can save your money and travel?"

Sara cataloged all the reasons she shouldn't accept his offer. She'd only met Corbin two months ago, and they shared little in common. Plus, her mother had fixed them up. Still, his kisses melted away reason.

The first month passed without incident. Corbin attended classes during the day, while Sara worked at a bookshop a block from the ocean. She finished work at four and rushed back to the apartment to cook dinner. Then they concluded the night with sex that must have kept his neighbors up past midnight.

Then their relationship changed. Corbin tasked Sara with washing his laundry, a job she accepted at first. After all, she was living rent free. But if work ran late, and she didn't return home in time to cook his meals or clean his clothes, he scolded her.

Corbin called her a worthless moocher and nicknamed Sara the *bed-and-breakfast girl* to his friends, claiming she was a freeloader and only good for one thing. Disgusted with his attitude, Sara packed her belongings while Corbin attended school, intent on moving out without telling him. But the professor canceled class that morning, and Corbin caught Sara carrying the last box through the living room.

He slapped the box from Sara's hand and spilled her belongings over the floor.

"Where the hell do you think you're going?"

"I'm moving, Corbin. You obviously don't want me around, and I'm tired of the things you say about me. I'm leaving."

Danger flickered in his eyes. "Oh, no you aren't. I let you live rent-free for three months, and this is how you repay me?"

He stepped closer. Sara backed away until the wall trapped her. Corbin loomed over Sara. She felt certain he'd strike her. As she braced herself, he turned and kicked the box across the apartment. It ricocheted off the wall, skidded over the couch, and struck a standing lamp, which toppled over and crashed against the floor.

"Shit. Now look what you made me do."

As he knelt beside the mess and shoveled glass into the waste basket, Sara gathered her clothes into her arms, leaving her shoes and a photograph of her family behind. She ran for the door and escaped into the hallway before he realized she'd fled. He swung into the corridor and shouted at her to stop. Another door opened, and a curious woman peeked her head outside to check on the commotion. Realizing he couldn't chase Sara in front of witnesses, Corbin slammed the door and allowed her to escape.

Over the next month, Sara's phone rang every hour until she blocked Corbin's number. She stayed with a girlfriend from high school for two weeks. The same car rumbled past their window every night, always disappearing before Sara read the license plate. Three times she spied Corbin inside the bookshop, pretending to browse, his eyes flicking toward her as she worked behind the desk. Humiliation prevented Sara from moving home. She paid for her share of the rent and said goodbye to her roommate, thankful to put Southern California in the rear-view mirror. That was the last she'd heard of Corbin Berriman until today.

"Please tell me you didn't give him my number."

"No, but I thought you might call him, Sara," Mom said, placing the dinner dishes in the cupboard. "You two were perfect for each other. Corbin manages an investment firm in Encino."

"Good for Corbin."

"Whatever happened between you two? I never approved of you putting your studies off, but I felt secure after you moved in with Corbin. He cared for you. Eventually, you'll get over your ridiculous desire to explore the world. If I were you, I'd marry Corbin."

"Marry Corbin? Why would I ever marry him?"

"You could enroll in school. With the money Corbin makes, you won't need a scholarship."

"I didn't date Corbin for his money."

"Did I say you did? Don't be so confrontational, Sara. Your father and I only want what's best for you, and Corbin always protected you." Mom sighed. "If you were still with Corbin, you wouldn't be in Nowhere, Texas."

No, she'd be dead by now.

Sara eyed the clock. "Is there anything else, Mom? There's a storm watch. I shouldn't be on the phone."

"Texas weather is dangerous. We don't get tornadoes in California."

"You're right. Except the ground opens up and swallows everyone. Oh, and the wildfires. Nothing like watching your neighbors lose their homes."

"Don't be smart, young lady. There's always a price to living in paradise. Do you have enough money to eat?"

"Yes."

"Are you sure? You sound like you're holding back. Is that infernal car still running?"

Sara bit her lip. All she needed to do was tell Mom about the Jetta, and her parents would wire the money and solve all her problems in a heartbeat.

"Running fine. The Jetta will last a lifetime."

"I can't believe the wheels haven't fallen off. All right, then. Don't be a stranger, Sara. Your father and I worry."

"I won't, I promise."

She set the phone aside and eyed the screen until it turned black. Rain splattered the windowpane, and the clouds over the city churned and swirled.

What had Logan said about hunting on the Caprock? Without an operable car, Sara couldn't check on Logan and make sure he hadn't gotten himself into trouble. Was he stuck outside in the storm? Every spring day, the dry line, a thick layer of desert dry air, rolled out of New Mexico and slammed into tropical humidity over Texas. Resultant storms grew to the stratosphere and brought high winds and torrential rains. She hoped Logan knew green skies meant hail, and a low cloud on the southwest flank of a thunderstorm portended tornadoes.

Sara pulled the shade over the window and blocked out the rain. If Logan had a death wish, there wasn't much she could do about it.

But as the wind whipped rain and hail against the apartment complex, she couldn't stop worrying about him.

———

The storms that rolled through Dusk Corners muddied the fields and formed a temporary creek in the center of Main Street. The sun peeked out from behind the clouds as water gurgled into the sewers.

Wolf shaved over the sink. The razor bit through his flesh between his chin and neck. After pressing a piece of toilet paper against the wound to stop the bleeding, he dried his face and returned to the bedroom, where his window overlooked the sleepy Texas town.

Wolf counted the cash in his wallet. Depending on how long he stayed at the Irvin Hotel, he might run out of money. Not that he didn't have plenty stored away, but accessing his money could be challenging. He hid behind two-dozen fake identities and stored considerable sums of cash and investments in various overseas LLC accounts. Accessing the funds brought risk. The FBI searched for him, and if they were smart, they'd follow the money trail.

When his money supply ran low, he eschewed hotels, choosing to stay in private residences. Wolf had his techniques down to a science. He targeted upper-middle-class homes isolated from neighbors. After he established the homeowners were out of town or on vacation by following their social media accounts, he broke inside. Almost every house he chose provided reliable, fast internet service, so he could research the killers he tracked. Though he trespassed, he always left the house in better shape than he'd found it. He cleaned up after himself and repaired issues with the home—clearing rain gutters, fixing wiring issues that might become fire hazards, tightening loose screws on window locks. He doubted the home-owners even knew anyone had broken inside after they returned from their trips.

Breaking into houses didn't seem wise in West Texas. Wolf didn't buy into the stereotype that asserted everyone in Texas owned a gun. He'd traveled the world, and the people of the southern plains weren't any different from those in New York or Paris. They shared the same values and fears about the future. But there were too many farms outside Dusk Corners, and farming didn't afford vacation days. Wolf didn't expect he'd find vacant homes in this region.

He password-locked his computer and moved to the door-way, listening for the proprietor downstairs. Except for the metronome-plunk of water dripping off the roof, quiet blan-keted the hotel. Wolf descended the stairs. Nobody manned the check-in desk, and the stolen Jeep Wrangler remained the only vehicle in the parking lot. Even Chapman's truck had disappeared.

Wolf stepped outside and hopped over a puddle. The humidity hung like a wet blanket over the town. He stopped on the sidewalk and glanced left and right. At the edge of town, two men in cowboy boots strolled into Miller's Pub. Wolf headed in their direction.

Eight people—six men and two women—sat at the bar. Wolf expected classic country on the jukebox: Hank Williams or

Johnny Cash. Instead, Aerosmith's "Sweet Emotion" rolled through the establishment.

A heavyset man with tree trunks for arms nursed a beer and glared at Wolf. The mustached barkeep wore a flannel shirt with the sleeves rolled up to his elbows. A tattoo of Marylin Monroe adorned the bartender's left arm, and a pencil jutted from behind his ear.

"What can I get you?"

Wolf leaned against the bar. "Do you serve dinner?"

He wasn't hungry, and the gurgling in his stomach made him think he'd vomit anything he ate. But he imagined Renee urging him to eat before he collapsed.

"Sandwiches and burgers. I'll grab you a menu."

The barkeep knelt behind the bar and dug out a menu. Wolf felt eyes on him as he considered his options. There weren't many places Brady Endieveri and Sheila Jarvis could have visited in Dusk Corners besides Miller's Pub. But how would Wolf broach the subject? If he posed as an FBI agent or a private investigator, he'd spook the customers. Better to stick with the story he'd told Chapman and keep his lies straight. Word traveled fast in places like Dusk Corners.

A grizzled man with a five-o'clock shadow stared as Wolf waited. "You visiting family or passing through?"

Wolf turned his head. "I'm meeting with my niece and her boyfriend."

The man nodded and sipped beer from a bottle.

Wolf scanned the menu. He doubted he'd keep a greasy burger down, and every food choice came with fries or potato chips.

"I'll take the turkey on wheat bread."

"Lettuce and tomatoes?"

"Splendid."

The bartender entered a small kitchen off the bar. A fat

woman with an overbite sat on the heavyset man's knee and whispered into his ear. Wolf read her lips. She told the man that Wolf looked like a cop.

Five minutes later, the barkeep returned with Wolf's turkey sandwich. As the menu promised, a side of potato chips came with the sandwich. A toothpick skewered the bread, and a pickle lay beside the sandwich.

"Seven dollars," the man said.

Wolf handed him a ten-dollar bill and told him to keep the change. He picked up the sandwich and raised an eyebrow. These weren't thinly shaved slices from the grocery store, but a thick chunk of smoked and brined turkey breast. Wolf bit into the sandwich and wasn't disappointed.

The others stopped paying attention to Wolf and mingled. The overweight lady dropped two coins into the jukebox and queued a Garth Brooks song. She began dancing and wagging a finger at her man, enticing him to join her.

Wolf set the empty plate aside and gave the bartender a thumbs-up. When the man retrieved the plate, Wolf pulled out the photograph of the missing college students. The smile melted off the bartender's face.

"Do you recognize the students in this picture?"

The bartender used a rag to wipe a smudge off the bar. "Sorry. Those look like city kids. Why would they come through Dusk Corners?"

"They were on their way to Roswell from Lubbock. Perhaps they passed through town and stopped for a drink."

"Are you a cop? Does Sheriff Rosario know you're here?"

Wolf had only talked to a few people in town, and already two had mentioned Rosario. It sounded as if the sheriff ran the county with an iron fist.

"I'm not with the police. The girl in the picture—her name is Sheila Jarvis. She's my niece. The man she's with is Brady

Endieveri. They're college students in Denver. They were supposed to arrive in Roswell for a music festival, but never made it."

"I'm sorry about your niece and her boyfriend, but they didn't visit Miller's. Hell, you're the first out-of-towner to pass through these doors in months. I'd remember them if they'd stopped in."

"Fair enough. Maybe you saw their vehicle in town. Brady drove a blue Ford Focus."

"That doesn't ring a bell. There are multiple routes from Lubbock to New Mexico. Highway 6 is just one option. They'd be better off sticking to the interstate."

"True, but this is the most direct route."

The bartender slid the photograph back to Wolf. "Sorry, but nobody like that stopped in Miller's. Did you check the hotel?"

"Yes. I have a room in the Irvin Hotel for three more nights. Sad to say, the owner didn't recognize them."

The man scratched his forehead. "Once you leave Dusk Corners, towns are few. If you break down, good luck finding a garage."

"That's what I'm worried about. You know kids. They don't care for their vehicles."

The bartender bobbed his head. "You can say that again. My cousin's kid ruined his Chevy because he never changed the oil. Stupid bastard broke down thirty miles outside of Amarillo. If it were my kid, I'd have told him to buy a bus ticket. I'm not driving all the way to Amarillo to bail you out." The bartender hooked a thumb at the customers. "You're welcome to ask around, but nobody here saw those kids. Better take this matter to Sheriff Rosario. He knows these roads like the back of his hand."

Wolf thanked the bartender. He showed the picture to the

patrons. Few gave it more than a cursory glance, and nobody recognized Brady and Sheila.

He stepped onto the sidewalk and stared down the lonely strip of blistered macadam known as Highway 6. In the distance, the road forked. The dying sun painted the horizon in blood.

"I saw those kids."

Wolf spun around and found the lanky, hoary man from the bar. Wolf hadn't heard the man approaching over the music.

"You saw my niece and her boyfriend?"

The man took the picture from Wolf and tilted it into the sunlight. "Didn't see their faces, but their car came through town. Must have been last Monday." He held out a hand. "Seth Fonda."

"Don Weber," said Wolf, shaking Fonda's hand. "You're sure it was them?"

"Blue Ford Focus with Colorado plates. I wouldn't have given the car a second thought, except the damn thing was burning engine coolant. Heard what you said in the bar about kids not maintaining their vehicles. I have to believe the car was making all sorts of noises, and they must have smelled the coolant. It's surprising they made it from Lubbock to Dusk Corners in this heat."

"Which way did they drive?"

"That way," Fonda said, pointing his finger into the setting sun.

"Toward New Mexico."

"If you say so." Fonda's lower lip quivered as he wiped sweaty hands on his shirt. "There's nothing but open land between here and the border, and ain't none of it safe to drive."

Fonda spat.

"Why isn't it safe?"

"You break down outside Dusk Corners, and it's you against

the scorpions and tarantulas. And you never know who might come along."

"What do you mean?"

"Just saying the countryside ain't just families and farmers. Outsiders have a strange way of disappearing on the Caprock. Now, if you beg my pardon, I need to get home before the wife gets some fool idea in her head that I'm seeing a younger woman."

More questions swam in Wolf's head as Fonda walked away. Something frightened the man and caused Fonda to glance toward the setting sun with a wary eye.

The Devil's Rock killer was out there somewhere. And the FBI couldn't find him.

10

The slash of orange on the eastern horizon portended the coming day, though it was still too dark to see beyond the waves. Scarlett Bell's legs ached. Her bare feet pounded the shoreline, the Atlantic chill catching her ankles when the tide pulled the breakers over the beach. She preferred to run in the dark, hours before the beach clogged with tourists, and the summer heat became too much to bear. At the top of the beach, condos rose in black rectangles against the starlit sky. No lights shone through the windows. Beside the condos, the silhouettes of eastern redbud flowers danced in the ocean breeze. Bell couldn't smell their sweet fragrance, with the onshore wind pouring off the Atlantic.

A lead profiler with the FBI, Agent Scarlett Bell had garnered national attention over the last several years. She possessed a sixth sense for catching fugitives, and her track record far surpassed that of her colleagues. Her high cheekbones and blonde hair, tied in a ponytail this morning, afforded Bell a celebrity status she'd never asked for. Tabloid photographers followed her every move, and photographs of Bell covered magazines in grocery store checkout lines. Bell wanted none of this. She preferred to work in anonymity and never felt comfortable in the spotlight.

A crab with snapping claws skittered across the sand. She gave it a wide berth and continued down the shore, her beach condo a mile ahead. She'd already run eight miles, and the sun wasn't due to rise for another hour.

Exercise quieted her restless mind. When she was nine, a kidnapper murdered her childhood friend, Jillian Rossi, along a creek that ran behind their houses in Bealton, Virginia. That nightmarish summer, the same man captured Bell before she fought him off and escaped. Throughout her teenage years and into adulthood, she'd repressed the memory, never certain if she'd dreamed the abduction. She spent years in therapy with Dr. Morford as she vied to unlock the secrets to her past. But only one man understood Bell and helped her overcome her demons.

Logan Wolf.

A shiver ran through Bell. She hadn't seen Logan Wolf since he rescued Bell and her partner, Neil Gardy, from the mass murderer who'd killed Wolf's wife. Bell wanted to help the fugitive. Don Weber, then the deputy director of CIRG, had set up Wolf and framed the former BAU agent for his wife's murder. Now that the truth was out, Wolf's name should have been cleared. Except Wolf never stopped butchering murderers. The entire FBI was searching for Wolf, and if they found him, Wolf wouldn't survive the encounter.

Bell ran faster. Her arms and legs pumped, and the wind chilled her flesh as sweat poured off her body.

She slowed to a jog when she arrived at the condo. For a long time, she leaned over with hands on her knees and caught her breath. She'd replaced the traditional lock set with a keypad entry, and now she punched in the code and unlocked the door. Inside, gray light filtered through the sliding glass doorway to the deck. She opened the cupboard and removed a brass frying pan and slicked the surface with nonstick cooking spray. After she set the pan aside, she diced onion, tomato, and mushrooms, then added a handful of spinach. She cracked three eggs over the pan, added three egg whites and feta cheese, and mixed the ingredients. Setting the pan on the burner, she sprinkled black pepper over the omelet.

A bottle of chardonnay stood on the counter. She stared at the wine, remembering when she'd returned from an investigation and found the bottle on the kitchen table with a red bow wrapped around the neck. Bell didn't know how Wolf broke into her condo. She wouldn't share the entry code with him, and she never found a jostled window or a broken lock. Wolf was a ghost, a phantom who walked through walls. Doors didn't stand in his way. The fugitive serial killer always left her gifts—philosophy books, burner phones, exotic foods, fine wines from across the globe, and once a Peruvian blue passion flower, which still grew in a pot beside the deck door. Bell concealed a wicked karambit knife in her bedroom closet. She'd discovered the blade in her refrigerator beside a pristine cut of Wagyu beef. Someday, she'd ask an FBI trainer to teach her how to use the blade.

Bell had learned to trust Wolf, even after the former BAU agent kidnapped Bell and demanded that she profile his wife's killer. There was something undefinable between them, a bond that surpassed mutual respect. They were two lost souls struggling to survive in a world that refused to understand them. Tragedy had forged Wolf, and that's why the serial killer empathized with Bell, who'd entered law enforcement because she'd lost Jillian.

She slid the omelet from the pan to the plate and dabbed ketchup over her breakfast. Doing so always caused Gardy to twist his mouth when they traveled together.

"You put ketchup on everything," Gardy would say, pointing his fork at her plate. "Steak, eggs. I bet you pour ketchup over oatmeal when nobody is around."

She didn't, though her parents loved to tell everyone how Bell used to eat ketchup sandwiches—two slices of white bread, with her favorite condiment spread in the middle.

Bell lifted the bottle of wine and pursed her lips.

"How do you break inside, Logan?"

She carried the plate to the bedroom and ate in front of the computer, one hand balancing the plate while the other typed on the keyboard. Seven weeks had passed since she'd heard from Logan Wolf. No calls on the burner phone, no wine bottles or strange foods he'd picked up during his travels. On more than one occasion, Wolf had contacted Bell with information about a case she was working on. How Wolf found out about her investigations, she could only guess.

She twisted her hair around her finger and tugged. It was only a matter of time before Wolf's luck ran out. If the FBI didn't capture him, he'd encounter a more devious killer. That thought seemed unimaginable to Bell. Wolf was a machine, the perfect killer. Yet she recalled something her high school volleyball coach had told their team after they won the league championship.

"No matter how skilled you are, there's always someone who is better. Respect your opponent. It only takes one loss to end your season."

Bell finished breakfast and set the dish on the desk. She sifted through the encrypted messages Wolf had sent two months ago. He'd pursued a rapist and strangler in Nevada, a man the BAU had tracked for two years. The local police found the man with his throat slit and a sack placed over his head—Logan Wolf's calling card. Forensic evidence linked the dead man to the strangulations, closing the two-year investigation.

Her phone hummed on the desk, and for a heartbeat, she wondered if Wolf was calling. Except he'd never call on her mobile phone, only on the prepaid burners he collected. She read Gardy's name on the screen and answered.

"Isn't it a little early to phone your friends, Gardy?"

"You're up by five every morning. Stop pretending I ruined your beauty sleep. If I had to guess, you already ran ten miles and finished breakfast." He yawned. "I don't understand how you do it."

"Early to bed, early to rise. You remember the saying. And I only ran eight miles this morning."

"You're getting soft."

"I can still kick your butt, Gardy."

He snickered like Muttley, the cartoon dog from Bell's youth. "No arguments here."

"So, why are you calling? This better not be about another case. I have four days off, and I intend to make the most of them."

"Not another case. You blew out of the office yesterday without saying goodbye."

"Like I said, I have a rare four-day break, and I want to enjoy myself."

"I hope enjoying yourself doesn't entail spending every day in front of the computer, tracking your benefactor."

Bell shifted her jaw. How did Gardy know?

"I'm right, admit it."

"Kreskin strikes again."

"Not really. I came looking for you at lunch yesterday, and you'd left your browser open. I could only think of one reason you'd research active serial killers the BAU isn't pursuing."

"Gardy, that's creepy. I don't appreciate people reading through my browser history."

"That's your business. I swear I didn't go through your

history. All I saw was what you'd left on the screen. Bell, he isn't a stray dog you can take home and rehabilitate. I worked beside Logan Wolf when I first entered the BAU."

"Yes," Bell said, swiping the hair over her shoulder. "You've told me the story many times."

"Even before Renee's murder, I didn't trust him. Nobody got inside the head of a killer like Logan Wolf."

"Sounds like a hero to me."

"Or maybe it takes a killer to catch one."

"Wolf wasn't born a killer. Don't forget he saved our lives, Gardy."

"I remember. But he could have cleared his name and rebuilt his life. Instead, he became nothing more than a vigilante murderer. That makes him dangerous and untrustworthy."

"If you're finished with throwing Wolf under the bus, I have dishes to wash."

Gardy sighed. "You're not taking this seriously."

"What do I need to do to get you off my case?"

"Tell me you're spending your days off on the beach, relaxing in the sun and reading a book."

"You read my mind, Gardy. That's exactly what I'll be doing."

"Right," he said, drawing the word out. "So if I stop by for dinner one of these nights . . ."

"You'd better call ahead. I want to visit my parents in Bealton."

"So you won't purchase a plane ticket and fly off to meet Hannibal Lecter?"

"Scout's honor."

"Hmm. All right, but I'll check on you."

"I wouldn't have it any other way."

She ended the call and grinned. Gardy cared too much, and that's what she loved about him. She also understood why Gardy didn't trust Logan Wolf, and why he wanted to protect

Bell from the fugitive serial killer. She'd never told Gardy about the gifts, or that Wolf broke into her condo whenever he pleased. If Bell had, Gardy would have stationed an agent outside her door.

Bell opened a digital document and listed the known serial killers active in the United States. At any given time, thirty to fifty serial killers stalked the country. That number had been declining for decades, but it was still disturbingly large. She eliminated cases the FBI was actively involved in, then she settled on a handful of murderers. Her gaze landed on the Devil's Rock killer, who'd evaded the authorities for a decade, far longer than any known murderer.

She called up another window and logged into the FBI system. From here, she queried an offshore account Wolf used to move money. Wolf wasn't aware Bell had linked him to the account, and she'd kept the information to herself, lest her colleagues close in on the fugitive. According to his financial records, Wolf withdrew funds in Minnesota six days ago, then in Colorado three days later. He was heading south.

Two college students from Denver had vanished last week, and the tabloid media believed the Devil's Rock killer, dormant for three years, had abducted the students. Wolf must have investigated Colorado and gathered information about the students and their whereabouts. He was the deadliest assassin she'd ever encountered. But she sensed something ominous on the horizon, a monster Wolf might underestimate. She worried about Wolf, and not just because he was in over his head with the Devil's Rock killer. She flashed back to the security footage from a convenience store in Pronti, Kansas, the home of a murderer known as The Skinner. Video surveillance captured Wolf inside the store, grabbing stomach medication off the shelves. He'd seemed peaked and weak, a shell of his former self. Was Wolf dying?

Bell logged on to her airline account and purchased a round-trip ticket to Amarillo. From there, she'd rent a car and drive toward the Caprock. With any luck, she'd find Wolf before he got himself into trouble.

Now all she had to do was save Wolf's bacon and capture a mass murderer before the FBI figured out what she was up to.

11

Puddles glistened and mirrored the hazy blue sky as Wolf stepped out of the Irvin Hotel after a night of fitful sleep. He'd spent half the night hunched over the toilet, with a stabbing pain in his stomach. Now the pain subsided to a burning tremor, a warning to watch what he ate for the next few days.

While he wandered through the town, a red-haired man with a limp turned the corner. Wolf's hand moved toward the hunting knife he kept hidden inside his pocket. The man glanced up in surprise and crossed the road, putting as much distance as he could between himself and Wolf.

Pinching the bridge of his nose, Wolf leaned against the building and gathered his breath. He pictured an abandoned warehouse ten miles outside of Cleveland, washed in lunar silvers beneath a sickle moon. That had been fifteen years ago. During a nightmarish nine-month period, dozens of prostitutes vanished from the streets. Local authorities ignored the disappearances—the transient whores had moved to different cities or shacked up with their drug suppliers—until public outcry demanded the police take action. After failing to solve the mystery, the police contacted the FBI, who sent Logan Wolf and his partner, Agent Leland McIntyre, to Cleveland. McIntyre had only worked five months with the BAU, and Wolf feared the man wasn't prepared for the horrors that awaited them in Cleveland.

It took Wolf four days to track the killer to the warehouse, which sat at the center of the disappearances. A homeless man spotted a light on the warehouse's fifth floor and alerted the police. While McIntyre circled the warehouse, Wolf entered through a first-floor window, where someone had pried a board free.

On the fifth floor, the stench caused Wolf to double over and wretch. Two dozen bodies were strewn about the room, some posed and lifelike, staring at Wolf with blank, accusatory eyes, gazes which demanded answers. Why hadn't he saved them? Why had it taken so long for Wolf to discover their final resting place?

Each woman's neck lolled and twisted at a grotesque angle. The killer had crept up behind them and broken their necks, then dragged them to his secret den in the forgotten slum.

Wolf removed his gun and swung it across the room. Rats skittered through the walls. The warehouse smelled of urine and death.

An unseen door imploded. The beast lumbered into the room, furious at Wolf for invading his space. There was no reason in the man's eyes, no sense of right or wrong. Wolf fired his service weapon and struck the murderer in the chest and shoulder.

He kept coming.

Wolf fired again. Each blast lit the room and revealed more decaying bodies.

The man stood six inches taller than Wolf. He grabbed Wolf's head. A split-second before the monster snapped Wolf's neck, the agent fired at close range and knocked the killer backward.

Responding to the gunfire, Agent McIntyre burst into the room. His mouth hung agape as he took in the carnage. McIntyre froze, not reacting when the murderer climbed to his feet and stalked after the rookie BAU agent. The killer would have butchered McIntyre, but Wolf pulled the trigger. The bullet blew through the killer's head and felled the beast.

When McIntyre regained his senses, he joined Wolf, who knelt over the killer. McIntyre flicked on his flashlight.

The killer's unblinking eyes stared up at them. He wore a mess of red hair that burned in the light.

Now Wolf leaned against the building and rubbed his eyes. He hadn't thought about Cleveland in years.

Why did the Devil's Rock murderer remind him of Cleveland?

SARA'S WALLET was six-hundred dollars lighter when she picked up the Jetta from the mechanic. He'd warned her the car had, at most, five thousand miles remaining before it kicked the can. If she was smart, she'd take whatever she could get for the Jetta and use the money for a down payment on something new. Excellent plan, except Sara didn't have money for a new car.

As she drove to her apartment, she imagined herself at her parents' doorstep, bags dangling from each hand. Mom and Dad would take her in. No doubt they'd kept her room impeccably clean, ready for the day she returned, defeated and contrite for being a fool. The frustration coursing through Sara caused her to press down on the accelerator, and she braked before she clipped the bumper of a pickup truck in front of her.

She turned off the thoroughfare. Her apartment loomed at

the end of the road. The limitless Texas sky framed the building, making the apartment appear puny in comparison.

Her thoughts returned to Logan. The strange man understood the risks he was taking. He could handle himself. No matter what happened, it wasn't her problem. Yet he'd invaded her dreams last night. She'd awakened after midnight with a scream held behind her teeth. In the dream, Logan lay in a puddle of his own blood, his mouth moving, but no words emerging. His hand reached out for hers, as though he needed to tell her something while he still had the chance.

Instead of driving into the parking lot, Sara executed a three-point turn and drove toward the highway.

"This is stupid," she muttered.

There was no stopping her once she decided. When she'd first encountered Logan, he'd denied being a cop and fed her a story about hunting in West Texas. She couldn't picture him with a rifle, faking duck calls or firing at deer. It wasn't even hunting season. He'd lied to her.

She knew where Logan was heading—the Devil's Rock.

The evening news reporters never stopped talking about the two missing students from Denver. Was Logan researching the murders? The closest town to the Caprock was Dusk Corners. It seemed like a long shot that she'd find Logan there. But where else would he stop?

Sara set her GPS. An hour later, Highway 6 brought her into Dusk Corners.

She slowed the Jetta to a crawl as she marveled at the town, which appeared straight out of a black-and-white western movie. She eyed the fuel gauge, which sat at a quarter-tank full. She'd expected to find a gas station here. No such luck.

Empty sidewalks bordered the street. A five-and-dime store with boarded windows stood to her left. Beside it, a vacant lot littered with rubble gave way to miles of open land. She parked along the street and stepped out of the Jetta. The noonday sun wrenched the sweat from her body and sapped her strength. She shielded her eyes when a gust of wind kicked up dust and grit.

To her right, she spied a vintage hotel with six pillars along the front. Sara crossed the hotel parking lot, which held only one vehicle, and it wasn't Logan's Jeep Wrangler. On a whim, she entered the hotel. A bell jingled when she pulled the door open, and a white-haired man with a horseshoe mustache looked up from the counter. He glared at her as Sara approached. The nameplate on his desk read *Pete Chapman*.

"Must be my lucky week," Chapman said. "Two out-of-town visitors in two days."

Hope swelled in Sara's chest. "Who was the other visitor?"

Chapman watched her from the corner of his eye. "Seems everyone who steps through my door is full of questions. You interested in a room?"

"I'm looking for someone, a person who must have stopped here."

"I'm not in the people-finding business. But if you need a clean, quiet room while you search for your friend, I can oblige."

Sara considered asking for Logan by name and stopped herself. Instinct warned her that Logan, who struck her as secretive, wouldn't appreciate Sara using his name. Maybe he really was in law enforcement and working undercover.

"If you please, sir. The man I'm looking for is my father."

"Your father, eh?" Chapman said, giving her a disinterested sigh. He pulled out a ledger and ran a finger down a row of numbers.

"Yes, my father."

"Why do you believe your father rented a room?"

"Because he traveled to Dusk Corners and there's no other place to stay."

"I won't give out information about my guests. That violates their privacy."

Sara doubted this man gave a damn about privacy, yet he refused to budge.

"It's important I contact him."

"So call him."

"I can't. He's stuck in his ways and doesn't own a phone."

Chapman slammed the ledger shut. "This isn't my problem. If your father rented a room, then he'll be along soon. Rent a room, or be on your way. You're welcome to wait for your father in the parking lot."

"So you're admitting my father is staying here."

"I'm not."

Below the counter, her hands clawed at her shirt. She needed a convincing story.

"Listen, I need to contact my father because I'm pregnant. I realize you're under no obligation to help me, but my father needs to know. My mother passed, and he's the only family I have."

The man ruffled his hair. He opened his mouth, stopped and closed it, then started again. "You say you're pregnant?"

"Yes."

"And you believe your father is staying here, but you have no way to contact him."

"That's correct."

"Describe your father."

Sara leaned her forearms on the counter. "Black hair like mine and deep-blue eyes. He's about so tall." Sara raised her hand several inches above her head. "Please, I'm sure he stopped here."

Chapman's eyes shifted. "I can't confirm he's your father, but a man drove out of the parking lot about an hour ago and headed west."

"Did he say when he'd return?"

"I didn't ask. As I said, you're welcome to wait in the parking lot—"

Sara rushed out of the hotel before Chapman finished. She hurried back to the Jetta and drove out of town, following Highway 6, the only road leading west. With Dusk Corners fading in her mirror, she scanned the horizon. There was nothing beyond the town, no vehicles, no people. Just parched clay and scrub meadow for as far as her eyes could see. It occurred to her that this pursuit was utter lunacy. She barely knew Logan, and despite Dusk Corners being the only town west of the Devil's Rock, she had no proof he'd come this way.

A fork in the road appeared as Dusk Corners vanished behind her. The sign for the highway leaned sideways, ravaged by recent storms. A leafless tree blocked the sign, making it easy for drivers to mess up and take the wrong road. She paused at the fork and considered which way she should drive. The highway would take her to New Mexico. The road to the left might go anywhere. An armadillo skeleton lay beside the road. Flies picked the remains off the carcass.

Sara backed up and took the unmarked road, a feeling of desperation to find Logan dragging her into the unknown.

12

Sara felt like an idiot. After an hour of aimless driving down the back roads of West Texas, with the creeping sensation of someone watching her the entire time, she returned to Dusk Corners. She hadn't found Logan, and she'd resigned herself to believing he wasn't in Dusk Corners. She'd guessed wrong. For all she knew, Logan was hunting out of season somewhere between Lubbock and Midland.

But as she passed the Irvin Hotel, she recognized the Jeep Wrangler in the parking lot. Sara slammed the brakes and stopped the Jetta along the curb. She hopped out of the car and noticed a man's silhouette in the Wrangler's front seat. Logan.

He opened the door without looking up and crossed the lot.

"Logan, stop."

His head swiveled, and she was sure his hand groped inside his pocket for a hidden weapon before he recognized her. Who was this guy?

"Sara, what are you doing here?"

"Trying to find you."

"Are you following me? You really shouldn't."

"I wanted to thank you for helping me after my car broke

down. It's fixed, by the way. I don't expect it will last through summer, but I—"

"You shouldn't be here."

"I just need to talk to you. It won't take long."

He shifted his feet and glanced at the hotel doors.

"Hey," she said, touching his forearm. He flinched as though shocked. "I'm your daughter."

"Come again?"

"That's the story I gave the sketchy hotel dude. He wouldn't confirm that you'd rented a room."

"So you told him I'm your father?"

The toe of her shoe scuffed the blacktop. "It was a dumb lie, but it was all I could come up with."

Logan blew out a breath and rubbed his eyes. "I'm not getting rid of you, am I?"

"Nope."

"Then I suppose I have no choice." He swung his head toward the sidewalk as two men passed. "We can discuss this situation in my room. For a town this small, Dusk Corners has too many eyes."

Sara followed him through the doorway and across the lobby. The proprietor watched them as they climbed the stairs. Their shoes clomped against the wooden steps as she chewed her lower lip. She had no direction in her life. By now, Sara assumed she would have figured out who she was and enrolled in school, satisfying her parents. She was a vagabond and never stayed in one place longer than several months, and it wasn't because she wanted to see the world. If that were the case, she'd backpack across Europe or rent an apartment in Hawaii. Instead, she worked a dead-end job in Lubbock, Texas. She owned nothing of worth, and now that the car repair had drained her bank account, she wouldn't be able to pay her rent. Traveling with Logan intrigued her. Like Sara, Logan lacked direction. It made sense to pool their resources. And she liked this guy, as much as it shocked her to admit it. She'd felt drawn to him the moment he approached her outside the diner, almost as if they'd met before.

Logan worked the key into the lock and pushed the door open. A bag lay on the bed. Two rumpled shirts and a pair of pants spilled over the blankets. Logan snatched up a pill bottle beside the pillow and stuffed it into his pocket before she read the label.

He closed his laptop, but not before she noticed the dead bodies on the screen. Crime scene photos. She covered her mouth.

"You really are a cop. Either that or a fed."

Logan didn't answer. With a trembling hand, he pushed the computer against the wall and pulled the shade on the window.

"You're not on a hunting trip; that's for certain. Why can't you just be truthful with me?"

"Why do you need to know? We only met yesterday."

"Are those pictures from the Devil's Rock murders? I read about the two missing college kids. If you're a federal agent, shouldn't you have a partner to back you up?"

"You ask too many questions."

He removed his jacket and draped it over the chair. His navy-blue t-shirt clung to his chest and arms, accentuating his physique.

"I worried about you, and since you lied to me about owning a phone, this was the only way to reach you."

"So you followed me through West Texas."

"I trust you, Logan. You're the first guy who did something nice for me and expected nothing in return."

"I gave you a ride. That's all. You're smarter than this, Sara. I could be a rapist. You shouldn't accept rides from strangers. It's not safe."

"Then you shouldn't offer rides. Maybe I'm the dangerous one. But you trusted me. I guess it's time we were truthful with each other." She offered her hand. "Hi. I'm Sara Brennan from Los Angeles, California. I drive an unreliable Volkswagen Jetta, and I'm an office temp in Lubbock. And you are?"

"I already told you my name."

"Logan, right. What do you do for a living, Logan?"

He turned away and peeked around the shade, studying the town.

"Fair enough. You don't have to tell me. But you shouldn't stay here alone. Not in West Texas. Do the people you work for know you're here?"

Again, no answer.

She placed a hand on his back. He swung around. Danger lingered in his gaze. But there was something else—a vulnerability Sara hadn't recognized until now. Though she didn't wish to pry, it was obvious tragedy had struck Logan. She thought of Corbin and all the misogynistic, untrustworthy men who'd taken advantage of her. Logan was different. His eyes met hers, and her heart beat faster. This was insane. She'd fallen for the guy.

"I wish you'd return to your home," he said, his voice a tick above a whisper.

"I can't until I tell you what I came here to say."

"And that is?"

"This."

She pressed her lips against his. He fought for a second and stopped. After the kiss, he held her at arm's length.

"Why did you do that?"

She pushed his hands away and kissed him again. This time, he didn't resist. His lips were warm, and his solid chest brushed against hers. Her hands groped his back.

Sweeping the bag off the bed, he lifted Sara and placed her on the mattress. She gasped as his hand ran beneath her shirt.

WOLF'S EYES flicked open to Sara curled beside him. The light spilling between the shade and jamb told him a few hours had passed since she'd found him in the parking lot. She murmured in her sleep and tugged the covers over her bare shoulders.

He lay back on the pillow and stared at the ceiling. She reminded him so much of Renee. The mannerisms, the nonstop pursuit of the truth. This was the first woman he'd slept with since he lost his wife eight years ago. He'd never even kissed a woman or considered dating.

And that scared Wolf. The last woman he'd cared for died because of him. Sara had her life ahead of her. The last thing she needed was someone like Logan Wolf messing things up.

He eased the covers off his body and climbed off the bed, clenching his jaw when the springs squealed. Behind him, Sara continued to sleep, snoring softly as he padded across the floor and retrieved his clothes. His stomach cramped. He fished the medication out of his pocket and popped the last pill, swallowing it dry. It slid down his throat like a lit match.

In the bathroom, he assessed the face in the mirror and wondered how much longer he had. The pain came more frequently. There was something festering and growing inside him, and he doubted there was enough time for a doctor to turn back the clock. Perhaps it was a blessing Renee left him first. As much as he missed her, he couldn't bear the thought of dying and leaving her alone.

He rinsed his face and dried it on the towel. Sara stirred on the bed, and Logan tensed, knowing he'd made a mistake. For eight years, he'd concealed his identity and evaded the authorities. Now, during a regrettable twenty-four hours, he'd given a young woman his first name and invited her into his bed. What was he thinking?

He forced himself to smile and returned to the bedroom, where Sara hung her legs off the mattress and rubbed the sleep out of her eyes. The light sneaking into the room confused her. The woman wasn't sure why she'd awoken to the afternoon sun blazing outside the window. Wolf pulled the shirt over his head. She padded across the room and hugged him. He dropped his head, unsure where to place his hands as she nuzzled his chest.

"That was amazing," she said. He didn't answer. Agreeing might convince her to stay longer, and he wouldn't allow it. "I hope the manager didn't hear us. After all, I claimed you're my father. Creepy."

"I gather the manager hears everything."

She met his eyes. "Does he spy on his guests?"

"Something like that. His opinion doesn't matter. I have three more nights booked, unless I complete my work sooner. After that, I'll never cross paths with Mr. Chapman again."

"You didn't give him your name, did you, Logan?"

He turned away. "No."

"But it's a hotel. Certainly, he required identification." She rounded Wolf and faced him. "So you travel with fake identification, and now you're searching for those missing college kids. I pegged you for law enforcement, but I don't believe that's correct. Who are you, Logan?"

"Who I am isn't important."

"I want to understand what you do and who you are." He arranged his belongings in the bag. "You seem like you're in a hurry to get out of here."

"I told you yesterday. I came here to hunt."

"You don't sound like a hunter."

Logan raised his brow. "And what does a hunter sound like?"

"Not like someone who's pairing wine with his meal. Are you here to hunt the Devil's Rock killer? You're some kind of vigilante."

"Stop asking questions you don't want answers to."

"That's it, isn't it? You're going after the guy who killed all those people on the Caprock, and you don't want the cops to find you."

It occurred to Wolf how easy it would be to pluck this loose thread and eliminate the one person in the world—beside Agent Scarlett Bell—who knew his secrets. How Sara had figured everything out in twenty-four hours, he didn't know. But killing her wasn't an option. He cared for Sara. Wolf assumed she'd gather her belongings and rush out of the room, afraid he'd murder her before she made it to the car.

She didn't. Sara turned his chin toward her.

"Take me with you."

His mouth went dry. "What? No, that's not an option."

"Why not? I can keep a secret."

"You're not coming with me. Forget it. Drive back to your apartment and pretend you never met me."

"If you're going after the Devil's Rock killer—"

"Did I say I was? You arrived at that idea on your own. I drove to Texas to escape from reality for a few days. Go away."

She flinched as though slapped. "I slept with you, Logan. That's all you wanted from me? Sex? Thanks a million for being like every other macho jerk in the world." Sara's eyes misted over. "You used me, and now you're throwing me out of your bed."

"You're wrong. I'd never take advantage of a woman."

"Then prove it and give me your number. Don't lie. You own a phone. I bet it's inside your bag."

She reached for the bag, and he pulled it away.

"You won't let anyone close to you," she said, grabbing her

keys off the nightstand. "Fine. Go off and hunt, Logan, if that's why you're here. I won't bother you again."

"Sara, be reasonable. Don't leave like this."

She slammed the door. He stood in place and listened as her footsteps thumped down the stairway. Then he didn't hear her anymore.

Wolf whipped the bag across the room. It crashed against the headboard.

He always drove away the people he cared about.

13

The old house lacked air conditioning. Between May and October, when the Texas heat refused to relent, the home's interior felt like a wood stove.

Jacob lay on the cot and watched a winged bug on the ceiling. The insect was unlike any he'd seen before, with turquoise-green scales, over-size eyes that jutted in opposite directions, and translucent wings. He might have considered the creature beautiful. But as it crawled across the cracked ceiling, he wanted to snag the insect and tear its wings off. Slowly. Let the insect suffer, then snap the head off its neck and toss the remains through the open window.

The ceiling groaned when Balor's weight shifted inside the attic. Jacob imagined his brother standing at the window as he always did, staring into the distance, as though waiting for an invisible sign. One of these days, Balor's girth would prove too much for the attic floor, and he'd smash through the ceiling and crush whatever lay below, including Jacob. The fall wouldn't hurt Balor. Nothing did. Jacob once saw Balor drive a nail through his finger while they repaired a loose board in the cellar. The monster didn't scream or wave his hand and fling blood over the walls. Instead, he raised the skewered finger in front of his face and cocked his head, as if piecing together a puzzle.

They'd been on the run since Jacob turned sixteen. Balor was twelve then, and already a foot taller than Jacob. And that was the issue. The boy kept growing and growing, eating the family out of house and home. Busy drinking away their problems, Mother and Father never cared for their children. They rarely called Balor by his name, referring to him as *the freak* whenever the boy turned his back.

Jacob and Balor grew up thirty minutes north of the Texas–Mexico border. Neither attended school. Mother claimed she homeschooled the children, but she couldn't be bothered. Twice a year, she filled out progress reports and sent them to the education department, answering test questions for Jacob and Balor to prove they'd learned something. That kept the authorities at bay, though child services stopped by after several months with concerns. The closest neighbor, a farmer named Clinton, lived a half mile away. He claimed to hear Balor crying and yelling at night.

The social worker who arrived assumed she'd find bruises and lacerations on Balor's body. She didn't. There was no evidence Mother and Father beat their youngest child, because they never physically harmed him. The bruises were mental. Balor screamed for reasons Jacob never understood. Sometimes the boy lumbered outside while everyone was asleep and yelled until his voice fell hoarse.

One month after Jacob's sixteenth birthday, his parents returned home from the bar and discovered a dead cat in the living room. The stray had wandered the property for months, and now it lay on the living room floor with its head twisted one-hundred-eighty degrees. Balor knelt over the cat and didn't respond when their parents demanded answers. That was the night Mother and Father couldn't bear living with Balor. The boy frightened them. Father threw Balor out of the house. The boy didn't fight back. Had Balor done so, he could have snapped Father's neck as easily as he had the cat's. Balor didn't understand the ramifications. He stood in the yard like a statue until Jacob came to him. Jacob couldn't let his simpleton brother wander into the night, so he ran away from home and took Balor with him.

The brothers hitched rides in the backs of hay carts and tractor trailers until they reached San Antonio. Jacob got an overnight job stocking shelves at Walmart, earning just enough money to afford a room at the YMCA. Jacob lied about his age, claiming he was eighteen. He didn't need to. The oaf manning the desk never asked Jacob for identification.

The room wasn't large enough for one boy, let alone two. Cockroaches crawled up and down the walls, and the bunk-bed mattresses stank of puke and urine. All day and night, a slender boy in the next room named Phillip moaned and orgasmed. That was the first time Jacob learned about male prostitution. Morgan, the twenty-something man on the other side of Jacob and Balor, left his door open at all hours of the day. Whenever Jacob passed Morgan's room, the man slumped on the floor with glassy, slitted eyes. Track marks dotted his arms, and when he spoke, it was always in a whisper. Morgan always invited Jacob inside. The man reminded Jacob of the witch from *Hansel and Gretel.*

A shared bathroom and shower stood at the end of the hallway. Jacob didn't trust the showers and often went days without washing until his coworkers complained about the stench. The showers weren't safe. The men who used them were older and bigger than Jacob, and they leered at the boy while he stood nude under the cold spray.

One morning, he returned from work before dawn. He

hadn't showered in a week, and his skin itched so much that he was convinced microscopic bugs were wriggling on his flesh. Everyone in the complex seemed to be asleep. Without waking Balor, whose legs hung off the child-size bunk, Jacob grabbed a towel and a bar of soap and hurried to the showers. He almost wretched when he stepped inside. Someone with diarrhea had filled the toilet without flushing. A flaxen river flowed across the tiles from an overflowed urinal. Jacob walked on tiptoe across the mess and didn't remove his sneakers until he reached the showers.

The frigid spray hit him like tiny ice shards. He scrubbed his body and watched the doorway.

As he rinsed the soap off his face, two shadows filled the entrance. He recognized both—Phillip, the boy who whored himself out next door, and a greasy-haired man from down the hall. Before Jacob could call for help, the man grabbed him from behind and covered his mouth while Phillip punched Jacob in the ribs and drove the air from his lungs. Together, they pulled Jacob to the dingy floor and forced him face-down. The aroused boy unzipped his pants and entered Jacob, while the man kept a hand clutched over Jacob's mouth. The shower continued to spray, with the water running over Jacob's nose and cutting off his air passages. They didn't just mean to rape him. Jacob's attackers would suffocate him.

Phillip pumped his hips and drove Jacob's face against the tiles. They were laughing, even as the boy climaxed. Jacob didn't care if they killed him. He no longer wanted to live.

His eyes drifted shut as he waited for the madness to end. A screech shocked him awake before the greasy-haired man landed in a heap on the floor. The older attacker stared unblinking with his head twisted and pointing in the wrong direction. Phillip's weight lifted off of Jacob. A horrible snapping sound came from behind. Phillip flew and crumpled against the wall.

Jacob scrambled to his knees and found Balor standing over him. In a matter of seconds, the twelve-year-old had murdered Jacob's attackers. Balor extended a meaty hand and hauled up Jacob, whose blood pooled on the floor and circled the drain. Jacob leaned against his brother and panted. It took him several breaths before he comprehended what had happened. Fury burned through his body. He wanted to chop his foes into pieces for what they'd done.

But Jacob was out of time. Soon, his neighbors would awaken and check on the clamor. After they found the dead bodies in the shower, the police would come. There would be questions. The cops wouldn't care that the two attackers had raped Jacob. They'd focus on the murderous twelve-year-old, who almost never spoke.

Jacob grabbed his brother's hand and pulled him out of the bathroom. Balor shuffled behind, stalking past doors that might open at any moment. The monstrous boy didn't care—didn't understand—that they were in trouble. Jacob grabbed his wallet and filled a bag with a change of clothes. They escaped into the predawn cold and never stopped running until they hitched a ride to Austin.

After hiding out all day outside Austin, Jacob spied an empty horse trailer attached to a rusty pickup truck parked at a twenty-four-hour gas station. Keeping his brother quiet, Jacob led Balor into the trailer and closed the door. They hunkered down amid the hay and manure, as horseflies buzzed around their bodies and bit hard, sucking the blood from Jacob's arms and legs. They remained silent until the driver returned and the truck started moving. Balor fell asleep in the corner.

Hours later, Jacob awoke to a truck door slamming. It was dark out, the stars sharp and a silent fog crawling over the plains. Jacob jostled Balor, who muttered in his slumber and turned away. Finally, Balor opened his eyes. They climbed out of the horse trailer. A silo ascended into the night like a silent behemoth. The truck and trailer stood outside an open barn, where horses slept behind closed stalls.

Jacob didn't know where they were, though the flat expanse of land told him they were near the Texas panhandle, a million light-years from the Mexico border. The police must have been searching for the boys. Jacob didn't feel the least bit of guilt. His body filled with power whenever he pictured his broken foes. In this world, only the strong survived. Kill or be killed.

Tasked with putting food on the table and a roof over their heads, Jacob worked construction jobs until he saved enough money to exit the cheap apartment merry-go-round and buy a little house on the Texas Caprock, a million miles away from humanity. The location was perfect. Society wouldn't understand Balor or give him a chance. Here, they could hide from the human race and only venture into the cities when they needed to. Balor was thirteen then. One evening, while Jacob slept off a difficult day hauling lumber, he awakened to Balor in the backyard. The boy had found a dead deer on the prairie, its innards trailing out after a predator with claws and fangs had gotten the best of it. Somehow, Balor had dragged the dead beast from the thicket to the yard, where he used a saw to remove the antlers. Jacob watched Balor through the window while the boy studied the antlers and placed them atop his head, like some insane headdress. Ever since, Balor had continued to bring antlers back to their home, butchering deer when he couldn't find one already dead.

Balor enjoyed killing. As did Jacob. And there was no greater game than man.

Now the trapdoor to the attic opened. Balor's weight dropped and landed in the hallway, rattling the walls. On the ceiling, the strange insect opened its wings and flew through the window, as though it sensed the monster's presence.

Every time Jacob killed, he remembered the people who'd wronged him and left him for dead. His parents, the rapists, the world which tossed Jacob and Balor aside. He'd attained an unquenchable taste for murder. The world deserved pain, and he lived to deliver it.

Outside the window, a crow perched on the tarp-covered car and squawked. Jacob smiled.

The time had come to kill again.

14

S ara refused to let Logan off easily.

　　She parked the Jetta in an alley between a closed five-and-dime store and an empty husk of a building. From here, she observed the Irvin Hotel parking lot until Logan exited the lobby. He paused before he climbed into the Jeep Wrangler. Sara ducked when Logan's head swiveled around, as though he sensed someone spying on him.

The Jeep's engine fired, and the brake lights ignited. Sara waited until the Jeep turned down Highway 6 and exited Dusk Corners.

After Logan's vehicle became a pinprick on the horizon, Sara turned the key and pulled out. She kept her distance. Even hanging five miles behind, she'd be easy to spot in Logan's mirror. She longed for trees and hills and roads that didn't continue arrow-straight into the sun.

As she followed Logan, she studied the terrain. Every few miles, she passed a farm or a sleepy home. The land appeared identical in all directions. She tilted her head. Who was Logan? He couldn't be a police officer or an FBI agent. Logan didn't drive a law enforcement vehicle, and he certainly didn't act like any cop she'd ever known. A private investigator? No, that didn't ring true.

The word *vigilante* kept surfacing in Sara's mind. If Logan was a vigilante, he might be dangerous.

Except he'd helped Sara after her car broke down. She felt an unexplainable connection to Logan, and she didn't regret making love to a man she'd only met yesterday. Remembering sent heat through her cheeks.

In the distance, Logan turned down a farm-to-market road and passed a tractor motoring along the shoulder. Sara slowed, not wanting Logan to spot her in his mirror. The sun glinted off the Jeep's roof, making the Wrangler appear like a shooting star.

Another turn, and Logan rocketed past pumpjacks working in a field of clay. It seemed Logan was treating the area like a grid, marking off each quadrant as he drove. A chill raised goosebumps on her arms. Was he really searching for the Devil's Rock killer? If so, how did he expect to identify the man?

Off to the west, a dust plume rose off the land. Sara assumed another car was kicking up dust, but no vehicle emerged on the horizon. Having almost lost sight of Logan, she concentrated on the road and increased her speed.

Fifteen minutes later, Logan returned to Highway 6 and headed west. When he reached the fork in the road, he veered left and followed the path Sara had taken earlier. She allowed him to race ahead. Wind gusted across the plains and rocked the Jetta, nearly pushing her off the road. She gripped the wheel and regained control of the car, breathing hard.

Checking the sky, Sara considered the puffy cumulus clouds near the Texas–New Mexico border. The strange dust plume had grown. No vehicle could have kicked up that much dust, which extended toward the clouds and curled over like a clawed hand. Sara swallowed. If Logan didn't turn soon, he'd drive into the dust storm.

A second tractor passed Sara, this one headed eastward. The farmer, a bronze-skinned man with a hat angled over his forehead, honked his horn and pointed behind him at the onrushing cloud of dust. Sara raised a hand in acknowledgment, but didn't turn around. A part of her wanted to step on the accelerator and catch up to Logan. He'd be furious that she'd followed him, but Sara had spent several months in West Texas and experienced too many dust storms. The worst storms blinded drivers and toppled cars with severe winds.

Sara blinked when Logan's Jeep vanished. She couldn't tell if the plume had consumed his vehicle. The storm was close now and barreling down the road like a runaway train. Sara checked the mirrors and didn't see the farmer anymore. If only Logan had given Sara his phone number.

She arrived at an intersection and checked in both directions. A blinking yellow traffic light warned her to maintain caution, but she didn't see another vehicle for miles, including Logan's Jeep. She'd lost him.

Sara turned and realized she didn't recognize her surroundings. She raised herself up on her seat and searched the mirror for Highway 6 or some familiar landmark. Beside the road, a lone tree leaned over in the wind, its branches and leaves tearing as the storm closed in. Now the sun vanished. She held her breath as the horizon disappeared behind a blood-red wall of dust and clay. Sara slammed the brakes and turned around. The dust storm cut off all escape routes. As she executed a three-point turn, the rear tires caught and spun on the gravel shoulder.

She zigzagged across the blacktop while sand and rock pelted a stop sign. Overhead, a traffic light swung and whip-snapped. Dust choked the air and turned day into night. A sudden blast of wind threatened to flip the car. She screamed and wrestled with the steering wheel. Sand and tumbleweeds ripped across the Jetta's hood and smothered the windshield. The car hit something solid in the road and bucked up. When the tires crashed down, she spun the wheel in the opposite direction.

She needed to stop. Driving blindly would get her killed.

Sara kicked the brake a second too late. A sense of weightlessness shot butterflies through her stomach. Then the car dropped into a ditch and pitched forward, slamming Sara's head against the steering wheel. Blood poured from her nose as a shrill whine tore through the engine.

The wind's roar came from all directions. Sara covered her ears and cried, unable to see past the hood. Clay and sand choked the air like a swarm of bees. She'd never considered herself religious, but in that moment, she accepted she was in God's hands. The wheels spun when she stepped on the gas. It was impossible to see the dashboard lights through glassy eyes, though the red and orange warning lights told her there was a serious problem with the car.

Sara had two choices: try to drive the Jetta out of the ditch, or wait the storm out. The latter seemed like an obvious choice, except the shrieking wind threatened to roll the car over. By now, sand and clay were filling the engine.

Using her shirt, she wiped away blood and tears. An impenetrable red wall shot across the car, the gale a devil's scream. She covered her ears and willed the madness to stop. It didn't. A road sign she couldn't read tore from the earth and ripped past her windshield, missing the glass by inches.

Then it became deathly quiet.

After the storm abated, Sara sat ramrod straight with both hands squeezed around the steering wheel. The sky cleared. To the east, the wall of red advanced on Dusk Corners.

"Texas," she said to herself. "I have to get the hell out of here."

Her voice sounded impossibly loud inside the car. A nervous chuckle escaped her parched throat. She shifted into drive, rocked forward, then reversed. The Jetta's wheels spun on silt and sand. Now that the dust had cleared, she noticed the car's front end had lodged against the upper half of the ditch, suspending the Jetta.

Sara stomped the gas pedal and attempted to free the car. The wheels refused to catch.

Now what? Nobody knew she was out here. Not her parents, not the police, not even Logan. The temperature rose inside the car as the air conditioner refused to turn on.

The engine shut down. Her eyes darted between the ignition and the dashboard's warning lights. Sara twisted the key. Nothing happened. The Jetta had died on this desolate road in the middle of nowhere.

She pounded the steering wheel and cried in frustration. Unable to start the car, she'd need to walk back to Dusk Corners. Except she didn't know where Dusk Corners was, and she couldn't find her phone. The damn thing must have fallen under the seat when she stupidly drove into the ditch. Her best chance of retrieving the phone was to climb out of the car and shove her arm beneath the seat.

Sara pushed the door open. With the bottom of the door jammed against the ditch, she squeezed through the opening, straining and crying when her hip caught. She'd almost escaped the trap when a motor rumbled behind her. Thank goodness someone had come along to help.

"Please, I'm over here," she said. "I lost control of my car and can't start the engine."

She craned her head and spotted a dusty black Dodge Ram parked in the middle of the road. The doors opened, and two men stepped out. A skinny man leered at Sara with hungry deviance coloring his eyes. The other towered over the truck, like a giant from a childhood nightmare. The humongous man clutched a knife.

Sara screamed.

15

S carlett Bell wheeled her carry-on through the Amarillo airport and down a polished corridor. The plane had encountered turbulence before landing, and her stomach continued to flutter from the pitching and jostling. She skipped the sandwich kiosk and opted for a ginger smoothie. The girl who blended the smoothie couldn't have been older than eighteen. She wore her purple hair in a bob, the bangs dangling over one eye. Her nose was pierced, and a punk rocker with a spiked hair adorned her shirt. Bell dropped five dollars in the tip jar. She sipped the drink as she followed the signs through the concourse.

Her phone hummed with received messages. Gardy kept checking in on her. By now, he'd figured out that Bell wasn't spending a relaxing day on the beach or visiting her parents. She switched her phone to silent mode and kept walking.

Halfway through the concourse, she passed a miniature mall selling overpriced luggage, clothing, and jewelry. To her right, a sitting area with dozens of open chairs beckoned. She slid into a seat and opened her laptop, which connected to the airport's free Wi-Fi. A teenage boy with braces watched Bell from beside his mother, who read a gossip magazine. Bell ignored the boy and turned the laptop away from his prying eyes. She skimmed her notes and followed Logan Wolf's money trail from the northern plains southward, unable to prove the fugitive was tracking the Devil's Rock killer. Her instincts filled in the gaps. She knew Wolf better than any FBI agent. He was heading to the caprock.

Bell perused her bookmarks and opened a website run by amateur sleuths. She'd learned about the site from a teenage girl named Scout Mourning, who Bell was helping prepare for a future FBI career. The website specialized in tracking fugitives on the most wanted list. Bell sifted through the forum with a critical eye—the excitable posters often exaggerated, and much of the information turned out to be unreliable. After typing Logan Wolf's name into the search bar, the screen filled with results.

"You have quite a fan club, Logan," Bell said, smirking.

She scanned the sightings and drummed a nervous foot against the carpeted floor. These were false leads. One member claimed he'd spotted Wolf in California seven weeks ago, the same week Wolf had accessed funds in Georgia, thirty miles south of where the FBI discovered another dead serial killer.

A recent message pulled Bell's attention. The sleuth mentioned a television interview with the owner of a Texas diner, where a man resembling Logan Wolf supposedly ate lunch. According to the report, Wolf left the diner with a young woman and drove out of town in a Jeep Wrangler.

Wolf was a loner, and Bell couldn't picture the fugitive dining with a woman, let alone leaving with her. But the location seemed right. Bell searched Google and found the diner on the map just north of Lubbock. Though it seemed risky for Wolf to enter a diner, even serial killers needed to eat. Bell marked the location and connected the dots between Colorado and the northern plains. If the report was valid, Wolf might have arrived at the caprock yesterday.

Closing the laptop, Bell wheeled her luggage past the baggage claim area. She rented a car and crossed the parking lot, where she loaded her bag into an SUV with a dented bumper. The Caprock murders had occurred in Pronghorn County.

Wolf was the proverbial needle in the haystack. In order to track Wolf, she'd need to find his target: the Devil's Rock killer.

Not expecting an answer, Bell dialed the last number Wolf had given her and tapped her foot as the phone rang in her ear. No answer. By now, Wolf had disposed of the prepaid phone and purchased another. He'd share the number with Bell when he needed her for something, and not until then. And that made her wonder how much he'd already learned about the Devil's Rock killer.

Google told her the county sheriff's name was Edward Rosario. Bell backed out of the parking space and drove to the highway. The sheriff wouldn't appreciate the FBI showing up on his doorstep without an invitation, but he'd just have to deal with it.

But how would she introduce herself without alerting Quantico that she was researching a murder case off the books?

WOLF EASED the Jeep out of the old barn. He'd spotted the dust storm raking the plains and driven inside the barn to escape the weather. The two-story house beside the road stood in disrepair, with missing shingles on the roof and a broken window along the side of the house. The home appeared abandoned.

Sand and clay covered the stone driveway like fallen snow. The Jeep's wheels spun on the grit before catching and carrying him back to the road. Wolf stopped at the next intersection. A snapped wire lay across the road, sparking and hissing dragon's fire. He backed up and turned around, choosing an alternate route back to Dusk Corners.

He drove with the windows open and the afternoon heat blasting through the vehicle. There was too much sand plastered against the side windows to observe the countryside. He checked the mirror as he tracked toward Highway 6 and rubbed the leg of his pants. Before the storm struck, he'd glimpsed Sara's car following him. She'd stayed several miles behind, but nobody followed the serial killer without him noticing. Now the road was empty.

He swung the Jeep around and retraced his route, finding no sign of the Jetta. Then he crisscrossed farm-to-market roads, concentrating on the area worst hit by the storm. Sand and clay lay across the blacktop. He slowed the Jeep and cleared the obstruction, cursing beneath his breath. Why did Sara insist on following him? Even worse, what if she told the police?

She wouldn't. Though they'd only known each other for a short time, Sara wouldn't turn on him because he'd offended her.

She wanted to accompany him. What if he'd said yes? Wolf didn't wish to spend his remaining days alone. Yet he couldn't accept Sara's company. Every law enforcement officer in the United States was searching for him, and his work was too dangerous.

He rubbed his belly when the stabbing pain returned. In a fantasy world, Wolf located the Devil's Rock killer and ended the nightmare. He took Sara by the hand, and together, they traveled the country and settled somewhere far from murder and tragedy. He used his underworld connections to establish a new identity. Maybe there was a future with Sara, the woman who reminded him so much of his dead wife.

Wolf saw no sense in imagining the impossible. If whatever ailed Wolf didn't kill him this year, the job would.

After another hour of scouring the countryside, Wolf drove back to Dusk Corners. As the Jeep approached the hotel, he hoped he'd find Sara's Jetta in the parking lot. He'd apologize, and she'd forgive him. Whatever happened next, he'd accept. But the Jetta wasn't in the parking lot when Wolf stopped the Jeep.

Inside the lobby, he approached the desk and asked Chapman if Sara had returned to the hotel.

"You mean your daughter?" Chapman asked with a tight smile.

"She drove west before the storm hit. I'm worried she got trapped."

"She didn't stop by the hotel, Mr. Weber. If she's missing, contact the sheriff."

"Listen, if she stops by while I'm out, tell her to wait. Give her a key to my room."

"As you wish, but a missing woman is a police matter."

16

Pete Chapman busied himself behind the check-in desk until the man who called himself Don Weber climbed the staircase and closed his door. The hotel proprietor set his pen down and padded silently to the staircase, where he ensured Weber wasn't in the hallway, listening.

For twenty-two years, Chapman had owned the Irvin Hotel. Before that, his father had run the place, after Granddaddy Chapman founded the operation in 1962. The hotel did a fair business, reeling in the occasional traveler on his way to New Mexico. During hunting season, he sold out for three weeks. The business paid the bills and kept food on the table. Chapman had no aspirations of becoming rich or selling out to Hilton or Marriott, though the big chains sent representatives every few years to make him an offer. He was used to strangers visiting Dusk Corners. But he didn't trust this Don Weber fellow, and he didn't believe the woman who'd visited was his daughter. If Weber was shacking up with a mistress and cheating on his wife, Chapman didn't care. That was Weber's business. Chapman just didn't want Weber in his hotel. The stranger seemed untrustworthy, the shady type who'd jam a knife into

Chapman's ribcage when he turned his back. Plus, Weber had mentioned those missing kids from the news. Nobody should ask about a couple of missing college students except cops and reporters, and Chapman didn't reckon Weber was either.

Sheriff Rosario was a no-nonsense lawman. He'd want to check up on Weber and find out why the man was really here. If Chapman identified a potential problem for Rosario, the sheriff would remember Chapman's good deed. It paid to have friends in high places.

He grabbed his cell phone and stepped outside, then punched the ten-digit number on the keypad and waited.

"Pronghorn County Sheriff's Department," the woman said. "How may I direct your call?"

"Put me through to Sheriff Rosario."

"The sheriff is busy this afternoon. Who may I ask is calling?"

"Tell him Pete Chapman from the Irvin Hotel is on the phone."

Silence followed. Thirty seconds later, the sheriff answered in a gruff voice.

"Sheriff, this is Pete Chapman."

"Who?"

The proprietor cleared his throat. "Pete Chapman, from the Irvin Hotel." After Rosario didn't respond, he added, "In Dusk Corners on Highway 6."

"Right, I remember you. Why are you bothering me? My hands are full this week."

"There's a guy staying at the hotel that you should check into."

"Is he causing trouble?"

"He's an out-of-towner named Don Weber. Came into Dusk Corners yesterday and booked four nights. He's snooping around, and I don't trust him."

Rosario harrumphed. "Probably a news reporter. They're like roaches. Once you see one, you can bet there's a hundred more hiding beneath the refrigerator."

"I don't think he's a reporter."

"Law enforcement?"

"Doesn't seem the type."

"You trained in spotting law enforcement, Mr. Chapman?"

Rosario's curt reply hung suspended like a guillotine. Chapman hadn't expected the sheriff to blow him off.

"Well, uh, no. But he had a woman up to his room. Claims she's his daughter, but they don't look a bit alike, and I gather he's fond of her."

"So he's banging some hookup he met. Unless he committed a crime—"

"Don't you want to know why he's here, Sheriff? He leaves the hotel for hours at a time, driving west on Highway 6. Then he returns and locks himself in his room. There's nothing west of Dusk Corners except farmland and prairie. What do you suppose he's doing out there?" Rosario didn't take the bait, so Chapman added, "He asked about those two college kids that disappeared between here and Roswell."

Rosario fell silent. Chapman could hear the gears churning inside the sheriff's head.

"He's looking into those missing college kids, you say?"

"Weber showed me a picture of them. Asked if they'd rented a room at the hotel on their way to New Mexico. I said they hadn't, but that didn't satisfy him."

"Four nights. That's a long time to stay in Dusk Corners outside of hunting season. Tell you what, Mr. Chapman, you got me interested in this fellow. As I said, my plate is full today. No chance I'll make it out your way before tomorrow or the next day. Whenever Weber comes and goes, note the time and save it for me."

"I can do that, Sheriff."

"Good, Chapman. And if you happen to know the make and model of his vehicle . . ."

"I got it right here. It's a black Jeep Wrangler."

"Got the plate number on this Jeep Wrangler?" The hotel proprietor read the number to Rosario. "If Weber checks out early, I want to know about it. You got that, Chapman?"

"Right away, Sheriff. Anytime you need a second set of eyes in Dusk Corners, all you need to do is ask."

"I'll keep it in mind."

Before Chapman could reply, the sheriff hung up.

17

Sara's arms stretched until she feared they might tear from their sockets. She blinked, took in the dusty, unrecognizable room, and blinked again. Where was she?

She struggled to lower her arms, but a long rope, which looped over an industrial-size hook on the ceiling, bound her wrists above her head. Across the room, the largest set of deer antlers Sara had ever seen hung on the wall, the tips like knives. Goosebumps covered her body as she stared at the antlers, as though the great beast they'd belonged to would smash through the wall and reclaim them, then set its sight on Sara. Hazy light filtered through a dirty window, marking the time as morning, meaning she'd slept a long time. Unspoken evil pervaded the room. It tainted every inch of plaster and floorboard and draped like a shroud over Sara. Intuition told her unspeakable things had happened in this room.

She recalled the dust storm and the Jetta breaking down after she crashed into the ditch. A truck stopped in the road, and two men climbed out of the cab, one so humongous she'd thought she must be dreaming. The monstrous man carried a knife. Sara shut the door and engaged the locks before a fist shattered the window. That was the last thing she remembered. They'd kidnapped her.

Sara tugged on the bindings. The ropes provided enough slack for her to wander several steps to either side of the hook. There wasn't a bed in the room. A wooden chair with one leg shorter than the others wobbled against the wall. A chemical toilet festered behind her, drawing flies.

She gagged when the stench of vomit hit her. After her attackers tied her in this room, she'd puked, though she didn't remember when. Dream-like memories drifted back to her— Sara screaming as they dragged her down a dimly-lit hallway, a skinny man with a scar down his face binding her wrists with the rope and warning her not to fight.

Every inhalation made her ribs ache. She'd broken two ribs after falling off her bicycle when she was eight, and figured twice as many ribs had shattered when the men dragged her through the Jetta's window.

As a curious fly buzzed outside her ear, a scorpion scurried across the bare floor and stopped inches from her sneaker. Sara kicked at the scorpion, which raised its stinger and poised for an attack. Another kick, and the scorpion shot off into the far corner of the room.

A closed window hung against the near wall. She strained against the ropes, but they stopped her two steps from the pane. Her head spun, and she wanted to vomit again. Sara swallowed the bile and crouched until the dizzy spell passed. It had to be eighty-five degrees in the room. No air conditioner or wind to help her breathe. Sweat trickled down her brow and burned her eyes. Overhead, the ceiling groaned as a great weight shifted. Her mind wandered back to her childhood and the *Three Billy Goats Gruff* fairytale that always gave her nightmares. Now she imagined the hungry troll above the ceiling, waiting for Sara to escape and wander past, so it could devour her, bones and all.

Footsteps in the hallway pulled her back to the present. They paused outside the door before the knob turned.

She retreated until the ropes prevented her from escaping. The door swung open and revealed the skinny man from the Dodge Ram. A bucket dangled from one hand. His eyes ran up and down Sara's body while he lingered in the entryway. Slipping into the room, he placed an index finger against his lips and edged the door shut. There was a bolt on the door, and he turned it.

The kidnapper crossed the room, still holding the bucket. Sara's lips quivered. Now he stood face-to-face with Sara, his breath stinking of steaming carrion on a hot summer's day.

"Get away."

"Shh," he said, stealing a look over his shoulder. "You need to be quiet, so he doesn't hear you."

"So who doesn't hear me?"

"My brother."

A sheathed knife jutted out of the man's pocket.

"Why are you doing this? You can't just grab stranded motorists and take them home. The police will search for me."

"Keep your voice down. If he finds out you're awake, he'll kill you."

"Your brother? Why would he want to kill me?"

The man lifted a shoulder and smirked, unveiling yellow, crooked teeth. "He doesn't trust strangers." The man touched her face with a scabby thumb. "But I do, and I won't let him hurt you. My name is Jacob. What's your name?"

Sara didn't want to tell him her name, as if doing so would lend him unlimited power over her. With her hands tied, she couldn't defend herself. Jacob caressed her cheek.

"Tell me your name."

"Amy," Sara said, reciting the first name that popped into her head.

His hand moved around her neck and squeezed, cutting off her airflow. "Don't you lie to me. Your name is Sara Brennan, and you live in Lubbock. I read your driver's license. You're a long way from home, Sara Brennan."

He released his grip. Sara hacked and coughed as she sucked air into her lungs. He covered her mouth with his palm and placed his forefinger against his lips again.

"I warned you to be quiet." He held his palm in place until the coughing fit ended. "Are you finished?"

She nodded.

"There's no reason to lie. I won't hurt you as long as you cooperate. We'll have lots of fun, you and I. I know what women like."

Not taking his eyes off her, Jacob bent down and reached inside the bucket. He squeezed water from the sponge and stood.

Jacob shook his head and said, "You made a mess of yourself. Don't worry. I'll clean you."

He brushed the dried vomit from her lips and cheek, wrung the sponge, and dabbed her face. The cool water lowered Sara's body temperature and stopped the room from spinning. He continued to clean her face and neck, then dropped the sponge in the bucket.

"Please let me go. I won't tell anyone, I promise."

"You're sweaty and filthy. That won't do."

His hands dropped to her hips and slipped inside the waistband of her jeans. Jacob's fingers crawled and groped like hungry spiders. As she sobbed, he unbuttoned her jeans and slid them down to her ankles. He wrung the sponge again and moved it up and down her legs, pausing at the tops of her thighs. It occurred to Sara that he'd tainted the water with her vomit, and now he was spreading the dirty sponge over her legs. Satisfied, Jacob turned his attention to Sara's shirt. He licked his lips.

"Stop. Don't do this."

"Let me clean you, so we can enjoy our time together."

He pulled her shirt past her aching ribs and yanked it over her head. The shirt dangled off her wrists, held in place by the ropes.

Sara winced. "It hurts."

"If you're a good girl, I'll untie you. Would you like that, Sara?"

She hated when he spoke her name. Every time he did, it defiled her.

The emaciated man scrubbed her skin with the sponge, leaving the bra in place. She expected he'd remove the bra next. He circled behind and hovered over her shoulders, his hips pressed against her. Gently, he sponged off her back while he ground his hips, panting.

Above them, footsteps trailed across the ceiling. Jacob froze.

He grabbed Sara and spun her around to face him. "I can't stop him if he comes for you." Jacob brushed his hand over his face and glanced away, carrying on a conversation with himself. "This isn't fair. I haven't had enough time with her."

Sara thought of Logan, the mysterious man who'd claimed he came to West Texas to hunt. Though he refused to acknowledge he was tracking the Devil's Rock killer, he never denied it. Sara had never depended on anyone, let alone a man she'd just met, to take care of her. But now she squinted her eyes shut and prayed Logan would hear her plea from across the plains and save her. Were these the men Logan hunted? For nine years, the newspapers had claimed a single murderer stalked the back roads of the Caprock. What if they were wrong? What if there were two killers? Brothers. The possibility that she'd fallen into the hands of the men who'd terrorized the state for almost a decade rocketed Sara's pulse. When her eyes popped open,

Jacob was staring at her. Perhaps she could fool him into letting her go.

"Untie me. Let me go before your brother takes me. I'll run away and wait for you. We can be alone, just the two of us." Hope sprang in Jacob's eyes. "There must be someplace safe for me to hide nearby. Tell me, and I promise I'll wait for you."

"You'd do that for me?"

"You seem like a nice guy, Jacob. I'm sure you don't want to hurt anyone. Tell me where to go. Just untie me before your brother comes."

His Adam's apple pulsed. Sara was certain he'd untie her before Jacob drew his mouth firm and wagged a finger.

"Oh, no, you don't. I won't let you fool me." He unsheathed the knife and set the blade's edge against her throat. "I'll cut you and watch you bleed. Then I can do whatever I want to you. You ever have sex with the dead, Sara? The body stays warm longer than you'd believe."

Jacob squeezed the knife, ready to open Sara's throat. He stopped when a squealing noise pulled his head around. It sounded as if a door had opened . . . the trap door to the attic.

The kidnapper's lips peeled back. "Or maybe I'll let my brother finish you off. You shouldn't have lied to me."

18

L ogan Wolf turned onto his side and blinked. After a night of tossing and turning, he'd forced himself to sleep for two hours this morning. A migraine throbbed behind his eyes as he squinted at the light washing over the window.

He lifted himself onto his elbows and waited until the haze of exhaustion faded. His laptop stood open on the desk, the Devil's Rock case files displayed on the screen. Wolf massaged his temples and thought of Sara, still worried she'd broken down or lost her way in the dust storm. That didn't explain why he hadn't found her car after retracing his route. He hoped she'd given up following him and left, figuring Wolf wasn't worth the effort after the way he'd spoken to her. But Sara wasn't the type to surrender easily.

As Wolf dropped his legs off the bed, he spied a folded sheet of paper sticking out from beneath the lamp. He hadn't noticed the paper last evening, when he'd felt too sick to think straight. Plucking the paper between his thumb and forefinger, Wolf identified the Irvin Lodge emblem across the top. The paper had come from the complimentary memo pad.

He unfolded the note and focused his eyes. Someone had scrawled a phone number across the page in a woman's handwriting. Yesterday, before Wolf woke up beside Sara, she'd scribbled her number on the memo pad and left it for him to find. He set the paper on the nightstand and dug through his bag for the burner phone. Sara wouldn't want to speak to him after the way they'd left things yesterday. At least he could confirm she was safe and inside her Lubbock apartment, even if she cursed him for his callousness.

Moving his vision between the screen and the paper, he entered the number and pressed the phone to his ear. The phone rang until Sara's voicemail greeting invited him to leave a message. He paused, unsure of what to say. A beep announced it was time for him to talk or hang up.

"Sara, it's me. Logan. I found your number. You probably don't want to speak to me, and I don't blame you after the way I acted. Please call and let me know you made it out of the storm yesterday."

He pressed the END icon and chided himself for not apologizing. Maybe he should call her back.

No, it was better to give her time. Sara would return his call when she was ready. If he didn't hear from Sara by this afternoon, he'd call again. Wolf folded the paper and slid it inside his wallet. As he sat down at the desk and skimmed his case notes, his gaze drifted back to the burner phone, willing it to ring.

The Kimberly Ripa case file dated back six years. In her photograph, she wore blonde curls down to her shoulders and a genuine, kind smile that invoked trust in others. The twenty-nine-year-old woman was unmarried and sang with the church choir.

Sheriff Edward Rosario of Pronghorn County had investigated the murder. Rosario stated in his notes that he believed the killer had abducted Ripa from her home, though the sheriff's department never found evidence of a break-in. In the West Texas countryside, people trusted their neighbors. It wouldn't surprise Wolf to learn that many left their doors unlocked.

He copied Kimberly Ripa's address and called up the location on a map. The house was a twenty-five-minute drive from Dusk Corners. A property records search confirmed the house had never sold.

Wolf shut down the laptop and considered whether it was safe to leave the computer unattended inside the hotel room. He'd secured the computer with a sixteen-digit password. If the hotel proprietor snooped inside Wolf's room, he wouldn't be able to crack the password.

When Wolf crossed the lobby, Chapman glanced up from the check-in desk.

"Morning, Mr. Weber. Ever locate your daughter?"

"I'm still searching," Wolf said, exiting the door before Chapman could interrogate him further.

The GPS directed him southwest of Dusk Corners, past the barn he'd hid inside to escape yesterday's dust storm. He studied the clouds as he drove, wary of more violent weather. The forecast on the radio called for severe storms by evening.

Kimberly Ripa's house was a brown ranch-style home two miles from the nearest town. The closest neighbor lived three-quarters of a mile away. Wolf pulled the Jeep into the driveway and stepped onto the crumbling blacktop. Weeds shot up in the middle of the driveway, and a gopher hole lay beside the house. As Wolf shielded his eyes from the sun, a tanker truck blasted past, followed by a farmer dragging a hay cart. In the distance, a metallic-green Camaro raced down a stretch of open roadway. Between the agriculture, tanker trucks, and kids hot-rodding, it wouldn't be easy for the killer to observe Ripa without drawing attention.

Wolf peeked through the living room window. Plastic

sheets covered the furniture. Shadows blanketed the rear of the room and the hallway leading deeper into the home. After he peeked over his shoulder, Wolf slipped on gloves and tested the door. Locked. Before he could pick the lock, another tanker truck thundered down the road. Wolf slipped around the house and checked each window, searching for a way inside.

After rounding the home, he found a small grove clustered at the back of Ripa's property. Here, the trees grew thick enough to conceal the killer while he'd spied on Ripa, except the only window looked into the kitchen. The yard rose in elevation by fifteen or twenty feet between the house and the grove.

Wolf ensured nobody stopped to see who had parked in the driveway of the abandoned home. The lawn grew past his knees, yellowed and withered, the weeds choking out the grass and sprouting like insurgent soldiers. A decaying picnic table stood behind the house. The wind had flipped the benches over. Bumblebees flared in an angry cloud as he approached. He noted the ground nest and avoided the bees, pushing through the overgrown yard until he reached the grove.

Bushy junipers crowded against bur oaks. The temperature dropped fifteen degrees inside the grove, though it was still hot enough to slick his back with sweat. Above his head, a woodpecker rattled.

Wolf closed his eyes and pictured the yard as the killer had. The killer would have stalked Ripa at night after she returned from work, sticking to the backyard to avoid being seen. In Wolf's mind, a light shone through the kitchen window, reflecting a yellow rectangle over the lawn, as May beetles and mosquitoes tapped against the glass, vying for a way inside.

The killer might have leaned against the bur oak that Wolf stood beside, one arm balanced on the trunk as he stared between the boughs. Wolf scratched a mosquito bite. He pictured Ripa at the sink, washing the dinner dishes, unaware of the madman lurking behind the trees.

Sheriff Rosario had photographed and measured two gigantic boot prints between the grove and the house, where rains had muddied and softened the earth. Wolf emerged from the grove and tracked through the field. After he located where Rosario had discovered the boot prints, Wolf realized he couldn't see into the kitchen. The window stood high off the ground. Even standing on tiptoe, he only viewed the top of the refrigerator.

He pulled a digital voice recorder from his pocket and lifted the microphone to his lips.

"The unsub is a large man, six-foot-eight or taller. He'd need to be to see inside the kitchen. The sheriff measured the imprints and estimated the boot size at twenty-four. But that was in the mud, and it's possible the prints expanded or the sheriff screwed up." Wolf drifted toward the back door. "The killer is disorganized. The extreme violence of the murders aligns with the Cleveland killer. This unsub can't control his urges, and he's prone to fits of rage. Except . . ." Wolf narrowed his eyes. "Law enforcement has been searching for the unsub for almost a decade, and nobody can find him. Disorganized serial killers don't clean up after themselves. They leave evidence behind. But this guy doesn't."

A black cloud moved over the sun and cast a long shadow across the land. Wolf picked the lock on the back entrance and stood aside when the door drifted inward.

"He watched Kimberly Ripa through the kitchen window. She didn't see him come out of the woods because it was dark, and the kitchen light was on."

Wolf knelt and touched the jamb with a gloved hand.

"No signs of forced entry. Ripa remained active in her church and trusted people. That's why she left the doors unlocked. The killer had watched her enough times that he knew the back door would be open, and the neighbors live too far away to hear screaming from inside the kitchen." Wolf loomed in the entryway. "Ripa saw him in the doorway and panicked. Before she reacted, he crossed the floor and knocked her unconscious, then dragged her away. Why didn't anyone notice his vehicle? He couldn't have taken her on foot."

Wolf ran his thumb over a chip on the counter. "The unsub has a low IQ and can't control his urges. Yet he never leaves evidence, and the police and FBI can't catch him. What am I missing?"

He raised his camera and shot photographs of the kitchen. After he retraced his steps to the forest, he took more pictures.

Wolf waited until the road was clear and pulled out of the driveway. He dialed Sara's number and got her voicemail again. This time, he didn't leave a message. He hoped she was back at her apartment and ignoring his calls, angry over their last conversation. The alternative was she'd gotten lost or stranded in yesterday's storm.

But if that was the case, why hadn't he found her?

19

Another message from Agent Neil Gardy buzzed on Scarlett Bell's phone as she sat in her rental vehicle outside the Pronghorn County Sheriff's Office. She sent an apologetic reply, lying that her phone had been recharging all morning. With the time zone difference, it was almost dinnertime on the east coast. Gardy wouldn't buy Bell's excuses, but it was the best she could come up with while she focused her energy on locating Logan Wolf.

The sheriff's office sat inside a long building, fronted by alpine-colored bricks. A fleet of brown-and-white SUV cruisers, bearing the sheriff department's logo, took up the parking spaces closest to the entryway. A newly planted cherry tree bloomed beside the walkway, and the sharp scent of black mulch rose to Bell's nostrils.

She bounced her knees below the steering wheel. Before arriving, she hadn't considered what she'd tell the sheriff when she introduced herself. She couldn't show Rosario a picture of Logan Wolf and claim Wolf was a missing friend. Rosario might recognize the fugitive from the most wanted list. She'd yet to concoct a convincing story to explain why she was in Pronghorn County and poking her nose into the Devil's Rock murders.

After a deep breath, she stepped into the parking lot and followed the concrete walkway to the doors. In the entryway, she pressed the buzzer and identified herself, displaying her FBI badge to a security camera mounted in the upper corner. A copper-skinned woman wearing a beige tulip skirt directed Bell down the hall, where two deputies in hats watched Bell until she stopped outside the sheriff's office. She wiped sweaty palms against her pants before rapping her knuckles on the door.

"Come in," a gravely voice said from behind the door.

Bell turned the handle. Inside, she found an impeccably clean office. Folders held every slip of paperwork. A cup held pens, and the IT staff had placed the computer beneath the desk, with only the flat-screen monitor, keyboard, and mouse visible. Placards and awards hung from the walls.

The man behind the desk had sun-parched, leathery skin and eyes that would make an eagle appear placid. Rosario appeared to be in his mid-fifties, close to his retirement age. Broad shoulders framed a powerful chest, and his long legs brushed the bottom of the desk. The chair squealed when he shifted his weight.

"Well," Rosario said, leaning forward. "I never requested FBI assistance. May I ask what you're doing in my county?"

"I'm not here on official business, Sheriff."

"You just happened to be in the area and stopped in to say hello? No matter." He directed a hand at the open chair across from his desk. "Where are my manners? Sit."

Bell dropped into the chair. The sheriff's gaze never strayed from her.

"My administrative assistant announced you as a federal agent," Rosario said. "May I see your identification?"

Bell removed her ID and handed it across the desk to Rosario.

"Agent Scarlett Bell, with the Behavioral Analysis Unit," he said, examining the ID, as though searching for a flaw. He gave it back to Bell. "Where have I heard that name?" Bell hoped Rosario hadn't read the exploitive tabloid articles. "You're not here to profile me, are you, Agent Bell?"

Rosario's stare burned holes through Bell, belying his grin.

"No, sir."

"Just a little law enforcement humor. People claim I take my job too seriously. They just don't know me well enough. What may I do for you, Agent Bell, and why are you in my humble county?"

"My family lives outside Amarillo," she said. "I'm on leave and visiting my cousins for a few days. I drove to the Caprock to ask about the unsolved murders."

Rosario's face changed, flashing anger for a split-second before he composed himself.

"The murders. You told me you aren't visiting on official business."

"I'm not."

"Then educate me, because I don't understand why you're in my office inquiring about my investigation."

Bell coughed into her hand. "I teach new recruits about criminal profiling. We're using the Devil's Rock investigation as a case study."

"A case study," Rosario repeated, drumming his fingers on the desk.

"That's correct."

"Then you don't need me. The FBI twice investigated the Caprock murders. Under my supervision, of course. You have access to the FBI files."

"I do, sir. Stop me if I'm wrong, but you're the only law

enforcement officer to investigate every murder. Therefore, you can offer insights and opinions that aren't available in FBI case files." Rosario didn't reply. "Your expertise is invaluable."

"Sounds to me like you're trying to catch a killer, not teach a course."

"Catching your killer isn't my job, Sheriff. Not unless you request my presence. But we'll study the case in class, and I'm happy to share our findings, even if they're unofficial. Anything I can do to help."

Rosario shifted his jaw and leaned back in his chair, fingers clasped behind his head. "I doubt a class full of trainees can shed light on our murders. But if you want my opinion, I'll give it to you. There is no Devil's Rock killer, Agent Bell. There never was, and that's why your organization can't catch him."

Bell blinked. "But there have been eight murders over the last nine years."

"Committed by different perpetrators, yes. See, that's where the FBI gets it wrong. You're no better than the media, fanning the flames and turning the murders into ghost stories. Pronghorn County has its share of challenges. Mexican cartels run drugs through Texas. Two militia groups cause trouble in the panhandle. And that's not including dangerous transients who move through the county."

"I don't understand. The female victims were raped, and every murder involved extreme violence. The killer impaled Riley and Luis Domin on stakes and severed Kimberly Ripa's head. That sounds like the actions of a deranged unsub."

Rosario shook his head. "Save the fancy jargon for Quantico, Agent Bell. We're not looking for one murderer, or unsub, as you insist on calling him. Multiple killers committed those crimes."

"Then why do the murders share similarities?"

"All violent offenders are the same. They care not for human life."

Bell sat forward and folded her hands in her lap. "Why would a militia group murder Riley and Luis Domin? Why would a drug cartel break inside Kimberly Ripa's house and cut her head off?"

"Maybe they all witnessed things they shouldn't have seen. You're over-thinking. If one killer murdered all those people, why does he rape the women he disfigures? He can't be lustful and repulsed at the same time."

Bell bit her tongue. Arguing would get her nowhere, though it shocked Bell that Rosario refused to acknowledge the obvious. One killer stalked the Caprock. For nine years, he'd evaded the authorities. Perhaps that's why Rosario clung to the multiple-killer-theory. He couldn't admit he'd failed to solve a famous case.

None of that mattered. Bell had come to Pronghorn County to find the killer before something terrible happened to Logan Wolf.

"That's a fair point," Bell said through gritted teeth. "I'll include your opinion during my next lecture. Off the record, of course."

"Given enough time, you'll see I'm right."

"Fascinating. Multiple murders committed in a single county created an urban legend."

"An urban legend, yes. That's a good way to put it."

Bell pointed at Rosario. "You know, I can teach an entire class about this topic: how the media influences law enforcement and public opinion, creating monsters where none exist. I never considered that the murders were unrelated."

"Now you understand what I'm up against, and why it's so difficult to catch these criminals."

"I'm curious, Sheriff. After you discovered Kimberly Ripa's body, how did you know the killer had abducted Kimberly Ripa from her home?"

"As I recall, there was no sign of a break-in. But I found boot prints in the mud behind her house." Rosario snapped his fingers. "You want more proof that different people killed those victims? I measured the boot prints from Ripa's backyard at size twenty-four. But there was a size-eleven sneaker print at the quarry when we pulled the Domin family out of the pit."

"I wasn't aware of that," Bell said, confused. "Why isn't the print size noted in the FBI case file?"

"Because it didn't fit your narrative. The agents expected a size twenty-four print, like the one I found at Ripa's house."

"Are you certain a quarry worker didn't leave the print? There's no guarantee the sneaker print belonged to the killer."

"Don't make the same mistake your coworkers made. The prints I measured from the Ripa and Domin cases were too dissimilar. Perhaps you believe the killer shrunk to half his height between the Domin and Ripa murders. That seem plausible to you, Agent Bell?"

"What about Brady Endieveri and Sheila Jarvis?"

Rosario folded his arms. "What about them?"

"They've been missing for over a week now. Is it possible the drug cartel or militia took them, too?"

"Or they're in New Mexico, sleeping off a bender. Check your facts. Endieveri and Jarvis were driving to a music festival in Roswell. You'll find enough narcotics at those festivals to keep a small country high."

"Why haven't they posted to social media or contacted their families?"

"I'm just as concerned as you are, Agent Bell. I sent patrol units down Highway 6 to search for their vehicle. Those kids aren't in my county. If they were, I'd have found them by now."

"Interesting. Highway 6, that's near Midland, correct?"

"Negative. Highway 6 runs through Dusk Corners and Joliet. If they were driving to New Mexico, they likely took that route."

Bell's intuition was correct. The college students had taken the interstate southwest of Lubbock, then switched to Highway 6 and passed through Dusk Corners. Rosario had just confirmed her suspicions without realizing she'd fooled him into divulging information about the case. The Pronghorn County murders clustered south of where Endieveri and Jarvis had vanished. That's where she'd begin looking.

"This has been most enlightening. I can't wait to present your findings to my class."

Bell stood from her chair, and Rosario rose to meet her.

"Always happy to help my law enforcement brothers and sisters. You'll be heading back to your family in Amarillo now?"

"After a bite to eat, yes. Well, good day, Sheriff. It was a pleasure."

She was halfway out the door when the tone of his voice shifted, the good-natured humor gone.

"Agent Bell, go back to Quantico. If I require the FBI, I'll call. Until then, there's nothing for you in Pronghorn County. Understood?"

"Yes, Sheriff."

20

S ara watched Jacob through the bedroom window. He stood in the yard beside the Jetta, with his hands on his hips. The Jetta had refused to start after she lost control of the wheel during the dust storm and drove into the ditch. Her kidnappers must have towed the car. Hadn't anyone noticed? Even on the barren roads west of Dusk Corners, someone must have seen.

Another bulk slumbered next to the Jetta. A tarp covered the unknown object, though the size and shape marked it as another vehicle. The car those two Denver college students were driving before they disappeared? What became of them, and was she next on the chopping block?

Sara tugged the ropes. The bindings burned and bit into her wrists, carving angry red stripes across her flesh. She struggled toward the door until the ropes stopped her. Sara reversed course and fought to reach the window. As always, she stopped two steps short of the glass. She thrust a foot out, hoping to kick the window. No luck.

The chemical toilet stank of urine and feces. She didn't want to peer inside. A bulbous fly crawled along the seat. Maybe she could stand on the toilet and reach the industrial hook screwed into the ceiling.

Sara lumbered to the toilet, pins-and-needles swarming inside her arms, her shoulder joints stretched and aching. Averting her eyes from the toilet's contents, she placed one foot on the seat before her sneaker slipped. She tumbled backward. Had the ropes not caught her, she would have cracked her skull on the floor. And wouldn't that have been a fitting ending? The girl who'd accomplished nothing in life, the daughter who'd disappointed her parents and allowed a spoiled, rich abuser to mistreat her for weeks before she fled, would fall and kill herself while trying to escape from two murderers. Had her life not hung from an unraveling tether, she might have laughed.

Sara closed her eyes and sobbed. While chasing after Logan, she'd been kidnapped by the men he was trying to find. The irony. She deserved to die.

Tugging the ropes, she pulled herself to her feet and climbed again. This time, she didn't slip. Sara balanced one foot on the seat, then brought the other leg up. Now she stood on the chemical toilet, her legs trembling as the ropes slackened. She imagined one foot slipping and plunging into the toilet. She tried not to look, yet it was impossible to avoid the reddish-brown mess putrefying inside.

Sara reached for the hook, which dangled off the ceiling six inches beyond her fingertips. She swung her arms and whipped the ropes, intent on unraveling the binding from the hook. After the first attempt failed, she tried again.

One section of rope twisted off the hook. It might take hours, but she believed she'd escape if she kept working on it.

Her arms gave way to exhaustion. She stumbled down from the seat and knelt beneath the hook. While she caught her breath, a floorboard groaned outside the door. Her eyes darted to the window and found Jacob, who was still deciding what to do about Sara's Jetta.

Sara recalled the monstrous brother blotting out the sky before he punched through the car window and dragged her out of the seat. She edged toward the wall until the ropes pulled her back. The doorknob turned.

Jacob's brother filled the doorway, his head brushing the top of the frame. She opened her mouth to scream, but nothing came out. He was a walking nightmare, an unimaginable devil. A thick beard draped off his chin and wrapped around his lips, framing his grin.

"Stay away," she cried.

He staggered through the doorway and took his time as he crossed the room. Sara wasn't going anywhere. Jacob had warned her to stay quiet, or his brother would kill her. She wished Jacob would return and stop the monster. A beast this size could rip her limbs off with his bare hands.

He tilted his head and studied her from the center of the room, still wearing the wicked smile he'd flashed from the doorway.

Then he burst forward like a train hurtling off the tracks. With outstretched arms and grasping hands, he lurched toward Sara.

The man's hands were larger than Sara's head. One claw wrapped around her neck and squeezed. Something clicked inside her throat as she gasped for air. His body shook with rage. Spittle drooled off his lips. He meant to kill her. All he needed to do was contract his grip, and her neck would snap.

Sara's eyes bulged. She felt the blood pooling in her face, her capillaries on the verge of bursting through her skin.

She kicked out and struck his leg. It was like kicking a concrete building.

The monster snickered and squeezed harder. Then a hand grasped his shoulder and spun him around.

"What are you doing? I ordered you to stay out of the room."

The beast whirled on Jacob. He grasped his smaller brother by the shirt, and Jacob slapped the monster across his face.

Silence filled the room. The two brothers glared at each other as Sara coughed. She bent over and wretched, but her stomach was empty.

"Go back to the attic, Balor. Do as I say."

Balor didn't budge. His hands closed into fists as he looked over his shoulder at Sara.

"She's mine, Balor. You don't touch her unless I give you permission." Jacob took a hesitant step toward his brother, the way the owner of a vicious, untamed dog would. "Why are you still here? I gave you an order. Go to the attic."

Balor's head fell. He seemed on the verge of obeying before his shoulders tensed. Jacob's mouth dropped open when Balor converged on him. The monstrous man grabbed Jacob by the shirt and tossed him across the room. Jacob landed in a heap and scurried away. Balor rumbled across the floor. He trapped Jacob between two pistons for arms, the monster's fists pressed against the wall as he imprisoned the smaller man.

"You can't hurt me!" Jacob yelled, pounding a fist against Balor's chest. "I tell you what to do. Obey my—"

Balor strangled Jacob with one hand, cutting off his brother's words. Jacob flailed and kicked at Balor, to no effect. Slowly, Balor lifted Jacob and pinned him against the wall. Jacob's feet dangled several inches off the floor. He gagged and struck out with his fists.

When Balor released his brother, Jacob crashed to the floor. The smaller man grasped his throat and spat blood.

"No," Jacob cried. "This isn't right. You can't attack me. I'm your brother."

Balor loomed over Jacob, unmoving.

"Who took care of you after Mom and Dad threw you out? That was me," Jacob said, thrusting a pointed thumb into his own chest. "*I* took care of you. *I* got you off the streets and kept you fed. And this is how you repay me?"

Jacob pushed himself onto his hands and knees and coughed out a red mist. He strained until he stood on wobbly legs, his knees buckling while he propped himself against the wall.

"Listen, I'm sorry for yelling. You can have the girl after I'm finished. Do you understand?" Balor didn't respond. "Please, just this once, let me have her. She'll be yours after, I promise." Jacob reached out with a cautious hand, as though Balor would bite it off. He placed the hand on Balor's chest and held it there, softening his words. "I always took care of you. I'm your big brother. Remember when those men tried to hurt us at the apartment, and you killed them? Who got you out of the city before the police came? Me. It was me, Balor. And when we took that pretty woman, and I couldn't stop you from tearing her head off. Who got rid of the body, so the sheriff wouldn't figure out you'd killed her? Again, I did."

Balor glanced away. Jacob drew his brother into his arms.

"You have to trust me this time. They're searching for us. We need to hide out a little longer, just until the excitement dies down. Nobody will remember a couple of out-of-state college kids." Jacob turned and pointed at Sara. "And they won't remember her, either. But you can't hurt the girl. Not yet. Not until I figure out what to do with the cars and the bodies. Do you understand why we need to be careful?"

Balor nodded and hung his head low. Straggly, oily hair dangled over his face. Balor turned away from Jacob. Sara thought the gigantic brother was crying until he flashed a secretive grin at her, grinding his teeth. Without another word, Balor feigned obedience and shuffled into the hallway. Before long, the trapdoor to the attic opened.

Jacob scrubbed a trembling hand through his hair and gave Sara an uncertain smile. The attic moaned under Balor's weight, making Sara believe the ceiling would crumble.

The smaller brother came to Sara. She pressed her back against the wall.

"See what I did for you? He would have killed you, but you're safe now."

"Thank you," she said, her voice hoarse.

He touched her shoulder. Then his hand drifted lower and brushed her breasts.

"I want sex now."

Her eyes flicked to his. "What? No."

"As repayment. I saved you."

Her hair swung as she shook her head. Sara struggled to lower her hands and block his advances. The ropes held firm around her wrists. She was powerless to stop Jacob, who dug his hands under her shirt and caressed her bare skin.

"I've been with women before and know what they like," he said. "I can make you happy. You'll see if you give me a chance. I'm not like my brother."

"No, Jacob. This is wrong and you know it."

His fingers twitched when they passed over her nipples. "But I want you."

"Just stop."

His hands dropped out of her shirt. Jacob slapped Sara's face and spun her head sideways. "Never disobey me, Sara. Not after what I did for you."

Her cheek stung, the ghostly imprint of his hand still burning her face. "I'm sorry, but I won't let you rape me."

"Bitch!"

He punched her with his fist, rocking her head back. Blood poured from her nostrils.

"I'm in charge. You don't question me."

Jacob grabbed Sara's chin and twisted it toward him. His knife appeared, the deadly blade tip a fraction of an inch below her eye.

"I'll cut your eyes out and feed them to Balor. Then I'll sever your tongue and make you swallow it. Never disobey me, you ungrateful whore."

He punched Sara in the stomach. She doubled over, unable to suck air into her lungs.

Sara curled on the floor as Jacob stomped across the room and slammed the door.

She knew he'd return soon. Next time, punishment wouldn't be enough to sate his urges.

21

Sheriff Edward Rosario watched Agent Scarlett Bell on the security monitor as she crossed the parking lot to her rental. He couldn't help thinking the woman didn't seem like an FBI agent. She had a firm backside, curves in all the right places, and a pleasing face, the sort of girl he could've taken home to his parents in his younger days and received unanimous approval. When she climbed into her vehicle—a rental by the looks of it—he wrote down the plate number.

He had too many strings pulling him. Those damn college kids that had vanished outside of Dusk Corners were eating at him. Despite what he'd told Agent Bell, he knew Endieveri and Jarvis should have surfaced by now if they'd spent the week getting high in Roswell as he'd theorized. No, they were somewhere in his county and never made it to the New Mexico border. He figured they'd turn up within a few weeks, and it wouldn't be pretty when he dug their corpses out of the prairie.

At the same time, there was a mysterious fellow named Don Weber hanging out at the Irvin Hotel in Dusk Corners. He needed to find out who Weber was and what the man wanted. And now this federal agent had shown up on his doorstep, asking questions about nine years of murders. He didn't believe in coincidences.

"Where are you headed, Agent Bell?" Rosario asked the security monitor.

When her brake lights lit up, he shut down the monitor and hurried down the hall, adjusting his hat as he jogged. He told his administrative assistant that he'd return in an hour or two, then picked out a vehicle, something nondescript that wouldn't invite attention.

Rosario waited until Agent Bell's rental turned the corner. After a tractor trailer passed, he pulled out of the parking lot in an unmarked cruiser and followed the FBI agent, keeping the truck between the two vehicles so he didn't spook the woman.

He'd seen through her paper-thin story. If he ran a background check on Scarlett Bell, he wouldn't find any family living in Amarillo. Furthermore, the lying agent wasn't teaching a profiling course to recruits. She'd come here to poke her nose into his investigation and stir up controversy. Rosario wouldn't allow it.

He'd won the sheriff position by a decisive majority, during a special election in 2001, two months after the World Trade Center buildings fell in New York, when all of Texas feared Bin Laden would send his suicide bombers through Mexico into Dallas, San Antonio, and Houston. Pronghorn County had needed a man who didn't fear the big bad wolf of terrorism, who understood peace wasn't possible until law and order were restored.

During his first week on the job, he'd tossed five locals into the clink for public intoxication at the county fair. He raised speeding ticket quotas, and his deputies complied. Revenues exploded, affording the sheriff's department a new fleet of cruisers.

Not that Pronghorn County needed a dictator with an iron

fist. The people required direction, and he was the man to show them the way.

Little of note happened during his first decade as sheriff. Just the usual small-town problems—teenagers drinking out by the quarries and drag racing between Joliet and the county border, the occasional weekend fistfight, domestic arguments.

Then nine years ago, after he'd won another landslide reelection, the murders started. Men and women with their heads ripped off their bodies, corpses bobbing in the muddy waters of the quarry pits, people abducted from their homes. Once, he'd believed a single killer hunted his county. But as the years passed, and he discovered more bodies, the evidence stopped adding up. The different shoe sizes gave Rosario his first clue. His second clue was the killer's inconsistent behavior— raping some victims, dismembering others. There had to be multiple murderers. That was the only explanation that made sense. Otherwise, he would have captured the perpetrator years ago.

Now Pronghorn County feared sundown. The same iron-willed, flag waving electorate that proudly spat in Bin Laden's face was afraid of the dark.

Worse yet, they blamed Rosario for the murders. He hadn't solved a single case, and genuine doubt grew over his chances in the upcoming election.

His county, like most of West Texas, had softened. Nobody cared about the oil fields drying up, or the energy companies fleeing to other countries. People wanted electric cars. They wanted to save the environment, even if it meant the oil and gas workers losing their jobs. And nobody feared the terrorists or believed they'd strike again.

Danger always hid in the shadows. It struck when you let your guard down.

Pronghorn County remained an unforgiving place. The river

cutting through the western half of the county flooded ruby-red during storms, the water choked with clay. During the summer, the temperature soared past one-hundred degrees. Crops withered. People collapsed from heatstroke when their air conditioners failed. Winters turned the highways into skating rinks and flipped eighteen-wheelers onto their sides. Decades before Rosario's reign as sheriff, everyone had envisioned Dusk Corners as the new county seat. That was before the energy market collapsed, and the oil industry abandoned the countryside outside of Dusk Corners.

Rosario tipped his cap to block the sun. A mile up the road, Agent Bell took a left and motored toward the truck stop below the interstate. If Rosario was a betting man, he would have placed a large chunk of change on the agent interviewing truckers about the missing college kids. His fingers curled around the steering wheel and squeezed.

The sheriff didn't oppose FBI involvement when necessary. He'd obliged after Kimberly Ripa's severed head turned up in a field, and again when the quarry workers discovered the Domin family skewered on wooden stakes. But he appreciated a heads-up before someone pissed in his latrine. Agent Scarlett Bell had attempted to pull the wool over his eyes and dazzle him with talk of unsubs and profiling mumbo jumbo. She'd lied to his face, and now she was driving south, instead of north toward Amarillo and her supposed family. Before long, she'd report to Quantico about the mythical Devil's Rock killer. A swarm of FBI agents would descend upon Pronghorn County and wrest away control of the investigation. Even after he solved the murders—and he would, if people gave him the chance—all the credit would go to the FBI, not the man who'd hunted the murderers for nine years.

Unless Agent Bell was here without her superiors knowing.

He bounced the idea around in his head as he drove. She

was driving a rental, not an FBI vehicle. Had the FBI sent Scarlett Bell to his county, wouldn't additional agents accompany her?

He picked up the radio and contacted his lead deputy.

"Beckley, give me everything you can find on Agent Scarlett Bell with the Behavioral Analysis Unit. What's she doing in my county? When did she fly in, and what airline did she use? If she has family in Texas, I want their addresses."

"Right away, Sheriff."

"And keep this on the down low, Beckley. Don't speak to Quantico until I give the order."

He set the radio down and pressed the accelerator. The more he pondered the sudden appearance of Agent Scarlett Bell, the stronger his conviction grew that she'd arrived without the BAU's knowledge. She was a rogue agent. He needed to find out why.

Agent Bell's rental became a speck on the horizon. He wouldn't let her get away.

Rosario closed the distance on Agent Bell, keeping vehicles between his unmarked cruiser and her rental. To his surprise, she passed the truck stop and took the entrance ramp to the highway. Maybe she really was driving back to Amarillo.

On the highway, Rosario weaved around a slow-moving Subaru and a pickup truck with a rusty bumper. He could see Bell's rental a mile ahead of him, the agent sticking to the speed limit, but aggressively shifting between lanes. Concerned Bell had spotted him, Rosario picked up speed. If he desired, he could place the red and blue lights on the dashboard and order her to stop. But he wasn't pulling over a local who didn't understand her rights. He needed to exercise caution with this woman until he figured out her motivations. Once he did, he'd squash her like a bug on his windshield.

Rosario blinked when Agent Bell's rental vanished. This

couldn't be. He'd seen her cut in front of a dump truck seconds before.

He drove faster and passed the dump truck, expecting her vehicle to emerge. It didn't.

He braked before he sped past the exit ramp, then yanked the wheel and motored down the only path Bell could have taken. A train of vehicles blocked him from turning left. The damn ramp needed a traffic light. He honked his horn, but nobody moved. Down the road, his target swerved onto a residential street.

Desperate, Rosario placed the lights on the dash and flicked the switch. He laid his hand on the horn, forcing a woman with two kids laughing in the backseat of a van to back up and give him room. His tires squealed as he forced his way into the intersection, almost clipping the van's bumper as he drew angry honks from impatient motorists.

Rosario whipped the unmarked cruiser around and raced toward the neighborhood where he'd last spotted Bell. As he turned down a road lined with middle-class homes and frequented by walkers and bicyclists, the rental took a sharp turn without braking. She'd seen him.

Another quick turn, and Bell doubled back, racing toward the highway. Rosario braked. The cruiser's tires caught the gravel shoulder and spun. Rubber shrieked against blacktop as he regained control of the vehicle.

He was too late. The rental vanished up the highway ramp, while another traffic glut formed ahead of Rosario.

The sheriff pounded the dashboard and cursed. He'd lost her.

22

The door down the hall clicked shut after a middle-aged couple dragged their bags into the room. Before they'd checked into the hotel, Wolf had watched them through the window while they unpacked their van. He heard them through the wall, dresser drawers sliding open, the clinks of clothes on hangers, the couple speaking at a polite volume.

Wolf pressed his thumbs against his eyes and willed his headache to go away. Sara's perfume still hung in the air. It was strongest on the pillow. The flowery smell followed him from the bedroom to the bathroom, where he splashed water against his face, then wiped himself dry with the towel.

Sara hadn't returned his call. Something was wrong. He should have turned around after he'd spotted her following him. She never would have listened to reason and left him alone, but he should have escorted her back to town and ensured she was safe. The dust storm had struck without warning, and after he found shelter and rode out the storm, she vanished.

Wolf opened his wallet and removed the slip of paper Sara had hidden beneath the lamp. He felt certain she wouldn't take kindly to another phone call. As he folded the note and slid it into his wallet, Renee's picture tumbled out and landed face-up in the sink. He fished the photograph out of the sink and held it in his palm. It was a picture of Renee from their honeymoon. Though she wore designer sunglasses, he saw her eyes smiling behind the frames. A crystal blue ocean sloshed in the background. He never remembered seeing her happier. There were no worries about the future, only an idyllic contentment, an undying belief that they'd be together forever. In a few years, they'd have a child. Maybe two. He'd win the CIRG deputy director position, and she'd write that novel she'd been talking about for two years.

Renee's father had never approved of Wolf. He said Wolf would give his daughter a hard life. He wasn't wrong.

Wolf lowered his head and closed his eyes, squeezing out tears that demanded escape. The stomachache returned, but he ignored it, the pain in his heart making him forget his indigestion. Wolf sat on the floor with his knees propped in front of him. He placed Renee's picture on his thigh and studied it through a curtain of tears.

"I'm so sorry I did this to you. To us." He wiped a hand across his lips and raised his eyes to the ceiling. "I can't do this much longer, Renee. The work, I mean. I wish to honor your memory, but I believe I've failed. Am I venturing down the wrong path?"

The beating of his heart was the only answer. He wondered if the neighboring couple listened and thought he'd lost his mind. He had, but that was years ago.

Renee kept grinning at him in the picture. He frowned. Why did Sara remind him of Renee? On the surface, they seemed polar opposites. Renee had blonde hair, Sara jet black. His dead wife's eyes mirrored the tropical ocean in the photograph, whereas Sara's bordered on obsidian. Renee had known who she was and what she wanted from life. Sara was a free spirit consumed by wanderlust.

Yet every time he thought of Sara, he pictured Renee.

His hands trembled and his mouth went dry as he contemplated how much he should tell Renee. Though Wolf had never spent a moment in church outside of his wedding day, he believed she could hear him. Since the murder, her guiding light had served as his moral compass.

"I met someone," he said, averting his eyes. He brushed his hair back. "Don't mistake my intentions. I miss you more than I can express. But I don't wish to be alone."

If his admission injured Renee, her picture didn't show it.

"She's a lot like you. I can't explain why, only that I know it's true. You'd enjoy her company, as do I." He wrung his hands. "Her name is Sara, and we made love. I'm sorry to sound so crass. But then I said something stupid, as I always do, and now I can't locate her. I'm worried."

Wolf yanked a tissue from the box beside the sink. After he wiped his eyes, he held Renee's picture.

"If I find Sara again, would it hurt your feelings if I spent time with her? I could use a friend. Haven't had one since I lost you."

He wasn't sure what he expected—Renee's voice to speak inside his head, the bathroom lights to flicker like a scene from a low-budget horror movie. He placed her photo inside the protective sleeve of his wallet and pushed himself to his feet, moaning when his back stiffened.

Wolf needed to find Sara.

He located the girl's number on his call list and pressed redial. As before, the phone rang seven times and kicked him into her voicemail. He'd already left a message the last time he called. His heart rate quickened when he imagined her lost in the countryside, the Jetta inoperable.

Wolf opened his laptop and studied a digital map of the murder locations. He overlaid a series of squares and marked

DAN PADAVONA

the quadrants he'd checked. There were still sixteen square miles of open land remaining. The undiscovered territory lay due west of where he'd last spied Sara's Jetta.

He checked the time. Back at Quantico, it was mid-afternoon. Every time he phoned his contacts inside the BAU, he risked someone intercepting his call. Anyone caught aiding Wolf would face criminal charges. There was only one man who could help him locate Sara.

Wolf cracked the door open and ensured Chapman wasn't in the hall, eavesdropping. Then he entered the bathroom and closed the door, easing it shut so he didn't disturb his new neighbors. He scrolled through his contacts and located Harold, the information technology specialist at the BAU. Wolf had dropped a prepaid phone on Harold's kitchen counter two months ago while the man was at work. He hoped his old friend carried the phone today.

Harold didn't answer the call. But ten seconds after Wolf hung up, his phone rang.

"Are you trying to get me fired?" Harold asked in a lowered voice.

Given the lack of voices in the background, Wolf assumed Harold had entered a closet or the storage room down the hall from his office.

"I trust it's safe for you to talk?"

"It's never safe, Logan. You know that better than anyone. Whatever you want, get to the point. Agent Gardy has been watching me all day. He thinks I can tell him where Scarlett is."

Wolf hesitated. "What about dear Scarlett?"

"Apparently, she told Gardy she was spending her four-day break on the beach. But she locked her condo and took her vehicle, and she's not answering her phone."

The first thought that popped into Wolf's head was Scarlett

had followed him to Texas. But he hadn't contacted Scarlett. How would she know he was in Dusk Corners?

"Did she mention her destination?"

Harold scoffed. "Even if she did, I wouldn't tell you. Get to the point, Logan. What do you need?"

"I'm searching for someone. A girl."

"Aren't we all?"

"No time for witty quips, Harold. I'm afraid I lost her in West Texas, outside of a town called Dusk Corners. I worry she might be stranded or injured."

"West Texas," Harold said, mulling over the location. "That's Devil's Rock territory. Jesus, Logan. Are you going after the—"

"I don't have time to explain. The girl gave me her phone number. I need you to trace her location."

"Technically, I need to go through the cell company to locate a phone."

"Technically, you shouldn't hobnob with a serial killer on the most wanted list. Yet we all make concessions and trust our maker will understand when we approach the pearly gates."

"Touché. Give me the information, and I'll see what I can do."

"Her name is Sara Brennan." Wolf read Harold her address and phone number. "Ping her phone and give me the location. This is a matter of life and death, Harold. If you fail me—"

"I know, you don't need to threaten me." Harold exhaled. "There's a staff meeting in ten minutes. They'll expect me to be there and will ask questions if I don't show."

"Come up with an excuse, then. I want the phone located."

"Give me time, Logan. I'll call you back when I find something."

Before Wolf could protest, Harold hung up. He trusted the information technology specialist would come through. He had to. Sara was running out of time.

23

S heriff Edward Rosario lit a cigarette and cupped his hands around the flame, shielding it from the incessant wind. He stood outside the door of the vacant five-and-dime store, his bulky frame reflected in twin windows to either side. The Irvin Hotel waited across the street, three vehicles in the parking lot, including a black Jeep Wrangler with out-of-state plates. Rosario took out his phone and snapped a picture of the Jeep. He'd check the plates after he returned to the office.

He puffed out a ring of smoke just as Pete Chapman hurried across the road. Chapman was a lapdog, and Rosario could do without the man's company. But lapdogs were loyal pets, and right now Rosario needed someone he trusted.

"Thanks for coming, Sheriff. He ain't left yet."

Rosario gestured with his cigarette at a second-floor window. A silhouette passed over the glass, appearing to pace.

"That the man you called me about?"

"Claims his name is Don Weber, like I told you."

"Any reason to believe he isn't who he says he is?"

"He showed me his driver's license. I don't allow anyone to

rent a room without identification. But there was something off about the license."

"A fake?"

"If it is, it's a damn good one."

"Weber still got that young girl with him, the one he brought to his room?"

"He claims she's his daughter. Now she's missing."

"Missing? Since when?"

"Since yesterday afternoon. One of those dust storms followed the dry line out of New Mexico. She was on the road when it hit."

Rosario dragged on the cigarette and tossed it on the sidewalk, stamping it out with his boot. "Weber go out searching for her?"

"Ever since Weber arrived, he's been in and out, like he can't sit still."

"Maybe he prefers fresh air to those box air conditioners you stick in the windows."

Chapman shook his head. "He drives west on Highway 6 and doesn't return for hours. There's nothing out there, Sheriff. Nothing for an out-of-towner to see."

"Tell me about the girl. Ever see her before?"

"Never."

"Describe her. She easy on the eyes?"

"Sheriff?"

"Good looking, you dolt."

The hotel owner shifted his feet. "She looks like one of those punk rockers. Hair chopped short and kinda spiky on top."

"Hair color?"

"Black. Too black, like she colored it."

Rosario wished he hadn't thrown the cigarette away so soon. He considered lighting another before Dr. Wilhoit's voice popped into his head, warning him to cut down. Rosario's great uncle had passed from lung cancer back in 2002, and the sheriff's older brother burned through a pack a day before he contracted emphysema last autumn. Instead, he bit his thumbnail down to the quick and spat the sickle on the concrete. Chapman turned his head in disgust.

"What about the college students Weber asked about?"

"He showed me a picture while I checked him in. I said I hadn't seen those kids."

"He tell you why he's looking for them?"

Chapman bobbed his head. "The girl in the picture. Weber says she's his niece."

"So one of the missing students is Weber's niece, and his daughter vanished west of Dusk Corners. This guy can't keep track of his family." Rosario dug a folded picture out of his breast pocket and opened it. "This the picture Weber showed you?"

The hotel owner jabbed a finger at the photograph. "That's the one."

"Answer carefully, Chapman. Is it the same photograph, or just the same kids?"

"No, that's the exact photo Weber carried with him."

"Hell," Rosario said, craving another cigarette. He was out of thumbnails to chew.

"Why is it important?"

"I'll ask the questions."

Rosario didn't tell Chapman that law enforcement circulated the picture. The TV and newspapers used a different photo, one supplied by the families. Not that Weber couldn't find either photograph on the internet. But if Shelly Jarvis was Don Weber's niece, why wasn't he carrying the photo from the families? It would be easy for Rosario to catch Weber in a lie. All the sheriff needed to do was look into Shelly Jarvis's family history. He doubted the girl had an uncle named Don Weber.

This damn Weber sounded like law enforcement—a cop or a fed. Either way, Weber was out of his jurisdiction and stepping on toes.

"What else has this guy been up to?" Rosario asked.

Chapman scratched his head and said, "Well, he stopped by Miller's Pub and questioned the locals about those students."

Rosario grabbed Chapman's arm and pulled him around. Chapman winced.

"You didn't tell me about the pub."

"Sorry, Sheriff. I meant to tell you on the phone, but I didn't want to waste your time. You said you were busy. Is it important?"

"If this guy interrogates people in my county, I need to know about it. Anyone give him an answer?"

"Donna Willis says nobody told Weber anything," Chapman said, staring down at Rosario's hand until the sheriff released his arm. "Then this other fellow, Fonda is his name, followed Weber outside. Donna eavesdropped from the doorway. Fonda claimed he saw the blue Ford Focus the students were driving pass through Dusk Corners."

Rosario spat. "Fonda is a worthless drunk. I'm surprised he didn't say a spaceship landed in the middle of the street, and little green men climbed out and ordered beers in Miller's."

"That's a good one, Sheriff."

Groveling prick.

The sheriff chewed the inside of his cheek. If Fonda had seen a blue Ford Focus in Dusk Corners, why hadn't he come forward days ago? After word got around the county that there had been a confirmed sighting of the vehicle, Rosario's approval rating would crater. Until now, there was no evidence that Endieveri and Jarvis had driven through Pronghorn County, only conjecture, though Rosario never doubted those students came this way. He never should have told that bitch BAU profiler that the students took Highway 6 through town. Looking back at their conversation, he realized she'd propped him up and stroked his ego until he opened his mouth like a fool. He'd show her who the real fool was.

With no thumbnails remaining, Rosario chewed a jagged fingernail on his index finger.

"Here's what I want you to do, Chapman."

"Anything."

"Keep a log under the counter. Note the times Mr. Weber comes and goes, and if anyone visits his room, snap a picture when they aren't paying attention. Can you handle that?"

"I won't let you down."

"Next time he drives away, unlock his room. I want to know what he's hiding."

Chapman stuttered. "But Sheriff, I can't enter a guest's room unless there's an emergency."

"I say there *is* an emergency, so you can enter. That good enough for you?"

"I'll get into trouble."

"With who? I'm the law here." Ignoring his doctor's advice, Rosario lit another cigarette. He inhaled and blew the smoke into the hotel owner's face. "You got a restaurant in your hotel, Chapman?"

"No."

"Good for you, I suppose. It would be a shame if a health department inspector made a surprise visit. You gonna check Weber's room?"

"Yes, sir. It won't be a problem."

"See that it won't be."

AGENT SCARLETT BELL drove with the window open a crack. The cool air pouring through the vents kept up with the Texas heat, but she wanted fresh air to ease her nerves. After the close call with the Sheriff, she'd sensed people watching her wherever she traveled.

Staying off the interstate, she passed the truck stop. If anyone had seen Brady Endieveri and Sheila Jarvis, it was a trucker. But she couldn't stop until she was sure Rosario wasn't following her.

The sheriff's words bounced around inside her head. The students had passed through Dusk Corners on their way to New Mexico. She checked her mirrors and found nothing but the open road behind her.

Bell stopped on the shoulder and punched Dusk Corners into her GPS. She'd reach the town in fifteen minutes if she took the interstate, twenty-five if she stuck to the back roads. She opted for the slower route and checked her messages, finding none. Her partner, Neil Gardy, must have given up trying to reach her. She dialed Harold, hoping the information technology specialist could feed her information on Logan Wolf's whereabouts. Harold usually played dumb whenever she was closing in on the fugitive. Was Harold protecting Bell from the serial killer, or had he forged a relationship with Wolf behind her back? The call went straight to Harold's voicemail. Bell set the phone on the seat and pulled off the shoulder.

She merged onto Highway 6. Except for the occasional billboard and long-haul trucker rocketing down the road, the highway seemed like a barren, alien planet. There were no advertisements previewing Dusk Corners. The welcome sign appeared without warning, as she cruised into a town that time had forgotten.

Most of the stores appeared as though they'd closed decades ago. Stout buildings with empty eyes peered at her as she followed the only road through town. There was a hotel to her right and a pub at the end of the road.

But it was the sheriff's cruiser hidden in the alleyway that stopped Bell in her tracks. She braked just in time to catch Sheriff Rosario in front of an abandoned store. His back was turned. The scrawny man Rosario spoke to peeked over the sheriff's shoulder, spotted Bell's rental, but continued talking.

Bell couldn't decide whether to continue forward and risk Rosario seeing her, or turn back and draw the other man's curiosity. She had to choose before the sheriff swung around.

Bell backed up and reversed course, her eyes glued to the mirror. Another close call. Nobody followed her out of Dusk Corners.

24

Harold hadn't called Wolf by the time the fugitive serial killer drove past another quadrant of farmland southwest of Highway 6, eliminating another area from his search radius. He was looking for the proverbial needle in the haystack, and knew the point would draw blood if he closed his fist over it. Even with the map of the murders and his power of deduction, he was flying blind. How would he find a murderer who'd evaded the FBI for nine years?

Two miles west of Dusk Corners, Wolf pulled over. The lights of the Irvin Hotel gleamed like a distant beacon as the sun descended behind him. After he called Harold and got his message again, Wolf slammed the phone on the passenger seat and cursed, wondering if someone at the FBI had learned the IT specialist was in league with the fugitive. Sara's phone would draw Wolf to her. If the location pinged in Lubbock, he'd confirm she'd made it home and was ignoring his calls. Wolf could accept that. He'd invited her anger. But if Harold located Sara's phone on the Devil's Rock, she might already be dead.

Gloaming turned the sky to a deep sea-blue. The first stars

were dagger sharp on the horizon and claiming the sky. Rolling the dice, Wolf called Sara again. A crazed section of this brain— as if a sane portion still existed—believed he'd hear her phone ringing amid the vast, open plains. But Sara didn't answer, and there were no phantom ring tones emanating out of the growing darkness.

He started the engine and drove into Dusk Corners, scanning the road for Sara's Jetta. When he pulled into the parking lot outside the Irvin Hotel, he didn't notice the cruiser with the sheriff's department emblem parked under a tree near the fence. As Wolf crossed the lot, the flare of a struck match parted the darkness. A man with a powerful physique puffed a cigarette and studied Wolf. Even before Wolf spotted the hat and badge, he'd pegged the figure as Sheriff Edward Rosario.

He kept his head down and pretended not to notice the sheriff.

"You Don Weber?" the gravely voice asked from the darkness.

"Who's asking?"

"Sheriff Edward Rosario." The sheriff, who stood three inches taller than Wolf and outweighed him by at least fifty pounds, stepped away from the building. His face was leathery from the unrelenting Texas heat, and the creases around the man's eyes marked Rosario as a veteran of the force, a sheriff who'd ruled over Pronghorn County for a long time. "You got identification on you, Don Weber?"

"In my wallet. Why? Am I under arrest?"

The sheriff waved the cigarette through the air, causing sparks to rain down. "Just wondering what business you have in my county. You a fed, Mr. Weber?"

"If I am, is it a problem?"

"If you're a fed, you'll produce your FBI badge, and then

we'll talk about why you're here, and why you're asking about those missing college kids. See, I figure you're either a fed or a reporter, because you don't strike me as a cop." Rosario walked into the light and stood over him, bullying his way into Wolf's space. "That right, Mr. Weber? You a reporter or a fed?"

"Neither. I'm searching for my niece."

"And your daughter, by the sounds of it. You have a funny way of losing your family, Don Weber. Now, I'll be seeing your identification."

Wolf reached into his jacket pocket. Rosario's eyes lit with anticipation. His hand rested on the grip of his gun, the sheriff hoping for an excuse to fire his service weapon. Under Rosario's watchful gaze, Wolf produced the fake ID and handed it to Rosario. Wolf paid top-dollar for his credentials. If Rosario walked the ID back to his cruiser and searched for Don Weber's name in his computer, the sheriff would find a complete back story on Weber, including known residences, his education background, and financial records. The computer would tell Rosario that Weber worked as a private investigator in Dayton, Ohio.

He removed the driver's license from its sleeve and handed it to Rosario. The sheriff switched his gaze between the card and Wolf several times before handing it back.

"This card a fake, Mr. Weber?"

"If it is, would I tell you?"

A sly grin curled Rosario's lips. "I suppose you wouldn't. Everything appears in order. But you still haven't told me the truth. That Jarvis girl isn't your niece, now is she? And the other girl, the one Pete Chapman says you escorted to your room, isn't your daughter. Not unless you like bedding with your daughter. You some kind of pervert, Mr. Weber?" Wolf lifted his chin. "No, I suppose you aren't. But it's strange how you keep misplacing family members. What do you do all day while you're upstairs in your room?"

"What I do behind closed doors is no business of yours."

"If you're poking your nose into my investigation, it damn well is. That driver's license appears legit, but then I don't see too many fake IDs, except when the kids buy beer on the weekend. And those fakes you can spot from a mile away. I hear the best IDs come from China these days. But I assume the federal government can produce something more . . . convincing." With the cigarette clutched between his fingers, Rosario poked Wolf in the chest. "That's why I'm sure you're a fed. Why don't you show me your badge, so we can get this over with?"

"I'm not a federal agent."

"Sure you are, Mr. Weber. Tell me, what's on the corner of Highway 6 and County Route 13?"

Wolf's eye twitched. He'd written the coordinates on the memo pad upstairs. "Did you enter my room, Sheriff? Or did you send Chapman to snoop around? That's an illegal search."

"Let's cut with the bullshit. Sheila Jarvis isn't your niece, no more than that girl you're sleeping with is your daughter. If you know something about Brady Endieveri and Sheila Jarvis, come clean. It's my job to bring those kids home to their parents. I'll ask you one more time. What's at the corner of 6 and 13?"

Wolf pulled his lips tight.

"Fine. You don't want to cooperate, then I won't afford you the hospitality a visitor deserves when he enters my county. I'll tell you what I think, Mr. Weber. You're working with that female fed who visited my office today."

Wolf drew in a breath. The female agent had to be Scarlett Bell. Somehow, she'd tracked him to Dusk Corners.

"Difference between you and her is, she had the balls to lie to my face about her interest in the Caprock murders. You just stand there with your lips glued shut. Tell me why the FBI is investigating missing persons cases under my nose?"

"I told you, I'm not FBI."

"I say you are."

"You can't smoke in my presence, Sheriff. I'm not privy to your local ordinances. But I'm certain your actions would be frowned upon."

With a chuckle, Rosario threw the cigarette on the blacktop and ground it under his boot. "You're a wise ass, too. Get out of my county and take your partner with you. The next time the FBI has business in Texas, you'll call me first, or there will be hell to pay."

"Should I have the pleasure of meeting a federal agent, I'll be sure to pass along your edict."

"Still with the smart talk. You speak like a Harvard grad, without the accent. Here's the deal, Weber. You have twenty-four hours to leave town. If I return tomorrow night and find you here, I'll deal with you as I see fit."

"Is that a threat?"

"You watch yourself, Weber. Not every Texan is as friendly as I am."

"It isn't wise to cross me, Sheriff. I've maintained my patience to this point, but I advise you not to push me."

"Ah, so now you're the one making threats."

"I don't make threats, my friend. I only keep promises."

Huffing, Rosario strolled to his cruiser and slammed the door. The tires spun on a patch of dirt and stone, then caught the blacktop with a shriek. Wolf didn't move until the cruiser exited the parking lot. The sheriff wanted Wolf to believe he was leaving, but Rosario would stay close and monitor Mr. Weber.

Wolf yanked the door open and angled toward the staircase. Chapman, working behind the check-in counter, lowered his head and scratched behind his neck when Wolf passed.

He twisted the key in the lock and opened the door, scanning the room for an intrusion. The memo pad lay beside the computer, where he'd left it. Nothing missing. He punched his password into the laptop and opened the security file, checking for any failed attempts to crack the code. It didn't appear anyone had tried. The room seemed untouched, except when he sniffed the air, he discerned Chapman's cheap cologne. The hotel proprietor had entered his room.

Wolf was so close to zeroing in on the Devil's Rock killer. Yet he couldn't stay at the Irvin Hotel. Not because Rosario's threat worried him, but because Chapman and the sheriff would watch his every move, making it impossible for Wolf to complete his mission. If Rosario ran the Jeep's plates, he'd discover the plates didn't match the vehicle.

Breaking into a vacant house wasn't an option, not with the sheriff following him around. But he couldn't leave until he finished the job and found Sara. Alive. He refused to consider the alternative.

Wolf shut down the laptop and slid it into the carrying case. He cleared the bathroom sink and swept his personal items into his bag. As he surveyed the room and ensured he'd left nothing behind, a stabbing pain shot through his abdomen. Wolf dropped the laptop case and slouched against the wall. He bit his tongue and willed the agony to stop, but it kept crashing down on him in torturous waves. A black haze clouded his vision, dropping him to one knee.

Gradually, the pain subsided, until he could stand and balance against the wall.

Collecting his belongings, Wolf cracked the door open and padded to the staircase. Below, Chapman had abandoned the check-in counter. Wolf descended the stairs, one hand clutching the banister in case the pain struck again.

Amid the thickening night, he checked the shadows for

hidden threats. The sheriff wouldn't leave so easily. Rosario was somewhere close.

Wolf slipped into the Jeep and drove out of the parking lot with the lights off. Arrowing into the undiscovered darkness, he didn't ignite the headlamps until Dusk Corners disappeared from his mirrors.

25

The hardwood floor hurt Sara's knees, but she wasn't strong enough to stand a second longer. Like a medieval torture device, the taut ropes pulled her arms toward the hook in the ceiling. Her head bobbed, eyelids fluttering as she fought to stay awake. Darkness had fallen over the house, so thick she couldn't see past her shoelaces. Jacob hadn't visited in hours, and the monster upstairs seemed to have fallen asleep. A long time had passed since Balor's footfalls last trailed across the ceiling.

She'd spent the final hours of daylight trying to whip the ropes and unravel them from the hook. Now, with her energy spent, she'd given up. There was no escape. She'd remain a prisoner until Jacob raped her or Balor broke her neck.

On the verge of drifting off, Sara snapped awake when a familiar sound pierced the night. It was her phone, ringing somewhere in the darkness.

She climbed to her feet and followed the sound until the ropes stopped her two steps from the window. The ringing came from outside. She'd forgotten about the phone. It tumbled off the seat when she crashed the Jetta into the ditch. Her kidnappers must have searched Sara for a phone, but never checked inside the car. Either that, or the phone was so entrenched inside the garbage that collected beneath the seat—discarded coffee cups, fast food wrappers, lost napkins—that they hadn't found it.

And now someone was calling Sara.

Her mother?

No, Logan. Even after she stormed out of his hotel room, he hadn't given up on her.

She clutched a thread of hope. If Logan wasn't a vigilante and worked in law enforcement, he'd have the means to track her phone's location.

The ringing continued. Overhead, Balor's weight shifted inside the attic. Had he heard? She willed the phone to stop before Jacob and Balor noticed. As long as the phone still had battery life, it would act as a beacon to her position.

The ringing stopped, the sudden quiet making her feel abandoned.

Please, let it be Logan.

Another thought. If Sara freed herself, she could call for help. She wouldn't have to run blindly through the dark countryside, wondering where she was. The built-in GPS would direct the police to her position.

Ignoring her exhaustion, Sara climbed atop the chemical toilet and jiggled the ropes, whipping waves down the bindings and toward the hook. She gasped when another knot unraveled. If she worked day and night, she might escape by tomorrow evening. Invigorated, she tried again, her sneakers slipping on the seat.

Footsteps in the hallway gave her a few heartbeats of warning before the door opened. Sara hopped off the seat and slouched against the wall.

She expected to see Jacob in the doorway. A shiver crawled

down her spine on spider legs when Balor's massive silhouette blocked the entrance.

The beast swayed in the darkness, his hands curling, as though he imagined them wrapping around her throat. She watched him through slitted eyes, feigning sleep and hoping he'd go away. Except he wouldn't this time. Balor intended to murder Sara while Jacob slept.

The monster took a step forward, careful not to alert his brother. One more step carried him into the center of the room.

Between the phone and the ropes loosening, Sara's hopes for escaping had grown. But now Balor would tear Sara apart before anyone rescued her.

Out of options, Sara shrieked until her lungs bled. A growl escaped Balor's lips, and the humongous man lumbered across the room. A shout pulled Balor's head around before harried footsteps pounded down the hallway.

Jacob spun into the room, breathless. To Sara's shock, he held a revolver in his shaking hands.

"Don't, Balor. We had an agreement."

Balor shook his head. Jacob swallowed and raised the weapon.

"Please, don't make me do this," Jacob said, aiming the gun at Balor's chest. "It's not time. She's mine until I give you permission."

Balor reached for the weapon, then hesitated when Jacob's arms stiffened, the man's finger resting on the trigger.

Sara turned away, expecting a deafening gun blast. None came.

Balor lowered his head and shuffled into the hallway. When the trapdoor to the attic opened, Jacob released a breath and lowered the revolver.

His gaze locked on Sara, who huddled on the floor and shook with terror. Jacob's mouth twisted with derision.

"Do you see what I do for you? And what thanks do I get? You're tearing my family apart. Balor is all I have left. I would have shot him to protect you. I would have shot my brother."

Jacob ran at Sara and booted her in the ribs. She cried out and curled into a ball.

"You good-for-nothing whore!" He kicked Sara again, sucking the wind out of her lungs. "You're just like all women. Poison. Every last one of you."

The heel of his foot caught Sara's chin and snapped her head back. Blood flew from her mouth as she gagged and clawed at the walls for purchase.

Out of his mind, Jacob stomped Sara's shoulder. She crumpled against the floor, a river of blood flowing off her lips. The madman stood above Sara, his foot raised above her head and prepared to crush her skull.

She wanted Jacob to finish the job and end this nightmare.

His breaths flew in and out of his mouth, crazed and out of control. With her hands bound, Sara couldn't shield herself from the beating.

She closed her eyes and prayed for death.

26

Sunlight painted the backs of Scarlett Bell's eyelids and kicked her out of a dream. She flinched and grabbed the back of her neck, her body stiff from sleeping in the rental car all night.

Bell blinked and gazed at the interstate rest area. Eight vehicles parked beside the building. On the far side of the lot, eighteen-wheelers formed a sleeping train. She yawned and scowled when her morning breath wafted back to her. A man in sunglasses exited the building with a Styrofoam coffee cup in his hand. Behind him, a couple emerged through the double doors, each holding a paper bag of something sweet. *Donuts*, Bell thought, her stomach grumbling.

She'd eschewed staying in a hotel, knowing Sheriff Rosario would phone every establishment inside his jurisdiction to find out where she'd holed up for the night. Now, as Bell massaged away a shoulder cramp and willed the pins-and-needles to leave her legs, she questioned her sanity for sleeping in the car.

Three voicemails awaited her—two from Gardy, and another from Quantico, asking where she was and ordering Bell to report back immediately. Like hell she would. What she did on her days off was her own business, even if she was tracking a fugitive serial killer and trying to keep him alive.

Bell stepped out of the car and cupped her elbows, expecting a morning chill, but the temperature was already approaching eighty degrees, a dire preview of the afternoon heat. Inside the travel center, she used the rest facilities and splashed water against her face. She caught her reflection in the dirty mirror and groaned. Her hair stuck out in multiple directions, as though she'd spent the night inside a wind tunnel. Bell raked her fingers through her hair until she appeared human.

After she cleaned up, Bell approached the donut shop and ordered a bagel with cream cheese and a black coffee. Thinking better of it, she told the skinny boy behind the counter, "Make it two coffees. It was a long night."

He nodded and took her money. The boy tossed a second bagel into the bag. *The kid must think I'm homeless*, Bell thought. She removed three dollars from her wallet, but he raised a hand and insisted the bagel was on the house.

"Hey, it's not my business," he said, lowering his voice. "But if you want to clean up for cheap, the truck stop down the interstate has showers. If you can raise fifteen bucks . . ."

"I appreciate the concern, but I'm okay. Really." To ease the boy's concerns and prove she'd meant what she said, Bell slapped a twenty-dollar bill on the counter. "That's for you."

"For what?"

"For caring. Consider it a tip."

She ate the bagel before she made it back to the car, then sipped coffee as she traveled. There wasn't a cloud in the sky, and the sea of blue extended to infinity over the flat landscape. While she drove, she kept checking the mirrors, expecting to see a sheriff's cruiser with flashing lights. Sheriff Rosario had no grounds to arrest Bell, but sometimes laws didn't matter in places like Pronghorn County.

She exited the highway and followed an unmarked road southwest of Dusk Corners. A prickle ran down her arms when she realized she'd entered Devil's Rock territory. This was where the college students had disappeared.

A silo rose in the distance. Beyond the structure, a dirt cloud followed a tractor motoring through a field.

Bell stopped the rental along the road and pulled the Devil's Rock notes from her bag. After skimming the case files, she set them on the passenger seat and touched her lip. A second later, she picked up the files and gave them another scan.

"None of this makes sense."

She'd profiled hundreds of murderers and never encountered a killer who fit this description.

"White, uneducated male, who lacks a firm grip on reality," she said, working on the problem aloud. "He's disorganized and violent. Yet the police and FBI couldn't catch him after nine years of searching, because he's too intelligent."

Bell snapped her fingers.

"Forget the intelligent part. It could mean he moves around a lot. That's the only way a disorganized killer can avoid capture." She sighed and rubbed her tired eyes. "Except he doesn't move around, because the murders cluster inside a tight radius."

She stepped out of the car and turned in a circle, her hand shielding her eyes from the sun.

"Where are you? And how do you know to clean up after yourself, even though you have no concept of right or wrong?"

Her mind returned to Highway 6 through Dusk Corners before the road shot into the great unknown. Truckers traveled Highway 6 between Texas and New Mexico. If Brady Endieveri and Sheila Jarvis had broken down, someone would have come along and helped. But nobody had found their blue Ford Focus. That told Bell they'd taken a wrong turn. Had they come this way?

Before she could talk herself out of it, Bell slid into the driver's seat and followed the dirt cloud to the farm down the road. Someone must have seen those college kids. How many Denver students took the back roads through this part of Texas?

A tall, red barn blotted out the sun. Rays jabbing through the window drew dust motes inside a hay loft. Though Bell couldn't see cows inside the barn, she smelled ripe manure. The farmer was a stout woman with a sun-reddened face. She climbed off the tractor without noticing Bell until the FBI agent honked her horn and waved a friendly hand over her head.

The farmer glanced around in suspicion. Then she wiped her hands on her blue jeans and plodded across a dirt driveway to where Bell stood along the road.

"Are you lost or something?"

"I'm looking for someone," Bell said, rounding the car.

"I'd say you work for Sheriff Rosario, but you don't talk like you're from around these parts."

"You're right about the latter. I'm an FBI agent," Bell said, skipping the preamble and lies.

She held up her identification, and the woman stood stone-faced, as though she'd seen a million such IDs.

"Probably looking for those students, am I right?"

"That you are."

"I'm Grace Langstaff," the woman said, offering a hand.

Bell shook the farmer's hand. "They were driving a blue Ford Focus with Colorado plates and have been missing for over a week. If I'm right, they took a wrong turn on Highway 6 outside Dusk Corners and ended up here."

"Everyone makes that mistake. There's a fork in the road

between Dusk Corners and Joliet. The scrub and trees grow past the sign, and nobody from the county will do anything about it."

"Please tell me you saw their car."

"I didn't," Langstaff said, flicking a blade of grass off her shoulder. "But the day those kids went missing, I heard a vehicle passing while I was working behind the barn. An awful squealing sound, almost like a hog running around with its throat slit. I don't get many vehicles out this way, so when one comes around, I notice."

"A squealing sound."

"Like something was wrong with the car."

That confirmed the theory that Endieveri and Jarvis experienced car trouble before someone with bad intentions came along.

"Did you see another vehicle? Someone following them?"

Before Langstaff could answer, a whooping sound swung them around. Lights flashed on the sheriff's cruiser. The man behind the wheel killed the siren and parked behind Bell's rental. Bell knew it was Rosario before he stepped onto the steaming blacktop.

"Don't tell her another word," Rosario said, pointing at Langstaff. "She's FBI and doesn't have jurisdiction in Pronghorn County. What did she ask you?"

Langstaff looked apologetically at Bell, who shrugged. Bell had nothing to hide. Langstaff might as well tell Rosario the truth.

"She asked about the kids from Denver," said Langstaff, staring at the tops of her boots. "I told her a car drove past the day they vanished. Figured it might help her find them."

"And did you spot a Ford Focus with Colorado plates?"

"Well, no. But I—"

"Then you didn't see them, now did you?" Rosario rounded

on Bell. "I should take you to the office and toss you in a cell for a few nights."

"For what reason?"

"For disobeying my order. I was clear, Agent Bell. You were to leave Pronghorn County and never return without my permission."

"It's a free country."

Rosario pulled his hat over his brow. "Only if I say it is." His eyes burned holes into Langstaff. "From now on, if anyone claiming to be a federal agent comes around and questions you, call me before you open your mouth."

Langstaff turned and walked back to the tractor, her shoulders slumped over, as if she carried a great weight.

"What now?" Bell asked. "Endieveri and Jarvis might have passed this way. We should look for—"

Rosario slapped the hood of Bell's vehicle. "You're leaving my county. Get in your car. I'll follow you to the border and ensure you don't get lost."

"You can't do this."

"The hell I can't. I suggest you start driving, Agent Bell, unless you want me to make good on my threat. I have no qualms over locking you up."

Bell pressed her lips together and turned toward the car.

"Oh," Rosario said, setting his hands on his hips. "Since it's obvious you aren't here on official business, maybe I should call your superiors at Quantico. Won't they love to learn that you're butting in on my investigation?"

"Whatever. You win, Sheriff. I'll leave."

"And tell your partner to get out of Dusk Corners."

Bell froze. Had Gardy followed her to Texas? "My partner?"

"Don't pretend that you're alone. You know the guy. Don Weber. Black hair, dark-blue eyes, talks like he reads too many books."

Logan Wolf.

Bell bit off her smile. Wolf was using the former deputy director's name.

"Where is he?"

"Staying at the Irvin Hotel. But you're leaving. I'll take care of your partner after I see you past the border."

27

S heriff Rosario bumped chests with a man leading his wife out of the Irvin Hotel. The man opened his mouth to protest, recognized Rosario's uniform and badge, and hurried away, with his tail squeezed between his legs.

Rosario had already wasted his morning escorting a rogue FBI agent out of his county, and he wasn't in the mood to deal with an intellectual snob like Don Weber. A deputy had spotted Agent Bell leaving the interstate rest stop after sunrise. After a few calls, Rosario figured out where Bell was heading—the Caprock, the assumed destination of his missing persons. It was a stroke of luck that Rosario spotted Bell's rental at the Langstaff farm. But now Agent Bell was out of Rosario's hair, and he could get back to work.

His first order of business, after he dealt with Weber, was to drive back to Langstaff's home and find out what she'd witnessed. Why the hell hadn't Langstaff contacted Rosario if she had information about the case? Now he had two problems: Langstaff, and that drunk idiot from Dusk Corners, Seth Fonda. Both claimed Endieveri's car had passed them.

Wait until the news found out.

Rosario groaned, knowing how these things always played out. After the media learned Fonda and Langstaff had information about the missing students, they'd wonder why the bumbling sheriff was out of the loop. The media would place Rosario in its crosshairs.

And that was the problem with news people. They wanted controversy and didn't give a damn if Rosario caught the killers. Better that the sheriff never apprehend the murderers. Fear sold newspapers and kept residents glued to their television screens. Devil's Rock was good for business.

He shoved through the doorway and marched toward Pete Chapman, who shrank as the sheriff approached. Rosario slammed an open hand on the counter.

"Where is Weber's vehicle? Is he out on Highway 6 again?"

"I—I don't know where he is," Chapman stammered.

"What do you mean, you don't know? I gave you one task—tell me when Weber comes and goes."

"I did as you said, Sheriff." The hotel proprietor's hand trembled. He reached beneath the counter and removed the list of times Weber had entered and exited the Irvin Hotel. "Here it is."

Rosario ripped the paper from Chapman's hands and raised it in front of his face. Damn, his eyesight kept getting worse. Rosario's doctor had prescribed bifocals during his last visit, but he couldn't keep the county safe with brittle glasses strapped to his face.

"What's with the last entry? It's from yesterday."

Chapman swallowed. "Weber took off sometime last evening. Just packed up his things and left his key on the counter. I checked his room. It's empty."

"Hell." Rosario cracked his knuckles. "And you're just telling me now? What good are you?"

"I figured you wouldn't care no more, on account of he'd left and was out of your hair. That's a good thing, right, Sheriff? Weber leaving and all?"

"Not if I can't find him."

"Maybe he went after that girl, the one he says is his daughter."

"It's not his daughter, dammit." Rosario paced the floor and muttered to himself, thinking out loud. "Do I have another missing person to find?"

"What's that, Sheriff?"

"I wasn't talking to you."

The sheriff slammed the door on his way out of the Irvin Hotel. Leaning through the open window of his cruiser, he grabbed the radio. Had the mysterious Mr. Weber hurt the woman he claimed was his daughter? Funny how people started disappearing when Weber was nearby. The man was somewhere in his county, and Rosario expected Agent Bell would disobey his orders and sneak across the border to meet up with Weber. What were they up to?

He wiped his hand across his mouth and contacted Deputy Beckley.

"That's right, Beckley. Agents Bell and Weber are on the run, west of Dusk Corners. If you see the agents, consider them armed and dangerous."

"Come again, Sheriff?" Beckley asked, the pitch of his voice rising an octave.

"You heard me. Agent Bell disobeyed a direct order to leave Pronghorn County, and Agent Weber, if that's his real name, threatened me."

"He threatened you?"

"Last night, after I told him to pack his belongings and stay out of our investigation."

Beckley paused before replying. "As you wish, Sheriff."

Rosario ended the transmission and studied the horizon.

The reddish-brown haze in the distance told Rosario that the dry line was kicking up another dust storm. The National Weather Service was predicting tornadoes and baseball-size hail by afternoon. Just what he needed.

The sheriff turned out of the parking lot and took Highway 6 to the fork, where he veered left toward the Langstaff farm. He'd never find those kids alive. But he'd be damned if he took the fall for not rescuing them.

28

The hair standing on the back of Logan Wolf's neck told him the Devil's Rock killer was near.

He stopped the Jeep Wrangler ten miles southwest of Dusk Corners and surveyed the land. After following Highway 6 to the fork, he'd taken County Route 13. He'd eliminated all but three quadrants of territory worth investigating, but he was almost out of time. Harold hadn't come through and located Sara's phone, and every call Wolf placed to the IT specialist went straight to his messages.

Wolf removed the laptop from its carrying case and called up a map. If he worked fast, he'd locate the killer before nightfall. How he'd recognize the murderer's house from the road, he wasn't sure, only that he felt certain he'd know it when he saw it. The house would be isolated and in disrepair. The victims' vehicles would be hidden near the house, concealed inside a barn or behind a shed. Wolf expected at least one upper-floor window lent advance notice should law enforcement approach the house.

Other than that, Wolf depended on intuition honed razor-sharp from hunting serial killers for the better part of his adult life.

And for being one.

As he directed the stolen Jeep toward the blazing sun, one eye pinned to the mirror and searching for a sheriff's cruiser, a sudden gust of wind threatened to shove him off the road. Wolf yanked the wheel and pulled his vehicle away from the ditch. Beside the road, a billboard with *Coye's Restaurant and Barbecue* scrawled in bold font rocked and swayed. Two smiling chickens in chef's hats held spatulas and forks, a sort of twisted animal cannibalism that brought a smirk to Wolf's lips.

He spotted the wall of red and brown rolling across the plains. Another dust storm. At the same time, a thunderstorm appeared near the New Mexico border. Lightning forked like dragon fire, and a swirling pendant snaked down from the clouds and tore across the countryside.

Wolf sought an abandoned house like the one he'd hid behind yesterday but found no candidates. The nearest residence sat several hundred yards away, with two cars parked in the driveway. He could ride out the dust storm, but the onrushing tornado wasn't a beast he wished to test. Even a moderate-strength twister possessed enough power to hoist the Jeep and toss it through the air like a child's toy. And this tornado headed straight at him.

SARA BOLTED AWAKE TO A LONG, drawn-out groan, like an old horror movie sound effect of a creaking door. But this effect encompassed the entire house, the noise tearing through every inch of wall and floorboard and sending a flutter down her spine.

She pushed herself up and stumbled toward the window

until the ropes pulled tight. The tarp covering the car in the backyard whipped and snapped, and the sky had turned black while she'd slept. A storm was coming, and this one would pack a wallop. Hours had passed since she'd last heard her phone ringing. Either her kidnappers had located the phone and disposed of it, or the battery was dead. Or maybe Logan had given up on finding her.

She shook the thought away. Logan wouldn't give up. A connection she couldn't explain existed between them. Under different circumstances, she could imagine dating Logan and even sharing a home with the mysterious man. A twist of fate drew them together, and she needed fate to intervene one more time and bring Logan to this house of horrors.

Something bounced off the roof with a dull thud. Then again. Hailstones, and big ones. Suddenly, Sara didn't want to be anywhere near the window, in case the wind burst through the glass.

It was then she noticed another knot had unraveled from the hook on the ceiling. Had she done that? If so, when?

Emboldened, she stood beneath the hook and jumped, trying to jostle the ropes. The angle was all wrong. She climbed onto the chemical toilet again, the smell making her eyes water as she whipped the ropes. Another knot sprang apart. The ropes continued to uncoil, giving her added slack. Another few inches, and she'd reach the window. Still, the ropes bound her wrists together. Unless she wanted to drag the ropes across the Texas Caprock, she needed to free her arms.

Another gust of wind rattled the windowpane and peppered the house with sediment. The sky was a deeper shade of black now. Purples and greens tinged the undersides of the clouds, which dropped and lifted with hypnotic violence. She knew a tornado was coming before the inhuman freight train roar screamed across the countryside.

Desperate to escape the storm, Sara shook the ropes and twisted another loop off the hook until her arms fell limp from overexertion. For the first time since the psychos tied her up, she lowered her hands to her sides. Her arms buzzed as the feeling returned to them. But the train sound grew louder, and Sara feared the house stood too close to the tornado's path.

A door burst open down the hall. Then Jacob's frantic voice called to his brother in the attic. Footsteps pounded toward her room.

Ignoring her exhaustion, Sara raised her arms above her head and hoped Jacob wouldn't notice the ropes had slackened. He threw the door open, glanced out the window, and hurried to Sara.

"Don't even think about trying anything," he said. "A twister is coming. We need to get to the basement."

Jacob's knife stuck out from his back pocket as he wrestled with the ropes around Sara's wrists. Her eyes locked on the knife. When he freed her hands, she'd have a split second to snatch the knife from his pocket and stab the maniac. Except Jacob couldn't unwind the knots.

"Hurry," Sara said, imploring him with her eyes. "The storm is almost here."

A shutter ripped off the house and whipped past the window. A chorus of shrieks emanated from above the attic— the wind was tearing the nails out of the roof.

Jacob cursed and worked faster, his fingers prying inside the bindings. Sara's heart fell when he grabbed the knife. Out of time, he sawed the ropes.

A desperate idea popped into her head. Insanity. It would never work.

Before she could talk herself out of it, Sara swung her arms down, pulling the ropes with them. Jacob didn't have time to react before Sara yanked back on the ropes and twisted them around his neck. He thrashed and screamed for his brother. The demon wind swallowed his cries.

They toppled to the floor, with Sara flat on her back and Jacob atop her and staring bug-eyed at the ceiling. She pulled harder on the ropes, strangling him. He gagged and writhed as she gritted her teeth and strained. He swung his elbow back and struck her temple. Her eyes lost focus. He tried again, and she twisted her head out of the way. The point of his elbow smacked against the floor.

The knife flew from his hand. Sara reached for the weapon, but Jacob twisted around with fury etched into his face. She wound the ropes around his neck and rolled him over, leaning back and tugging. Jacob's face turned red. His arms and legs beat against the floor as she pulled until he passed out.

After he stopped fighting and collapsed, she clutched the knife and sawed through the rope. Jacob had done most of the work when he'd attempted to free her from the hook. Two slices cut through her bindings.

She cried when the blood flowed back into her hands. Outside, the storm raged and screamed from the heavens.

Sara staggered through the doorway and collided with the wall when her legs gave out. Through the window in the front room, she watched a tree bend sideways and tear out of the ground. A swirling black mass rumbled across the road, the tornado choked with debris and shingles that must have comprised someone's home moments before.

Balor howled above the ceiling. He thumped toward the attic door, which stood mere steps behind Sara. The trapdoor opened, and the ladder extended. His bearded, lunatic face peeked through the opening, spotted Sara, and twisted with derision.

Sara lunged for the front door as Balor crashed into the hall-way. When she opened the door, the wind yanked it out of her hands and tossed it skyward. The storm shoved her against the wall while she turned and struggled along the outside of the house.

The tornado was almost on top of her when she broke free of the wind and sprinted out of the yard. Somewhere behind her, Balor burst through the doorway.

Then she became weightless. The storm snatched Sara and threw her toward the ditch as hail and rain pelted her body.

She struck the ground and lost consciousness.

29

The Jeep's rear wheels rose five feet above the road and smashed against the pavement. Wolf stomped the brakes, but the vehicle had a mind of its own as the storm manipulated the Jeep like a marionette. He held the wheel while the vehicle spun out and came to a stop in the middle of the desolate road. Hail the size of baseballs splattered against the blacktop. He'd lost the back windshield, where a gigantic hailstone busted through the glass.

A tornado swirled across the countryside about two miles south of his position. Thunder peeled and lightning stroked through the churning and twisting clouds.

He sat with his hands gripping the steering wheel, stunned he'd survived the storm. The hail stopped and the rain lessened as he eased the Jeep down the road, where melting hail turned the landscape into a scene from an apocalyptic winter.

Wolf wiped the sweat from his forehead and looked around, trying to get his bearings. Something sparkled along the road's shoulder, and it wasn't ice.

He shifted the Jeep into reverse and backed up. After he checked the sky for additional threats, he climbed out of the vehicle and knelt on the shoulder. Pellets of safety glass, and they hadn't come from the stolen Jeep.

Wolf turned around and spied two dark stripes along the blacktop that could have been tire streaks. The burnt rubber might have belonged to any vehicle, but Wolf believed Brady Endieveri and Sheila Jarvis had come this way. He was closer than ever to finding the Devil's Rock killer, but there was too much ground to cover.

Along the road, he pushed the tall grass aside and spotted three indentations in the mud shaped like shoe prints. Given their gargantuan sizes, he wasn't sure they were prints at all. Hadn't Sheriff Rosario found a size twenty-four shoe print behind Kimberly Ripa's house?

Stepping through the grass and wary of snakes, Wolf searched for additional prints. He pictured the lost college students stumbling along the road, with the monstrous killer steps behind. Had they broken down before the murderer found them? He located another print when the burner phone rang inside the Jeep. He jumped over the ditch and hurried back to the vehicle, hoping Sara was calling back to yell at him for being a jerk. Hope burgeoned that this was all a misunderstanding, and Sara was back in Lubbock and watching the storms through her apartment window.

He paused when an unknown number scrolled across the screen. After a moment of consideration, he answered.

"I take it you're still in Texas."

Harold's voice. Wolf clenched his hand around the phone.

"You were to call me yesterday, Harold. How long does it take to ping a phone?"

The IT specialist exhaled. "You're lucky I returned your call. I spent yesterday in the director's office getting grilled over who I was talking to inside the storage room. I had no choice but to dispose of the burner and purchase another. Everyone is watching me now, Wolf. I can't keep doing this."

"You can and you will."

"Why should I?"

"Because you're resourceful and efficient, my good man, and you believe in the cause."

"Bullshit."

"Is it now? If you didn't wish to help, you would have abandoned me years ago. But you never did. Face it, Harold. Had you the stomach and the skills, you'd follow the same path. Don't you lie awake at night, wishing you could rid the world of its nightmares?"

"Stop with the psychoanalysis. I located your friend's phone."

Wolf froze. "Sara's phone?"

"It took me this long to slip away and ping the location without someone staring over my shoulder. Do you want the coordinates or not?"

"Give me her location. Time is of the essence."

"Understand the limitations. I can get you within a one-mile radius with a high degree of certainty. But I can't—"

"The coordinates, Harold. You're beginning to tire me."

As Harold read the coordinates, Wolf repeated them to himself, memorizing the numbers until he pictured the digital map of the countryside and honed in on Sara's location. This was the break he'd waited for. He had one last chance to rescue Sara before the Devil's Rock killer turned her into another statistic.

"You got that, Wolf?"

"Loud and clear."

"The coordinates . . . that's the location of the Devil's Rock killer, isn't it?"

"It's better I don't give you an answer, Harold. It will keep you alive longer, and you can hang on to your precious job."

"But, Wolf—"

"Keep your head down. The FBI is onto you now. You won't hear from me for at least two weeks. In the meantime, keep yourself out of trouble."

Wolf tossed the phone into the car and punched the coordinates into his GPS unit. The map displayed a solitary road running through desolate land about five miles from his position. He cross-referenced the GPS location with the digital maps he'd downloaded at the Irvin Hotel and counted three residences within a one-mile radius. One house sat alone, with plenty of land on either side and a perfect view of approaching vehicles. The satellite image had been taken a year ago. It showed a dead tree in the front yard and a massive truck in the driveway. Between the leafless tree and the house, it would be easy to stash a vehicle in the backyard and conceal it from prying eyes.

Goosebumps prickled Wolf's arms. He'd found his quarry.

30

At fifteen minutes past seven o'clock, Sheriff Rosario took a radio call from Deputy Beckley. A half-hour before, after the deputy finished writing a speeding ticket on the interstate, he'd driven south toward Dusk Corners and glimpsed Agent Bell's rental creeping along the back roads, as though searching for something. The second Beckley turned onto the farm-to-market road to pursue Bell, she'd disappeared.

Rosario cursed inside his cruiser. If you wanted something done right, you had to do it yourself. Though loyal to the sheriff, Beckley was borderline incompetent and didn't stand a chance against a veteran FBI agent. It would be simple for Agent Bell to give Beckley the slip by driving into an open barn or parking the vehicle behind a thicket off the road. Like the idiot he was, Beckley probably drove past and never noticed.

Rosario felt as though the universe had shifted since sunrise. He sensed he was close to apprehending the maniacs who'd abducted those college kids. Rosario wasn't about to let Agent Bell or her partner disobey his orders and interfere in his investigation.

The sheriff fired his lights and siren and sped from the

interstate to Highway 6, where he followed the road into Dusk Corners. As he traveled, he replayed his discussion with Grace Langstaff, the farmer Agent Bell had questioned. According to Langstaff, she'd heard a squealing car pass her property on the day Brady Endieveri and Sheila Jarvis vanished. Langstaff never saw a blue Ford Focus. She'd been working behind the barn. The car could have belonged to anyone. Rosario's intuition told him the Denver students had passed the farm, but even the news media had to admit the evidence was flimsy. The reporters couldn't pin this screw up on Rosario. Now all he needed to do was pay Seth Fonda a visit and ensure the drunk understood what he'd seen. Or hadn't seen. Fonda was the only witness who claimed a blue Ford Focus had passed through Dusk Corners, and it would be easy to throw Fonda's reliability into question.

If Rosario solved the case, he'd salvage the upcoming election. And if the fates were on his side, and the sheriff found those students alive, he'd be a hero. The problem was, Don Weber always stayed one step ahead of the sheriff. What did Weber know?

His mind racing, Rosario stopped at the Irvin Hotel and found Pete Chapman at the check-in counter.

"I want to see Weber's room."

"But he left last night. I told you, he cleared out his belongings and took off."

"Will you open the damn room, or do I need to get a warrant?"

Chapman raised his hands. "No need for a warrant. I'll show you the room. But I'm telling you, there's nothing inside."

Rosario grumbled about incompetent deputies and hotel owners while he trailed Chapman up the stairs. The proprietor's hand trembled as he unlocked the door. Rosario barged in ahead of Chapman and swept his gaze over the room.

"Show me that picture again. The one with the intersection listed."

Chapman fumbled inside his pocket for his phone. "Here it is. There were two numbers on the pad. Thirteen and six."

"That has to be County Route 13 and Highway 6." Rosario removed his hat and fanned his face with the brim. "But I sent Beckley to the intersection, and he didn't find a damn thing. When I asked Weber about the location, he played stupid."

Rosario whipped the closet door open and beamed his flashlight up and down the walls. Finding nothing of interest, he moved to the bathroom. A black strand of hair lay between the tub and sink. Removing tweezers and a plastic bag, Rosario plucked the hair off the bathroom floor and sealed it inside the bag.

"Now we'll find out who you really are, Don Weber."

He scanned the bathroom for anything he'd missed. Then he entered the bedroom, lifted the mattress, and shone the flashlight beneath the bed. Rosario checked every inch of the room for a fingerprint. He found one on the nightstand.

Chapman leaned over Rosario's shoulder. "Is that Weber's print?"

Rosario narrowed his eyes. "It's too slender. If I had to guess, I'd say it's the girl's fingerprint."

"His daughter?"

"For the last time, she's not his daughter." Rosario paced. "I don't have time to lift that print. I'll send a deputy over. Until then, don't touch this room. Understood?"

"Yes, Sheriff."

"Now to figure out what Weber found at the intersection of 13 and 6. And when I get there, something tells me I'll run into Agent Bell."

"Who?"

"Shut up, Chapman. I'm thinking." Rosario's eyes drifted

across the room and returned to the nightstand. A memo pad with the Irvin Hotel's logo lay on the corner. "Is this where you found the note with the route numbers?"

"Yes. He must have ripped the sheet off and taken it before he left."

Rosario tapped his fingers against his leg. "You got a pencil in this room, Chapman?"

"Uh, no. I leave pens for the guests."

"Get me a pencil. You have one somewhere, right?"

"I, uh, I suppose."

"Then find it. I don't have all day."

While Chapman hurried downstairs, Rosario, wearing gloves, lifted the memo pad and stared. Someone had written a string of numbers on the pad and taken the sheet. After a minute, the hotel proprietor returned with a handful of sharpened pencils and offered them to Rosario.

"I only need one, you idiot," Rosario said, snatching a pencil.

Using the edge of the pencil, the sheriff drew with a light, sweeping motion.

"What are you doing?"

"Didn't you ever do this in grade school, Chapman? I'm figuring out what he wrote on the pad."

"You can see the indentations."

"That's the idea."

Satisfied, Rosario lifted the page and grinned. It was a ten-digit phone number with a California area code.

"Is that Weber's phone number, or the girl's?"

"Only one way to find out." Rosario pocketed the paper. "Remember, stay out of the room until my deputy sweeps for prints."

When he reached his cruiser, Rosario punched the number into his phone. After seven rings, a voice message played.

"Hi, this is Sara. Leave a number and I'll call you back.

Unless you're a mean person. Mean people suck, and I don't call them back." A giggle, then a flirty, "Bye."

Rosario ended the call.

"What's your last name, Sara? And why did you sleep with an FBI agent?"

With a grumble, Rosario radioed the office.

"Did Beckley return to the office?"

"Deputy Beckley should be back in five or ten minutes, Sheriff," the dispatcher said.

"Patch me through to Sharon."

"Yes, sir."

Sharon, Rosario's only female deputy, knew her way around computers, unlike his Neanderthal deputies. After Sharon answered, Rosario recited Sara's phone number and told Sharon to look her up.

A few key strokes later, Sharon said, "Sara Brennan. She lives in Lubbock. You want the address?"

"Give it to me."

Rosario copied the address as Sharon read it back to him.

"She a Texas girl, Sharon?"

"Graduated high school in Encino, California."

"California? Give me her parents' names."

She did.

He'd caught Weber in another lie. Sara Brennan wasn't Weber's daughter, and now the girl was missing. And what in the hell was Weber searching for on County Route 13? There was nothing out there but farmland, oil fields, and rattlesnakes.

Thunder rumbled west of town. Rosario peeked at the waving trees as a fat raindrop splattered against the windshield. Tornado warnings covered half the county, and the weather wouldn't let up until after midnight. That would make it difficult to locate Agents Weber and Bell. Rosario wasn't afraid of storms, but he'd lived his entire life in Texas and respected severe weather. He headed west on Highway 6.

Rosario turned left at the fork. Driving along an unmarked road until he reached County Route 13, he braked in the center of the road and stared. A chill rolled through his body, as if the cruiser stood at the gates of hell. The few trees left standing had been stripped of their leaves, the remaining trees flattened and thrown across the prairie. Wires lay across the road. Sparks hissed and rained fireworks into puddles. He stepped out of the cruiser, trying to remember if there had been houses along the road. If there had been, they weren't there now.

He ordered dispatch to send cruisers to his position, just in case the storms had struck residences. He didn't have time to search for survivors, not with two rogue agents somewhere over the horizon and dismantling everything he'd built during his two decades as sheriff.

"Nobody lives out here," he repeated, until the lie no longer festered on the tip of his tongue.

Daylight faded. Soon, darkness would descend upon Pronghorn County, and it would be just Rosario, the storms, and a pair of rogue agents chasing a phantom killer.

Movement pulled Rosario's vision down the road. He drew in a breath.

Agent Bell's rental.

Her car trailed down the Caprock three miles away. Rosario hopped into the cruiser and shifted into drive. It was already too dark to travel without headlights, but Rosario kept them off.

Agent Bell would never see him coming.

31

Outside a fast-food restaurant at the interstate rest stop, Scarlett Bell chewed a gristly burger slapped between two soggy buns. The soda helped her choke down the salty fries, but the caffeine made her restless and jittery. And at that moment, she needed to think clearly, even more than her stomach required food. The rest stop sat atop an incline a hundred feet above the highway, offering a westward view toward the New Mexico border. Lightning flashed through black, ominous clouds spreading across the prairie, and storm warnings kept interrupting the easy rock channel she played to relax her nerves.

Bell swallowed the last of the burger and wadded the bag before tossing it onto the floor beside the passenger seat, knowing she'd regret the fast food a few hours from now. Every burp would remind her of the greasy meal until she consumed something healthy, like a salad or a smoothie. As if she would find either at an interstate rest stop.

Spread out on the seat were notes on every murder from the Devil's Rock files. Combined with Grace Langstaff's belief that Brady Endieveri and Sheila Jarvis had passed her farm, Bell had

narrowed the search area to a ten-mile radius southwest of Dusk
Corners. That was too much area to cover in one evening, but
now that she'd confirmed Logan Wolf was nearby, all she
needed to do was follow the blood trail.

She left the rest stop and merged with traffic. The next exit
took her toward Langstaff's farm, a few miles from County Route
13. As she approached the farm, a fleet of sheriff's cruisers shot
toward Bell with their lights whirling and sirens shrieking. Her
heart climbed into her throat as she peered around, searching
for an escape route and finding none. The cruisers kept coming,
shooting down the road at eighty mph.

"I've done nothing wrong," she argued with herself. "They
can't arrest me."

But they could. Rosario would see to it, even though the
sheriff wouldn't have a leg to stand on after she contacted a
lawyer. Dragging the legal system into this mess wouldn't win
her any favors with the FBI. Rosario arresting Bell while she
investigated a murder out of her jurisdiction would be a public
relations nightmare. She set the car in park and waited for the
inevitable.

Instead of stopping and dragging her out of the vehicle,
they blew past, one after the other. Each cruiser's wake shook
the rental and sent shock waves through Bell's chest. After the
last of five cruisers rocketed by the rental, she swung around
and watched them through the rear windshield. It was then
she noticed the snapped power poles in the distance and the
barn crumpled on its side like a beached whale. The deputies
were responding to storm damage and hadn't even noticed
her.

Feeling stupid, she eased the car off the shoulder and
continued past the Langstaff farm, glancing toward the property,
but not seeing a vehicle in the driveway or a light inside. Bell
checked the map and turned left at the T. Her phone rang, and

she sent the call through the rental's speakers. It was her partner, Agent Gardy.

"Why are you in Texas, Bell?"

"Who said I'm in—"

"Cut the BS. A sheriff named Rosario called the office, asking why one of our agents was sticking her nose into his missing persons case."

"I can explain."

"Doubtful, but you can relax. I covered for you. Nobody needs to find out that you're in Pronghorn County. Where is he?"

"Who?"

"No more games. Logan Wolf. That's who you're searching for, right? Let it go, Bell. You can't trust him. He's just as likely to turn on you as—"

"You don't believe that, Gardy. Wolf saved our lives."

"That's no reason to put your life on the line and risk your career. If the FBI finds out you're aiding a fugitive, they won't just take your job. They'll lock you up."

"That's a risk I'm willing to take."

Gardy scoffed. "Why?"

"There's something wrong with him, Gardy. He's sick."

"You can say that again."

"I'm talking about his physical health. Wolf was there for us when we needed him. I owe him the same courtesy."

"Since the day I met you, you've never owed anybody anything. That's not how you play."

"Then maybe I care about the guy. Is that a crime, too?"

Several seconds of quiet played out, so Bell could replay her own words inside her head. Gardy always relied on this strategy when he couldn't get through to her.

"I wanted to talk to you face-to-face, but this will have to do for now," Gardy said. "Please understand. I don't hate Logan Wolf. In fact, I owe him my life."

"Then why won't you help him?"

"Just let me talk for once, okay?"

"Yeah, sure."

"There are some problems you can't fix, Bell, no matter how badly you want to. Wolf's train flew off the tracks when Renee died. That's not his fault, but it doesn't make him any less dangerous. You might see him as some kind of dark superhero, some avenging angel righting the world's wrongs. Or perhaps you think he's an injured mongrel dog that had once been someone's pet, a stray you can take home and train. Well, you can't. He'll turn on you when you least expect it. All the goodness inside Logan Wolf died a long time ago, and that's how he wants it. I won't sit back and watch my partner throw away her life to rescue a man who doesn't want saving."

"You don't know him the way I do."

"That's what scares me more than anything. How much contact do you have with Wolf? Be honest. I won't pass judgment."

"Like hell, you won't," said Bell.

"Tell me. A few times a year? Once a month? More?"

"Once every few weeks." When Gardy protested, Bell cut him off. "But not for a long time. He disappeared. That's not like him."

"I knew it. He visits your condo, doesn't he?"

"Not . . . when I'm home."

"You gave him a key?"

"Not exactly."

Gardy laughed without mirth. "What does *not exactly* mean? He breaks in?"

"Yeah."

"Yet you trust him."

"Wolf never betrayed me, Gardy. God knows he's had multiple opportunities to hurt me, if that's what he wanted."

"You two might have some twisted connection I'll never understand, but he'll land you in hot water when the FBI figures out he's been inside your place on multiple occasions, and you never reported him."

"That's another bridge to cross."

"There's a one-way ticket to DC waiting for you in Amarillo," Gardy said, his smile loud over the phone.

"What?"

"The plane leaves at midnight. That gives you enough time to pack and drive to the airport. First class, Bell."

"You had no right to book a flight in my name."

"Consider it a favor, one you'll thank me for after your drunken haze wears off. The party ends tonight. Cut bait and walk away while you still have your reputation."

"I wish you hadn't done that."

"Look, I can't hold off Rosario much longer. When he finds out I didn't pass his complaints on to the director, he'll push harder and take his argument straight to the top. You'll be in deep, and I won't be able to bail you out."

"I don't give a damn about Rosario."

"There's something else you need to know. Rosario collected hair fibers from Wolf's room at the Irvin Hotel. Don't worry. He still thinks the guy's name is Don Weber. Nice touch. But Rosario intends to send that sample in for DNA processing. Guess what name will pop up after the lab runs the test?"

"Oh, hell."

"Even if you keep protecting Wolf, you can't save him from Rosario. Now, do you want your name connected to Wolf when the cow patty wallops the fan? Or would you rather fly home while you can? Bell, I told Rosario you aren't working with this Don Weber character. I even covered for that ridiculous story you gave him about teaching a profiling course."

"Rosario bought it?" Bell asked.

"I doubt that very much."

Bell stared over her shoulder. The cruisers had stopped beside the storm damage. Deputies searched the wreckage for survivors, while a train of power company vehicles raced to repair the downed lines.

"Help me out one last time, Gardy. I swear I won't ask for another favor."

Gardy chuckled. "Right."

"Give me something new about the Devil's Rock killer."

"So you can save a fugitive? I won't."

"Come on. Have I ever let you down when you were in a fix?"

"What fix? Unlike you, I don't leap into pots of boiling water." Gardy exhaled, and Bell imagined him pacing inside his office with the doors closed, one hand glued to his forehead as he decided what to do. "There's nothing about the Devil's Rock murders you haven't already learned. But I gleaned one bit of information."

"Tell me."

"The BAU had me follow Harold over the last two days."

"Why on earth would you follow Harold?"

"I'll tell you what I found, and you can draw your own conclusions. Harold pinged the location on someone's phone earlier, but not before I intercepted the transmission. I checked the number, and it belongs to a woman from Lubbock named Sara Brennan."

"How would Wolf know Sara Brennan?"

"You tell me. Perhaps she's his next victim."

"Not unless she's a serial killer, herself," Bell argued. "You remember Wolf's credo. He doesn't murder innocents."

"Be that as it may, Harold located this Sara Brennan's phone, and I'm certain this has something to do with Logan Wolf and the Devil's Rock killer."

Bell touched her forehead. "That means Harold is working with Wolf."

"Seems you're not the only one Wolf swindled."

"Give me the coordinates, Gardy. If you don't trust my judgment, trust Harold's."

"What if the coordinates lead you to the Devil's Rock killer?"

"I don't care."

"I do."

"Sara Brennan might be in trouble. Did you share this information with—"

"Rosario? Please, I wouldn't help that cretin." Gardy clicked his tongue against the roof of his mouth. "I'll give you the coordinates on one condition."

"Anything."

"You board that plane at midnight and fly home."

"That's impossible. There's not enough time."

"You're testing my patience."

"I'll grab the first flight in the morning. Just read me the coordinates."

To Bell's surprise, Gardy complied.

32

Until now, Wolf had held firm to the slim hope that Sara had driven back to Lubbock. Harold's report had stolen that hope from him, and now he followed the GPS toward the coordinates the BAU IT specialist had given him. With the light almost gone from the sky, he searched the road for a stranded Jetta. Sprinkles pattered the windshield and ran in long streaks down the glass, interrupted by the swipe of the wipers.

The profile he'd constructed replayed inside his head—the killer lives in an isolated location in a home stricken by disrepair. This is the perfect place to hide a victim without drawing attention from the neighbors because there are none. The backyard provides privacy when the psycho stashes vehicles. He may bury some bodies on his property, so he may visit the victims and relive the murders.

Wolf wiped his eyes. A light shone in the distance, one yellow glow bleeding from a window along the front of the home. Wolf's heart pounded when he spied the house he'd seen in the satellite photo. This was it. He knew as soon as he saw the house that he'd found the Devil's Rock killer. Wolf swallowed. His achievement would be worthless unless Sara was alive.

He killed the headlights and slowed the Jeep along the shoulder. Checking the mirrors, he confirmed he was alone on the road. No witnesses. Nobody to phone the police if a stranger sneaked into the house and murdered the hostile inside. He noted the Dodge Ram parked in the driveway and cocked an eyebrow. Disorganized killers drove vehicles just like normal people, but despite the muddy exterior, this Ram appeared well-maintained. Someone had cared for the truck. The conviction he held for his profile wavered slightly.

Before the killer spotted him, Wolf pulled the Jeep off the road and parked behind two trees. He couldn't hide the Jeep from someone driving past, but at least the killer wouldn't see him coming.

Adrenaline thrummed on high tension wires through his body. The house stood a few hundred yards up the road, the faded white paint glowing as darkness seeped over the prairie. He slung raindrops off his face and eyed the sky with wariness when lightning stroked between two rain-swollen clouds. Running hunched over, he darted across the road, at one with the darkness.

Two shattered windows fronted the home. A checkerboard of shingles covered the yard.

Wolf crossed the property line and saw Sara's Jetta behind the house. The back tires were flat, and the front of the car hung ajar, as though someone had done a sloppy job of towing the vehicle. Beside the Jetta, another vehicle hid beneath a tarp. He checked the house for movement, then jumped over a puddle and ducked behind Sara's car. Testing the door, he found it unlocked. The killer had shattered the driver's side window. Safety pellets covered the floor. There was something glowing beneath the seat. After a quick glance toward the house, he fished his hand under the driver's seat and removed Sara's phone. He couldn't unlock the screen without her code, but he noticed an alert that Sara's mother had messaged her seconds before.

He silenced the phone and put it in his pocket. Then he peeked beneath the tarp. The Denver students' blue Ford Focus stared him in the face, and the stench that rolled out of the vehicle made his eyes water. There were enough flies buzzing inside the Ford to blanket the windows and seats with the disease-carrying insects. A man's body slumped in the back, his upper torso wrenched at an inhuman angle. The college student's pale face watched Wolf with dead, unblinking eyes. Where was his girlfriend?

Wolf turned away and started toward the house, sticking to the deepening shadows to avoid detection. There was a door off the back that appeared to descend toward a cellar. With a practiced hand, he moved the handle without making a sound. Locked. Wolf slid the lock pick into the handle and gave it a twist.

The mechanism popped, and the door swung open.

33

S heriff Edward Rosario crisscrossed the Texas Caprock in search of Agent Scarlett Bell and the man who called himself Don Weber. He couldn't decide if Weber was a dirty fed with a hatred for honest law officers like himself, or the devil behind the mask, a man who took women to his room and buried their bodies in the desert after he tired of them.

That afternoon, he'd spoken to an agent at the Behavioral Analysis Unit named Neil Gardy. Gardy backed up Agent Bell's story that she was researching the Caprock murders for a profiling course. Gardy also claimed Don Weber wasn't working with Bell, though Gardy remained evasive about who Weber was and why he'd come to Pronghorn County.

Rosario didn't believe Gardy. The FBI had entered CYA mode and didn't want to admit they were moving in on his investigation.

The sheriff passed a field of pumpjacks and spotted Agent Bell's rental cresting a ridge. Since Rosario had first spotted Bell outside Dusk Corners, he'd lost her twice. She was driving well above the speed limit and cutting across the Caprock as if she knew her destination. Rosario would nail her for speeding and interfering with his case. After he tossed her in a cell, she'd lose the smug certainty that Rosario wouldn't harm an FBI agent. He would. He'd broken stronger people than her. Forty-eight hours in a cage changed one's attitude and defined the pecking order.

Thunder rolled across the land. While Rosario pursued the FBI agent, his deputies busied themselves with wreckage between the highway and the Caprock. Three tornadoes had smashed his county, leaving nothing behind but splinters and lost hope. Power lines lay across multiple roads. When storms this powerful struck, it often took days before the utility company got the power working.

A call came over his radio requesting help. His deputies had come across a two-story farmhouse spun off its foundation. The home had been in the direct path of a killer tornado, and the deputies hadn't located the three children who lived there or their parents.

"Come in, Sheriff," Beckley's voice said through the speaker. "Repeat, we have an emergency at the corner of—"

Rosario reached over and flicked the radio off. The deputies and emergency workers would have to deal with the search and rescue mission. He had two rogue agents to apprehend, and the Caprock murderers were still at-large.

The hair strand and attached follicle lay inside a plastic evidence bag. He also had Weber's license plate and would run the number when he returned to the office. Soon, Rosario would know who Don Weber was and why he'd come to Pronghorn County.

It struck him suddenly. Bell had located the killers and wanted to beat him to the scene. She intended to rescue the missing students and steal the credit and fame. The sheriff didn't care about being famous. But Rosario knew how it would look if a single FBI agent usurped him and solved his case. He'd never recover. Good luck getting reelected.

As he closed the distance on Agent Bell, he narrowed his eyes. She'd taken an unexpected turn, heading away from civilization. Except for a few isolated residences, nobody lived in this area of West Texas. He picked up speed and gained on her vehicle. The FBI agent cruised two miles ahead of him now. Night spilled down from the sky, making it easy to track the vehicle's taillights. He kept his headlights off, so she wouldn't see him closing in on her.

Rosario pressed the accelerator until the engine roared and the cruiser shook. It was time to end this charade.

"You should have told me the truth, Agent Bell," Rosario said, drumming his fingers on the steering wheel. "Now you'll see how I deal with unscrupulous law enforcement."

34

S ara was adrift at sea. Wind and waves pounded her flesh as she clutched a piece of debris skimming the water. Behind her, the vessel she'd ridden sank into the ocean, only the hull visible as the water claimed the boat. She searched for other survivors who might be in the water, but saw only darkness above the breakers. The Pacific chilled her to the bone. Her teeth chattered, and water clogged her nostrils as she gasped and fought to stay afloat.

Exhaustion claimed Sara. Her eyes fluttered shut, the current dragging her under. A thunder blast ripped Sara out of her slumber, but when she blinked, she no longer viewed the raging Pacific, only a sodden prairie of clay. Muddy rivulets trickled around her.

The memory of Balor chasing her through the downstairs before the tornado struck brought Sara up to her knees. All around her, lightning strobed and rain hammered the earth. She lay five feet from a ditch clogged with debris and flooding waters. Had she landed in the ditch and lost consciousness, she would have drowned. Everything hurt, as though someone stabbed spears into her body whenever she moved. Panting, she searched for the house and found it a few hundred yards behind her. Except for broken windows and missing shingles, the house appeared untouched by the killer winds. Which meant Balor and Jacob might have survived. The dead tree that once stood in the yard had disappeared and left a deep gash in the earth. Branches lay everywhere, the old tree converted to kindling.

It took all of Sara's willpower to stand. A wetness dripped off her brow, and when she touched it, her hand came away red. The road extended for miles without a hint of civilization in the distance. She considered following the road and talked herself out of it. The brothers might climb into the truck and come looking for her. Sara remembered the phone inside the Jetta, but when she turned toward the house, a shadow moved across the window. She crouched low and hoped nobody had spotted her. Then, when the shadow didn't come again, she took off running toward a thicket several hundred yards into the prairie. If she made it there, she could cut back to the road with no one in the house spotting her.

As she rushed forward, the rain-drenched earth sucked at her sneakers and splattered her legs with mud. The soggy ground added to her exhaustion, but the pain seemed to lessen the more she moved her bones. At least nothing was broken. A miracle, considering how close the twister had come to engulfing her. Sara shot glances over her shoulder. Still no movement back at the house. She was going to make it.

Sara pushed through the trees and looked around. She felt the creeping sensation that she wasn't alone in the thicket and that someone was watching her. After she leaned against a bur oak and caught her breath, the thick canopy shielding her from the elements, she listened for the telltale footsteps of someone following her. But there was nothing but the wind whistling through the trees.

A gust released water from the leafy canopy. The droplets

cascaded down and soaked Sara's clothes. A branch snapped and pulled her head around, but nothing but shadows trailed her through the thicket. She hurried to the next tree and dropped to one knee, panting. Another branch snapped, and Sara's paranoia grew, encasing her up to her neck in frozen terror. But Sara was a big girl now, despite how her mother treated her, and she wasn't about to succumb to an overactive imagination. No one had chased her after she'd dragged her body away from the ditch. If Jacob or his demon brother had seen Sara, they would have left the house and come for her by now.

Unless they were already out in the rain and searching for her.

She got her bearings and cut through the trees, angling toward the road beyond the thicket. With any luck, she'd flag down a traveler who'd offer her a ride into town and call the police.

When she was almost out of the thicket, she saw the dead woman hung on crisscrossed stakes like a scarecrow. Her skin was as pale as Minnesota in January. Antlers, like the ones hanging in Sara's room of imprisonment, jutted out of the woman's head, where'd they'd been nailed into her scalp. A deep gouge ran across her throat, her shirt crusted with blood. Ropes bound her arms, and her neck lolled at a grotesque angle, so the woman's eyes seemed to look up at Sara, even though the victim's body was suspended a foot above Sara's head.

Sara gasped and backed away, unable to peel her gaze from the dead woman. This had to be Sheila Jarvis, one of the missing college students. Sara gagged and bent over, spilling what little she'd held in her stomach onto the muddy ground. When she turned back to Jarvis, a black and yellow insect the size of her thumb scurried out of the woman's mouth. The insect had wings and a deadly stinger, and the thought that something so repulsive had crept inside Jarvis's mouth caused Sara to shriek until her lungs went dry and refused to respond.

After the scream escaped her lips, Sara covered her mouth, realizing her mistake. The brothers must have heard. They'd come for her now.

Sara ran into the night.

35

The odor that struck Wolf at the top of the basement stairs reminded him of the death scent inside the Ford, except this smell was older, a nightmarish rotten meat stench baked into the concrete. He took one step and peered around the corner. Cloaked in shadow, the cellar waited in secrecy at the bottom of the stairs.

There was a red-stained hatchet on the floor. Blood spatter covered the walls, dry and black now and flaking off the concrete. He crept to the water heater and angled his head around the side. An ax rested against the wall, and a long metal table held deer antlers with deadly points. He grabbed the ax and lifted it. Hair and blood covered the edge of the blade. A frozen tremble rippled through his heart when he examined the hair color. If it was black like Sara's, he'd lose his mind. In the mottled dusky light that poured through the window, he studied the blade until he convinced himself the hair was blonde. It was hard to tell with all that blood. He set the ax aside and slipped the hunting knife from its sheathe. His other hand drifted to the Glock he concealed in his pocket.

A second stairway stood in the corner. Wolf listened at the

bottom, but the house remained deathly silent. Careful where he stepped and wary of the boards squealing beneath his weight, he ascended the stairs and nudged the door open. A hallway extended left and right. A living room without furniture comprised the front half of the house, with a kitchen across from it. Two bedrooms waited at the back of the structure, and a trapdoor loomed overhead. He stopped beneath the trapdoor, which ostensibly led to the attic. No sounds came from above.

He moved into the living room, staying close to the wall while a screaming wind ripped through the night sky. The kitchen held an ancient refrigerator and gas stove. Rust spots on the floor marked where the refrigerator had once stood before the killer moved it. No table or chairs. The house had one purpose: it gave the killer a place to slaughter his victims, with no one to witness his madness.

But where was Sara?

Wolf reversed course and stepped down the hallway, passing beneath the trapdoor again. Instinct stopped him. He reached for the trapdoor before a bang pulled his attention to the bedrooms.

On cat's paws, he checked the first bedroom. A twin bed was shoved into the corner, the sheets dingy and ragged along the edges. He located the source of the noise he'd heard. A broken shutter slammed the window when the wind gusted. Wolf released a held breath and swung his gaze around the room. More dried blood stained the floorboards, and another pair of antlers, like the ones from the cellar, lay on a table pushed into the corner. Sara wasn't here, nor was the Devil's Rock killer.

Wolf's face contorted when he entered the room at the end of the hallway. An industrial-size hook hung from the center of the ceiling, and flies buzzed around a chemical toilet. A pair of deer antlers with deadly points jutted off the wall, and a long rope hung from the hook. He imagined Sara bound by the rope.

Along the wall, he discovered more blood and an indentation in the plaster, as though someone had been beaten and tortured here.

Sara.

He sheathed the knife and opted for the gun. Fury overcame him. He wanted to open fire on the beast who'd done this and avenge the young woman. Was she alive?

A closet stood in the far corner. Wolf whipped the door open and searched inside. A few moth-eaten shirts dangled from hangers. An inch of dust tickled his nose. He hurried back to the first bedroom, the one which appeared lived-in. Here, the dresser held a pair of threadbare T-shirts and torn blue jeans. He was about to close the drawer before something struck him as odd.

Checking the shirts, he read the labels and held them up, measuring them against his body. They ranged from adult size small to medium. Wolf doubted the shirts were large enough to fit his body. The evidence no longer added up. The unsub wore a size twenty-four shoe and possessed brute force strength, enough to rip a woman's head from her body and drive wooden stakes through his victims. No way he'd fit into the shirts in this dresser.

What did this mean? Did the unsub have a son or an accomplice?

He chewed on the idea as he closed the drawer. An accomplice made sense. His unsub was disorganized and should have left evidence at the murder sites. Someone cleaned up after him, an organized killer who understood forensic evidence.

The wind shoved against the house and caused the joists to moan, the sudden disturbance drowning out all sounds as something shifted over the ceiling. Wolf directed the gun upward and fell silent. It could have been the breeze knocking over an object inside the attic. That was possible, as the broken windows would let the wind inside.

Wolf took nothing for granted. He circled back to the hallway and stared up at the trapdoor. A latch opened the attic from below. Nothing moved above the ceiling while he considered his options. His instincts warned him not to let his guard down. His priority was finding Sara alive, but he needed to search the attic, in case the unsub had seen Wolf approaching through the window.

Wolf ensured the hallway was clear of threats. Then he grasped the latch.

A scream stopped him before he opened the door. He threw his back against the wall and directed the gun left and right. It took him a second to determine the scream had come from outside.

He rushed to the room at the end of the hallway. The window opened with a squeal. Somewhere in the night, a woman screamed again. His gaze stopped on a thicket several hundred yards beyond the house.

Wolf kicked the screen out of the frame and climbed through the opening.

36

E very time lightning flashed, Scarlett Bell saw ghosts.

Monsters from her past rose out of the darkness and stood in the direct path of the rental's headlights, faces that would haunt her forever. Alan Hodge, the butcher who'd murdered teenage girls along idyllic Coral Lake in the Finger Lakes of New York. Derek Longo, the grocery market worker and serial killer who terrorized coastal South Carolina for months until Bell and Gardy finally caught him in the middle of a hurricane.

And The Skinner.

The psychopath from the plains of Pronti, Kansas, had evaded the FBI and avoided detection for a decade, stashing bodies in shallow graves behind his farmhouse and inside his barn. That was the first time Bell encountered Logan Wolf, also hunting for The Skinner. Wolf abducted Bell and brought her to a warehouse, where he offered to set Bell free if she profiled his wife's killer. Bell hadn't trusted Wolf. Why should she have after he kidnapped her? It took months before Bell trusted Wolf enough to profile Renee's murderer.

Now The Skinner case replayed in her head. It seemed so

similar to the Devil's Rock murders. The killer lived in isolation in the countryside, hiding from the law for almost a decade. As she scanned the shadowed prairie, she realized how easy it would be for the Devil's Rock killer to stay one step ahead of the FBI and sheriff's department. He could hide his victims on his vast property, or discard the bodies across the open land.

Bell believed the killer kept trophies. Body parts. Scalps, as Alan Hodge had kept. The Devil's Rock killer needed to relive his murders. She wouldn't be surprised to find he invoked some twisted ceremony after he stole a life. One significant difference separated The Skinner from this new killer. The Skinner, though demented, had been organized and intelligent. That's how he'd stayed ahead of the FBI. The Devil's Rock killer was disorganized, though just as difficult to catch.

Whether or not Bell's theories were correct, she'd know the house the minute she laid eyes upon it.

She checked the GPS coordinates and wondered about Sara Brennan. After speaking to Gardy, Bell had signed on to her FBI account and completed a background check on the woman. Brennan was only a few years out of high school and didn't attend college, despite exemplary grades. The girl bounced from one dead-end job to the next and currently lived in Lubbock, Texas, the third city she'd called home in the last two years.

What was a smart girl with a world of opportunity in front of her doing working menial jobs in Lubbock, when she should have been in some fancy lecture hall at Stanford or Berkley, or at an east coast college with ivy running over the buildings? And what did she have to do with Logan Wolf?

Bell had seen Brennan's picture. She was cute, if not beautiful, with a glint of adventure swimming in her eyes. Bell tried to picture Wolf cozying up to this girl and failed. The last person in the world to involve himself in a relationship was Logan Wolf. And even if he did, he wouldn't choose a girl half his age.

Or would he? How much did she know about Wolf and how his mind worked?

Bell kept returning to the possibility that Sara Brennan was the killer's latest victim. Somehow, Wolf had found out, and now he wanted Brennan's phone traced. This girl would lead Wolf to the killer.

Bell's heart ticked inside her throat. She was walking into a maelstrom. Not only would she encounter the Devil's Rock killer, she'd come face-to-face with the country's most dangerous fugitive. Though she'd developed a working relationship with Wolf, the serial killer was unpredictable.

Off the side of the road, the headlights picked out a dead calf beside its mother, both strewn on their sides, their torsos bloodied and bruised from hail and severe wind. Bell tried to look away, but the scene tugged her heartstrings and demanded her attention. The wipers swiped away another sheet of rain as a storm passed overhead. She focused on the monotonous sound of the wipers, taking deep breaths to calm herself.

A shape in the night caught her eye in the mirror. She looked over her shoulder and saw nothing but darkness and the open road behind her. As she traveled, she stole glances at the mirror, certain someone was watching her. Bell didn't dare increase her speed in the rain. Though the roads ran in straight lines through West Texas, she was unfamiliar with the territory.

The GPS announced that she'd arrived at her location. Harold guaranteed accuracy within a mile, which meant Bell might have some searching to do before she located Sara Brennan's phone. She stopped the vehicle and lowered the window, inviting the suffocating humidity inside, and dialed the number Gardy had given her. Sara's phone rang in her ear, but not outside the car. It was possible the girl had turned off the ringer, making it impossible to find the phone.

Bell glimpsed a house a half-mile down the road. She

wouldn't have seen it amid the darkness had it not been for the solitary light shining inside. This had to be it. She'd found the Devil's Rock killer.

Bell raised the window and shifted into drive, then checked the mirrors again, that unsettling sensation that someone was behind her pulling her attention away from her destination. As rain pattered the windshield, she turned her head just in time to spy an SUV, possibly a Jeep Wrangler, concealed behind a pair of trees on the opposite side of the road. Bell removed a flashlight, aimed it at the vehicle, and read the out-of-state plates. Wolf. He must have stolen the Jeep from another state. If Bell knew Wolf, he'd snatched a license plate on a different vehicle, so the police wouldn't identify the Jeep.

Logan Wolf must be inside the house. When she investigated, would she find her friend standing over the killer, or Wolf slaughtered and staring lifelessly up at her, as though wondering why she hadn't come sooner and saved him from his reckless behavior?

Bell switched the headlights off and coasted toward the house. Two bulks slept behind the home—cars. A tarp covered one vehicle. As she'd predicted, the killer stashed his victims' vehicles in the backyard until he found somewhere safe to dispose of them.

She reached for her gun a second before the red-and-blue lights ignited in her mirrors. They were so bright that she covered her eyes. A whoop of the siren, and Bell's heart leaped into her throat. How long had the sheriff's cruiser followed her?

Bell pulled over and waited. The sheriff had no right to treat her this way. She'd broken no laws, unless he'd caught her speeding several miles ago. If Rosario had, he would have ticketed her before now. This was personal. She hadn't obeyed his edict to leave the county, and now she'd pay the price for questioning the bully sheriff.

Rosario aimed the cruiser's brights through Bell's rear windshield, blinding her. She didn't hear a radio—curious, as Rosario's radio should have squawked with storm damage reports. Why had he turned it off?

Bell turned her head. She couldn't see past the headlight beams. Up the road, the killer's house waited. She clenched her hands and dug her fingernails into her palms. By now, the Devil's Rock murderer must have seen the flashing emergency lights and fled.

After an eternity, the cruiser's door opened. Rosario's silhouette was unmistakable as he approached the rental along the driver's side. He didn't hold his gun, but his hand dangled beside the holster.

"He can't arrest me," Bell repeated as Rosario moved along the car.

The sheriff shone his flashlight through the glass and motioned with his hand for Bell to lower the driver's side window. She complied.

"License and registration," Rosario grumbled.

"Is that necessary? You know who I am."

"License and registration, Agent Bell. Don't make me ask again."

While Bell dug her license out of her wallet, Rosario eyed her service weapon.

"Here it is," Bell said, handing her license over.

"You always carry a Glock-22 when you visit family?"

"I have a license for the gun, too. Do you need it?"

She reached for her wallet again, and he removed the weapon from his holster.

"Keep your hands where I can see them."

"But I'm only—"

"Do as I say. Now, slowly, hand me the vehicle registration."

"I'm driving a rental. This isn't even my car."

"The registration will be inside the glove compartment." Flustered, Bell shook her head and reached across the car. "Slowly, Agent Bell. You understand what the word means, right?"

Bell unlatched the compartment and dug inside, keeping her hands visible. Her pulse raced. Rosario wanted an excuse. To do what? Shoot her and claim he'd done so in self-defense? It took some searching before Bell located the registration. Rosario examined it under the flashlight for what seemed like hours.

"Sheriff, the Devil's Rock killer lives in that house."

"Quiet, Agent Bell."

"But he—"

"I told you to leave my county, and you disobeyed a direct order. Don't start with that profiling course garbage. I'm not buying it." Rosario met Bell's eyes. "Tell me who Don Weber is. Your colleague, Agent Gardy, lost his voice when I asked him about Weber. Yet Agent Gardy claims Weber isn't working with you." Rosario angled the flashlight beam at Bell's face. "Tell me who Weber is. I pulled hair follicles out of his room at the Irvin Hotel. You can't hide his identity forever."

"He isn't who you think he is."

"Not an FBI agent? Then what?"

"It's . . . complicated."

"Stop eluding my questions. I'll tell you what isn't complicated: you breaking the speed limit and driving seventy in a fifty-five. I clocked you outside Dusk Corners."

"Now isn't the time, Sheriff. The killer—"

"I told you to remain quiet. Shut your mouth until I ask you a question." Rosario glanced back at the cruiser and rubbed his chin. "You know what? I'm through playing games with you. Let's go, Agent Bell. Step out of the vehicle, nice and slow."

Bell's mouth fell open. "Are you arresting me for speeding?"

"For failure to comply to a direct order. We'll talk about the charges at the station." Rosario backed up and gave Bell room to open the door. He kept both hands on his gun, ready to squeeze the trigger if Bell flinched. "That's right. Keep your hands where I can see them."

Rosario grabbed Bell and swung her around, shoving her against the cruiser.

"Hey!" Ignoring her protests, Rosario frisked Bell and removed her service weapon. "You can't do this."

"I can do whatever the hell I want. I'm the king, and you're in my kingdom."

"When the FBI finds out how you treated their agent—"

"I don't believe the FBI knows you're here. Agent Gardy does, sure. But your superiors? Doubtful. You could disappear for a long time with no one noticing."

Bell swung her gaze to the house. Sara Brennan might be inside, injured and bleeding. "This is ridiculous."

"Follow me to my cruiser. Nobody ever accused me of not being a gentleman. I'll ensure you make it back to the station."

Before Bell could argue, Rosario shoved her into the back of the cruiser. He slammed the door a split second after she pulled her feet inside. Rosario hadn't cuffed her, hadn't even read Bell her rights. She pounded on the window.

"This is insane. Let me out of here."

"You be a good little girl, now. I'd cuff you, except I only have one pair, and I reckon I'll need them where I'm going."

Reality dawned on Bell. Rosario meant to apprehend the Devil's Rock killer alone, unaware that Don Weber was Logan Wolf.

"It's too dangerous, Rosario. At least let me watch your back. Don't go in there alone."

Rosario fixed the brim of his hat and grinned.

"Not to worry. Stay put, Agent Bell. I'll be back soon."

37

S ara's scream still echoed across the prairie when she covered her mouth. She froze as the shrilling wind sang dirges through the night sky.

Sara backed away from the scarecrow version of Sheila Jarvis's corpse. The dead girl's eyes continued to regard Sara with silent, haunted derision, as if there was something Sara could have done to save Sheila from this fate.

Backing away, Sara turned to run before footsteps raced toward the thicket. Each footfall splattered the waterlogged terrain and kicked up mud.

It was too late to run for the road. Sara's pursuer would spot her when she bolted from the thicket. She hid behind a tree and waited until the footsteps stopped outside the copse. Branches creaked above her head, and raindrops tumbled down from the canopy, soaking her through. At the edge of her vision, the scarecrow shifted with the wind, as though alive.

Dead leaves crunched underfoot behind her. Sara bit her lip to keep from screaming. Tears trailed down her cheeks and wet her lips with a salty tang as she reached into her empty pockets, praying for a weapon she might use to defend herself. Who was following her?

Balor? No. The man behind her was too light on his feet. It had to be Jacob.

When her attacker drew near, Sara darted to the next tree and placed her back against the trunk, prepared to run. Her body ached from Jacob's beating. In her condition, she couldn't outrun him.

Nobody moved inside the thicket for a long time. She almost convinced herself Jacob had given up and left to search the countryside. Then the hand clutched her hair from behind and ripped her backward.

Sara screamed and fell, the breath flying from her lungs when she struck the earth. Jacob drove his knee into her chest and tugged her hair. A lecherous smile curled his lips.

"You shouldn't have run, Sara." He swung his eyes to Sheila Jarvis's corpse. "See what Balor did to that girl? Can't look away, can you? You'll be next after I bring you home to my brother. But first, we have unfinished business."

He grabbed her breast and squeezed. When he snatched the collar of her shirt, Sara raked her fingernails across his eyes. Jacob toppled backward and cried out, one hand covering his face.

"You little bitch! You're dead now."

As he rubbed the agony out of his eyes, Sara scrambled to her feet and ran. She wasn't sure where the road was. The dense thicket confused Sara and stole her sense of direction. Jacob climbed to his feet when she broke out of the trees. A quick search of her surroundings, then she spotted the gray stripe of road in the distance. To Sara's shock, a vehicle sat along the shoulder down the road from the murderers' house.

Buoyed by the unknown vehicle, Sara sprinted across the

field. Behind her, Jacob panted and cursed. But he was faster than she'd expected and gained on Sara with every step.

His shoulder drove into the small of her back. Sara pitched forward and struck the ground, with Jacob's weight landing on top of her. She twisted and struggled as he grasped her wrists and pinned them down. Sara brought her leg forward and pried Jacob off her, kicking out with the heel of her sneaker and snapping his chin backward.

Jacob landed on his side and rolled over. Before Sara climbed to her feet, he grabbed her ankle and pulled her legs out from under her. Again, Sara found herself beneath Jacob. He twisted her onto her back and tore her shirt open while she struggled. When he groped at her bra, Sara punched his face and spun his head around, drawing blood from his lip. He spat blood and slid the knife from his pocket. The blade reflected Sara's terror-filled eyes as he raised the knife over his head.

Sara spun away, but wasn't quick enough. The knife plunged into her shoulder and drew a torrent of blood. She screamed. Jacob would rape and murder Sara under the starless sky, and no one would come to save her. The psychopath's hand covered her face and smothered her nose and mouth. She couldn't see Jacob bring the knife over his head for the fatal blow.

As Sara reached up to gouge his eyes again, Jacob vanished. She inhaled oxygen into her lungs and blinked when Jacob's body landed in a heap several steps away. There was someone else in the dark, a ghostly shadow that moved without making a sound.

Jacob scampered backward and blinked. "Who the hell are you?"

The figure darted at Jacob and swept a knife across the murderer's chest. The killer screeched and rolled to his side, covering his heart as blood welled between his fingers. Gasping, he struggled to his feet and retreated. The silent attacker lunged forward and swung his fist, connecting with Jacob's chin and spinning him around.

Sara dragged herself away from the fight. Dizziness and fatigue sapped her strength. She'd lost too much blood.

The unknown man spotted Sara and started toward her. She raised her arms in defense before she recognized Logan.

"Stay where you are, Sara. I'll get you out of here."

"Logan, how did you—"

Logan ducked as Jacob's knife whistled over his head. Jacob's momentum carried him forward. Before the murderer recovered, Logan twisted around and jammed his hunting knife into Jacob's chest.

The killer collapsed and lay twitching on the ground.

"Turn away," Logan told her.

She didn't understand why until he gave her a pleading stare. Sara grasped her shoulder and turned her head. A horrible ripping sound interrupted the wind, like a blade tearing through leather. Then a splash. Jacob gurgled, blood rushing out of his neck in a horrifying waterfall.

The plains and sky tilted and spun. Sara's eyelids fluttered as Logan's hands grasped her arms.

The last thing she heard was Logan begging her to stay with him before the night took her.

38

Invisible amid the darkness, Logan Wolf knelt beside Sara and wiped the hair off her face. The gusting wind whipped his black jacket. Rain slicked his face and ran in rivers over his clothing. Five steps away, the man who'd attacked Sara stopped convulsing and lay still. Wolf knew another killer was still out there, the beast with size twenty-four shoes, the monster who tore apart victims with his bare hands.

Something in the way the gray light illuminated Sara's face brought him back to the stormy, early summer evenings of his youth, when life was simple, and his only decision was who to ride bikes with tomorrow or whether to play pickup football or baseball. Humid, rainy evenings were meant for iced tea on the closed-in porch and board game marathons.

He'd met Renee on such a night. Faraway lightning, what the old timers referred to as heat lightning, had painted the clouds with purple and red tones as he strode hand-in-hand with this amazing woman, knowing he wanted to learn everything about her.

Now the fleeting light seemed all wrong. Corrupt and deceitful.

Wolf checked Sara's pulse. He was losing her.

"Sara," he said, leaning his head close to hers.

Her eyes blinked open for a moment and closed. The girl's skin took on a disturbing pallor, her face like a full moon as lifeblood bubbled off her shoulder and soaked her shirt. He removed his jacket and sliced the inner fabric with his knife. Then he tied the cloth around Sara's shoulder. The makeshift bandage wouldn't stop the bleeding, only slow it down. Sara needed a doctor, and he'd have to transport her to the city to find one.

Wolf stood and swung his gaze across the field. Two trees hid the Jeep Wrangler on the far side of the road. The walk back to the car was a mile or longer. Another vehicle caught his eye. It hadn't been there when he'd approached the killer's house. The night concealed the unknown vehicle, making it impossible for Wolf to gage the threat.

One lone light continued to shine from inside the house. He looked toward the Jeep, then back at the house. Even if he carried Sara to his vehicle, he'd need to find a hospital or an urgent care clinic. The nearest medical professional might be forty or fifty miles away. Sara didn't have that much time.

Wolf searched his pocket for the burner phone, but there was no coverage in the middle of nowhere. Maybe the house held a proper first aid kit or a landline phone. He hadn't noticed either in the house, but his focus had been on finding Sara. It wouldn't take longer than five minutes to carry her to the house. The unidentified vehicle along the road gave him pause. A new threat might await them when they arrived, and he still hadn't located the Devil's Rock killer, only his accomplice.

Careful to keep Sara's head and neck steady, unaware of the wounds she'd suffered during the attack, Wolf scooped up Sara and retraced his steps through the thicket. The trees cleared when the rain let up. Clouds raced across the sky in ragged shreds, the moon appearing and disappearing as he struggled to hold Sara while he searched for unseen hazards. This was rattlesnake country. Snakes rarely emerged at night, but the rain might have flooded them out of their dens.

Sara murmured something he couldn't understand.

"You're safe now, Sara. Hang in there just a little longer."

Her eyes shifted beneath the lids, and she issued a weak moan. He hoped Sara's bloodless face was a trick of the light. Otherwise, she might not survive the trip. Wolf couldn't lose her as he'd lost Renee. He'd failed them both. In his mind, he dropped to his knees and asked the sky why this kept happening to him, why every woman he cared about paid the ultimate price for the life he'd chosen. Without a choice, he struggled onward, determined to save the dying woman in his arms.

He was halfway to the house when a shadow passed over the window.

39

Rosario pictured Kimberly Ripa as he'd found her six years ago. He recalled turning away after he spotted the headless corpse. Maggots congealed inside the stump of her neck, and there was more blood soaking into the ground than he'd believed a body could hold.

So many of the victims maimed and disfigured.

Until tonight, he'd believed multiple killers had murdered Ripa, the Domin family, and too many others over the last nine years. The evidence pointed toward several psychopaths, not one. Gangs, the Mexican cartel, militia groups. Yet as he approached this lone house, set alone in the countryside, worry tickled the back of his mind. What if Agent Bell was correct and one killer had caused the endless terror on the Texas Caprock?

Rosario shook his head. He only had Agent Bell's word to go on. Just because she claimed this was the killer's house, didn't make it so. It was a fact of life in law enforcement that sometimes you'd be wrong. The difference between honest cops and federal suits was the police admitted their mistakes.

He clutched his gun and crossed the soggy lawn, careful not to tumble into the gaping hole in the center of the yard. A tree had once stood here, and now that same tree lay a hundred yards away in the field. The house might have appeared abandoned were it not for the light seeping through the broken windows. Around the corner of the house, a Dodge Ram 3500 dominated a dirt and stone driveway. Rosario cast a glance at the doorway, then wandered to the truck and peered through the windows. A crumpled fast-food wrapper lay on the floor. His eyes stopped on a dark splotch covering the passenger seat. It might have been blood. In the darkness, it might have been anything. He checked the doors and found them locked.

The sheriff returned to the house and stood beside the front door. Down the road, he spied his cruiser and the agent trapped in the backseat. A cage divided the front from the back, and the doors opened from the outside. Even if Agent Bell kicked the windows, she'd have a hell of a time breaking the glass. Rosario had witnessed a drunk man beat a cruiser's windows from inside with a wrench. Somehow, the arresting officer had missed the tool hidden inside the man's coat pocket. The wrench bounced off the glass and struck the drunk between his eyes, rendering him unconscious. Once the police tossed you into the backseat, you were there for the duration. Agent Bell wouldn't escape unless he opened the cruiser.

He listened at the door, which stood open to the screen. No sound came from inside.

Rosario peeked his head around the corner and edged the door open. Inside the house, he directed the gun over a room devoid of furniture. Wind through the shattered windows hunted through the home. A kitchen stood to his left, and a long hallway extended toward the back of the house. The shadows were too thick to see what lay beyond the corridor.

The sheriff considered announcing his presence and thought better of it. He'd followed Agent Bell to this house to rescue Brady Endieveri and Sheila Jarvis. And if Don Weber's supposed daughter was here, he'd save her, too.

Except it appeared no one was inside the house.

Rosario cleared the two front rooms and started down the hallway. The first bedroom he encountered held a bed and a dresser. Someone lived here. At the end of the hallway, he paused beside an open doorway and spun into the second bedroom. His mouth fell dry when he spotted the long hook and rope dangling from the ceiling. Discoloration on the floorboards drew his attention. He covered his nose and mouth when he passed a chemical toilet.

Kneeling beside the dark splotches on the floor, he shone his light and confirmed his fear. Blood, and a lot of it.

He followed the blood trail back to the ropes and hook. Someone had been tied and beaten in this room.

A monstrous shape on the wall made him jump. He raised the gun and aimed his weapon at the rack of antlers.

Rosario wiped his forehead with the back of his hand and cast the flashlight beam over the room. He searched for a wall switch and found one beside an open closet. The sheriff flicked the switch. Nothing happened. He ran his gaze over the bedroom and discovered someone had removed the bulbs from the light fixture.

A quick check of the closet revealed footprints trailing through a thick layer of dust. Given the clear indentations, it appeared someone had entered the closet in the last few hours.

Rosario's throat constricted. Something about the house set him on edge, as though eyes followed him.

Down the hallway, a third door waited beside an open bathroom. He gave the trapdoor in the ceiling little consideration. Rosario was too focused on this third door, which had to lead to the basement, as there hadn't been an entrance to the cellar elsewhere in the house. Every time he reached for the door, the old house groaned, as if someone raced up behind him.

Must be the wind, he convinced himself. The sooner he cleared this damn house, the better.

The cellar door swung open and revealed a stairway diving into shadows. He couldn't see past the first few stairs, and each wooden step appeared warped and splintered, too brittle to support his weight. Rosario flashed the light into the cellar and picked out a long table loaded with knives and a hatchet. He glanced behind him when the hallway made that moaning sound again.

A pull string dangled overhead. He gave it a yank, but the bulb didn't respond. Total darkness. Just Rosario and his service weapon against the cellar and whatever lurked inside. The sheriff wondered if he should call for backup. A ridiculous idea crossed his mind—maybe he should return to the cruiser and release Agent Bell. He'd feel more comfortable with a trained FBI agent watching his back. But he didn't trust the woman. Since she'd arrived in Pronghorn County, she'd done nothing but lie to him. Besides, he'd be a hero when he rescued the three kidnapping victims.

He followed the stairs to the concrete floor and swept the beam over the cellar. Something clicked outside of the light. He swiveled and aimed the gun toward the noise, the flashlight dancing in his trembling hand.

Just the water heater.

An object leaned beside the tank. He crept closer, not trusting the shadows. The light landed on an ax, its deadly blade crusted with dried blood and hair.

Rosario stepped backward and caught his breath until his head stopped spinning. Then he raised the radio and read his location.

"Right, the missing college students. I think they were here.

I've got a bloody weapon in the basement. No hostiles in the house, but I need backup. And a forensics specialist." The sheriff swung the flashlight beam across the floor and spotted more blood. "To hell with it. Send an entire team."

Rosario supported himself on the water heater until his legs steadied. Over two decades as sheriff, he'd never encountered this much blood. The fact that it was old blood, dried and crusted against the concrete walls and floor, didn't bolster his confidence. He wished he'd never entered this house.

A bang came from upstairs. He muted the radio and switched off the flashlight. Darkness lunged off the walls and drowned him. Rosario blinked, willing his eyes to adjust.

Dammit. He'd left the door open at the top of the stairs. If the hostile had returned . . .

Rosario crept to the staircase, careful not to bump into anything and give himself away.

As though the killer didn't already know someone was in the basement.

He stood against the wall with his gun trained on the rectangle of incandescent light filling the doorway. Holding his breath, he climbed the stairs one at a time, his body prickling with the fear that something had followed him out of the cellar.

Rosario swung through the doorway and cleared the corridor. His eyes landed on the two bedrooms. He didn't like this. The killer might be anywhere inside the unfamiliar house, and backup was at least twenty minutes away.

He wanted out of there. When his deputies arrived, they'd apprehend the murderer. Until then, he'd wait beside the cruiser, where he could monitor his prisoner with no one creeping up behind him. He turned toward the front of the house when the ceiling moaned and crackled. The unexpected noise froze Rosario, who lifted his eyes a moment before the trapdoor burst open.

The stairs swung down and clipped his head, opening a gash over his brow. Stunned, he stumbled and aimed his service weapon into the attic.

All went silent except for the night wind and the hammer of his heartbeat.

Rosario rounded the trapdoor, never lowering the gun as he stared up at the black hole.

Two monstrous hands plunged through the opening and grasped his head. He squeezed off three shots. The gunfire blew through the ceiling and missed their target.

Rosario yelled as the hands lifted him off the floor and dragged him by the head into the darkness. His legs kicked and scrambled to grasp the stairs. The shadow filling the trapdoor entryway was impossibly huge. Though he couldn't discern the monster's face, he sensed it grinning.

Then the hands clamped against his skull in a vise. He hung suspended from the attic, his skull popping and shredding in his ears.

Rosario screamed.

40

Wolf's arms struggled to support Sara as he staggered across the field. Tears streamed from his eyes and rendered the house in blurs, the yellow light inside darting back and forth.

"I did this to you, Renee," he sobbed, delirious. "I'm so sorry."

He wanted to drop to his knees and lay the young woman upon the earth, comforting her until she passed. Wolf was no longer sure who he cupped in his arms, only that he loved the woman and couldn't survive without her.

His blinded eyes caused him to stumble and veer off course. He rounded the house, uncertain why he was there or where he intended to take the dying woman. The ground tripped him up and tipped him against the outer wall. He leaned against the flaking paint, breathing in the fecund clay as rain pattered his face.

"This is my fault," he told the woman. "I'd give my life to save yours."

He kissed her forehead. Her skin tasted salty, too cold to support life. If he'd already lost her—

His eyes landed on the vehicle parked across the road. Reality forced its way past the frenzied veil clouding his thoughts, and he recognized the Pronghorn County Sheriff's Department emblem on the cruiser. He blinked his eyes, pushing away his psychosis, and spotted someone in the back-seat. A woman. She pounded the glass and seemed to shout his name, though it was too difficult to hear beneath the rain and wind. The blonde hair and haunted face pulled him out of his daze.

Scarlett.

The night's events hurtled back to Wolf. He stared down at Sara, her eyes closed and face pale. He leaned his head close to her nose and mouth. Was she breathing?

Bell hammered the glass again, and Wolf raised his head and struggled to the cruiser. The FBI agent pointed at the door handle.

He opened the cruiser, and Bell leaped out with the Glock-22.

"Is that Sara Brennan?"

Wolf hoisted Sara higher, afraid he'd drop her. "You know her name?"

"What happened?"

He sobbed and swung his head back to the house. Now he remembered why he'd come here. To locate a first aid kit and murder the Devil's Rock killer.

"Stab wound. She lost too much blood."

Bell regarded Sara with concerned eyes. "We have to get her to a hospital."

"There's no time. I need to stop the bleeding before I lose her." The choked sound that came out of his throat pulled her eyes to his. "Help me, Scarlett. I can't lose another one."

"Here," she said, propping open the back door to the cruiser with her leg. "Lay Sara inside and get her out of the rain."

"I can't let her go."

Bell touched his cheek. "Listen to me, Logan. You did a good job with the tourniquet and bought her time. The problem is, she needs an ambulance, and you won't find cell service out here. Sheriff Rosario will radio an ambulance and get help for Sara. But you can't allow him to see you. He's on to you, Logan. The sheriff isn't buying the Don Weber ID, and he picked your hair follicles out of your hotel room. Once he submits the evidence for a DNA test, the entire world will know you're in Texas."

"What are you suggesting?"

"Leave while you can. I saw the Jeep up the road. That's yours, I take it. Drive away before Rosario sees you."

Wolf lifted his chin. "Not a chance, Scarlett. I came here with one purpose—stop the madmen before they kill again."

"Madmen. There's more than one?"

"You'll find the first man near the thicket," Wolf said, tilting his head toward the prairie. "He stabbed Sara, but I assure you he'll not harm another."

"Where is the other man?"

"Inside the house, I presume."

Bell swung her eyes to the door. "Rosario is inside."

"Then I propose we—"

Gunshots. The blood-curdling squeal that tore through the house caused Bell's knees to buckle.

"Get her inside the cruiser," Bell said. When Wolf didn't respond, she placed a hand on his shoulder. "She still has time, Logan. But we need that ambulance."

With Bell's aid, Wolf loaded Sara into the cruiser and lay her on the seat. Another horrible scream came from inside.

Logan ran to the house with Bell behind him.

41

Haunting images of The Skinner played inside Scarlett Bell's head as she rushed toward the house, the FBI-issued Glock-22 in hand. Logan Wolf was first through the door, the serial killer not making a sound as he swept his own gun across the living room and kitchen.

Bell spotted Rosario's broken body in the hallway. She stepped past Wolf and hurried to the fallen sheriff, pulling up when she saw his disfigured head. Blood welled from the sheriff's mouth and ears, and his open eyes held a snapshot of his final terror-filled moments. Stairs dangling beside her climbed into the black unknown. She aimed her gun at the opening in the ceiling, then touched Rosario's neck and checked for a pulse.

Dead.

Bell turned around to warn Wolf, who'd vanished into the kitchen, when a hand reached through the opening and clutched her hair, dragging her off the floor. She flailed and twisted, crying out as the roots yanked out of her scalp. The arms jutting out of the darkness were preternaturally thick, more pistons than flesh and bone. With frantic desperation, she aimed her weapon at the opening and fired. The bullet whistled into the shadows and exploded through the attic.

"Scarlett!"

Wolf's shouts faded into the background as the beast dragged her into the attic.

Bell's head struck a joist and bent sideways. Her hands refused to respond as she lost feeling in her body. Beside her, the feeble light spilling up from the downstairs vanished as the Devil's Rock killer lifted the stairs and slammed the trapdoor shut. She begged her limbs to respond.

Bell stared into the darkness in shock. What was happening?

The monster tugged Bell up by her shirt and tossed her across the attic. She struck the narrow crevice where the roof met the floor. Her back wrenched. Bell's heart hammered in her ears as he stalked toward her.

When he was a step away, Bell pulled her knees toward her chest and kicked out, striking the killer's thigh. His leg gave out on him, and he dropped to one knee and grabbed an overhead joist to support himself. Bell took advantage of his injury and reached for her gun. It wasn't there. Panic surged on hot wires beneath her skin as she pawed blindly across the attic floor for the lost weapon.

Her eyes adjusted to the dark. A mattress that was too small to support the madman lay beneath a window, where gray light trickled into the attic. Thunder roared and lightning flashed on the horizon. She crawled toward the window while her attacker recovered.

Another flash of lightning revealed an impossible sight.

Human bones. Dozens of them strewn across the floor. Beside the window, a rack of deer antlers.

Beneath her body, the floor rattled as Wolf leaped and struck the trapdoor, searching for a way into the attic.

"Logan, I need help!"

The monster grabbed Bell from behind and hauled her into his arms. He swung her body like a child's toy and hurled her into the shadows. Bell's head and shoulder struck the floor. The attic tilted on its axis as the Devil's Rock killer lumbered after her. The gray light pulled his face into focus—insane eyes that craved murder, a thick beard dotted with dust and debris, sharp, crooked teeth tainted red with blood. He smiled, stalking with his clawed hands, reaching for her like a movie monster come to life.

There was no fighting a man of his size and strength. He'd crush Bell and break every bone in her body. With the beast looming over her, Bell kicked up and struck his groin. He doubled over. When he dropped his hands onto his knees, Bell snaked her legs around his head and twisted, determined to snap his neck. She torqued her body, a tactic that had ended many killers' lives. But he grabbed Bell and lifted her until she lost leverage and became a play thing in his grasp. The side of her head struck another joist. A rusty nail gouged her scalp and drew blood.

Then she saw it. The Glock-22, shimmering like an ancient artifact beside the trapdoor.

When he lifted Bell over his head, she twisted and squirmed out of his grasp. She dropped to her feet behind him. A round-house kick snapped the monster forward and bought her enough time to lunge for the gun. He turned and bellowed, rushing at her with alarming quickness, his body blotting out what little light filtered through the window.

Her hands closed over the gun as the floor rattled with his footfalls. She twisted toward him and squeezed the trigger.

The gun blast blew through his arm and knocked him backward. He shook it off and came at her again. She fired the Glock in rapid succession. The first two shots whistled past his head.

The third struck the monster's chest and dropped him to his knees.

Yet he rose again. Red soaked through his shirt as he shuffled across the attic with an unsteady gait.

Bell squeezed the trigger and blew a bullet into his shoulder. He kept coming. When she squeezed the trigger again, he slapped the gun from her hand and sent it spinning across the dusty floor.

The beast laughed and clutched her head, squeezing as she pounded his shoulders. He lifted her off the floor until she was face-to-face with the madman. Her eyes felt on the verge of popping out of her head. This was it. He was going to crush her skull, as he'd killed Rosario.

The trapdoor burst open. Logan Wolf climbed into the attic and called out to Bell. Incensed, the monster tossed Bell aside, where she landed in a heap, tears streaming down her face. As she pushed herself up to her hands and knees, Wolf fired his gun and knocked the monster backward, the killer's arms pinwheeling as he careened toward the window. The madman's shirt became a smock of gore, but he refused to fall.

The monster lashed out with a tree trunk arm and knocked Wolf's head sideways. Wolf stumbled against the wall. The former BAU agent punched the monster in defense. The fist struck the beast's chin to no effect.

Wolf shook away the cobwebs and aimed his gun. The gunshot drove the Devil's Rock killer backward. Wolf leaped off the wall and unsheathed the hunting knife.

When the madman lurched at him, Wolf ducked behind his attacker and grabbed the man's head, wrenching it backward. In one fluid motion, Wolf ripped the blade's serrated edge across the killer's throat.

The monster gurgled and collapsed, driving Wolf toward the window.

Bell jumped to her feet. "No!"

Glass shattered. The madman tumbled through the opening and took Wolf with him.

She ran to the window and spotted the killer's broken body on the ground, his head pointing in the wrong direction, legs and arms splayed across the muddy grass. Bell gasped when she saw Wolf dangling from the ledge. Before his grip gave out, she grabbed his arm and dragged him into the attic.

He collapsed and lay on the floor amid the bones and dust. Their eyes met, and she smiled.

"Thank you," Bell said, holding out a hand to help him up.

The relief on his face changed to concern. "Sara."

He jumped to his feet and grabbed his stomach, the sudden pain causing him to stagger against the wall. Bell supported him.

"What's happening to you, Logan?"

"It's nothing. We have to get Sara to a doctor."

"Someone might recognize you."

"That's a chance I'll have to take."

"You'd do anything for this girl, wouldn't you?"

Without answering, he struggled to the trapdoor. A kitchen chair lay beneath the opening, explaining how Wolf had broken into the attic and saved Bell from certain death. Sheriff Rosario sprawled in the hallway. Bell looked away from the dead man's mangled skull. That would have been her fate had Wolf not intervened.

Wolf and Bell limped together to the front door, supporting each other.

In an insane world, we'd make a helluva team, Bell thought to herself.

She held her breath as they exited the house. Half-expecting to find the Devil's Rock killer gone, she exhaled. He lay in the same position, eyes open and lifeless, reflecting the lightning.

Sirens approached through the countryside.

"The sheriff's department is coming," Bell said when they came upon Sheriff Rosario's abandoned cruiser. "We'd better leave before they arrive."

Wolf turned to her. "They'll catch up to you, eventually. You'll have some explaining to do."

"Once they see Rosario, they won't blame me for murdering the Devil's Rock killer."

"You don't think they'll wonder who aided you?"

As they limped back to the back door, she leveled him with a glare.

"As if I can't handle myself, Wolf."

"I never doubted you. Yes, I'm certain they'll buy your story of single-handedly thwarting a legendary killer. Won't the tabloids feast on this tale, dear Scarlett?"

Bell shook her head and smiled. "Wait until they learn that you're my secret weapon."

42

Sara hung limply in Wolf's arms as he lifted her out of the cruiser. The tourniquet slowed the bleeding, but her breathing was shallow, and the girl's pallor had worsened. Bell touched the girl's neck.

"Her pulse is weak. I'll find the closest hospital. We'd better take my car."

"Why?"

"You really want to park a stolen vehicle outside the emergency room, with half the county searching for the mysterious Don Weber?"

"I can't leave the Jeep here. They'll pull my prints off the interior."

Bell bit her lip. "Okay, fine. Put Sara in my car, and you can follow me to the hospital."

"I can't let her go again."

"You have to. We'll need to speed to reach the hospital in time. If a deputy pulls me over, I'll explain the circumstances. At least my vehicle is legal."

"You always think ahead, Scarlett."

Wolf set Sara in Bell's car. As the FBI agent slid into the driver's seat, Wolf leaned over and kissed Sara's forehead.

"You're almost home, my girl," he said, his throat constricting when her eyes shifted beneath their lids, as though answering him. "Ride with my dear friend, Agent Bell. I'll be right behind you."

Wolf didn't know Bell's destination. While they raced across unmarked country roads, he trusted she'd locate a hospital on her GPS. As they drove, his mind returned to the night he'd discovered Renee dead on the kitchen floor, the hollow pain that had followed him since. He didn't understand his connection to Sara, only that losing her would shred what little remained of his sanity. The doctors would save her. They had to.

The hospital was a ten-floor concrete building with three wings jutting in opposite directions. Outside the emergency room entrance, two orderlies helped a woman push an elderly man in a wheelchair through the automatic entry doors. The rental's tires screeched to a halt beside the curb. Bell rounded the car and lifted Sara out of the seat. Feeling helpless, Wolf abandoned the Jeep in the parking lot. Before he climbed out, he reached across the seat and grabbed a baseball cap and a pair of blue-tinted glasses. It wasn't much of a disguise, but it would have to do.

He caught up to Bell and took Sara from the FBI agent's arms. Carrying the girl through the entrance, his head swung back and forth until he located someone who could help them. The mustached orderly took one look at Sara and called for a doctor. Moments later, a medical team laid Sara on a gurney and rushed her down a hallway as Bell answered their questions. Wolf heard *stab wound* and *blood loss*, but nothing else. He was too focused on the unconscious girl to discern the conversation.

Outside a pair of double doors, the team ordered Wolf and

Bell to stay back. Bell flashed her badge, but the doctors refused to allow anyone to follow them to the operating room.

The hospital smelled of cleaning solution and lost hope. With nowhere else to go, Wolf trailed Bell into the waiting room at the end of the corridor. Thankfully, the room was empty.

Bell took the chair beside Wolf, who leaned over with his elbows on his knees, legs drumming to a frantic beat. She placed a hand on his arm, and his legs relaxed.

"So, I have to know. How did you meet this girl?"

Wolf wrung his hands and stared out the window. "Just someone I met during my travels, Scarlett."

"At a diner outside of Lubbock?" He turned to her, and she nodded. "A worker at the diner claimed someone who looked an awful lot like that fugitive murderer, Logan Wolf, stopped in and ate lunch with a pretty brunette with spiky hair. Sound familiar?"

"Someone recognized me?"

"You're famous, Logan. Dare I say even more famous than me. How did you come to know Sara Brennan?"

He dipped his head. "Her car broke down. I performed my gentlemanly duty and ensured she made it home."

"You were smitten."

"I don't believe anyone ever described me as smitten before your clichéd quip."

"She's beautiful. I don't blame you for taking interest. Don't look now, but the elusive Logan Wolf has a heart."

"You know me better than that, dear Scarlett."

"Yes, I do. You never stopped loving Renee, and if I had to guess, you saw something in this Sara Brennan that reminded you of your wife."

"Are you profiling me?"

Bell grabbed Wolf's hand and set it in hers.

"You really care about her, don't you?"

He didn't answer. Wolf wiped his eyes and pushed the hair off his forehead.

"She's in good hands, Logan. You did everything you could to save her."

He shook his head. "Did I? I led Sara into danger. Were it not for me, the Devil's Rock murderers wouldn't have taken her. I'm poison, Scarlett. Everyone I touch encounters the reaper."

"Then stop."

"I can't."

"Yes, you can. You're just too stubborn to give up. No matter how many murderers you eliminate, there will always be more. Society breeds them, and they multiply like roaches. Your work is done. Live your life."

Wolf leaned back in his chair and avoided Bell's gaze. If stopping was possible, he would have done so years ago. Was he as insane as the monsters he hunted? What endgame did he expect to achieve? No matter how many killers he murdered, he'd never hear Renee's voice again or feel her soft breath on his neck while they slept.

Wolf wasn't sure when he drifted off. His head snapped up when the doctor appeared in the doorway. The middle-aged doctor had kind, green eyes and blonde hair, and the stubble on his cheeks spoke to a man who'd worked long hours without a break. Beckoning Scarlett Bell with his hand, the doctor waited for the FBI agent to rise. Wolf followed Bell to the doctor, his mind racing.

"We're attempting to reach Ms. Brennan's family," the doctor said. "So far, they haven't returned my messages. Since you're the federal agent who brought Ms. Brennan in, I can tell you she's out of surgery and stable."

Wolf closed his eyes and leaned against the wall.

"She lost a lot of blood, but she's tough," the doctor continued. "We'll keep her until she regains her strength. It could be days."

"Can we see her?" Bell asked.

The doctor pressed his lips together. "You're not family. I take it a crime was involved and you need answers. But in her state, Ms. Brennan needs rest."

"We'll save the questions until she's strong enough to answer. Sara Brennan is very important to us."

The doctor looked from Bell to Wolf and tapped his clipboard against his thigh. "Two minutes. Not a second longer."

After the doctor pointed them to Sara's recovery room, Wolf and Bell hustled down the corridor. Outside the room, Bell set her back against the wall and waited.

Wolf cocked an eyebrow. "What are you doing?"

"Giving you privacy."

"This is unnecessary."

"Remember what the doctor said. Two minutes. I suggest you get to it."

The head nurse behind the desk watched with suspicion as Wolf slipped into the room.

He found Sara sleeping. Her breathing sounded better than it had before, and the color had returned to her face.

Renee hadn't made it to the hospital. She died long before the police arrived.

Wolf brushed Sara's hair off her forehead with his thumb. The girl shifted beneath the sheets.

"You made it, Sara. I never expected less."

Wolf fell into a chair and slid it beside her bed. Two machines monitored her vitals. Her heart pulsed with a regular pattern, like the beat of every song that ever made him smile. Unsure what to say or do, he slipped one hand beneath hers and clasped their fingers together.

"Were you to awaken, you'd admonish me for what I'm about to do. It's better this way. I'm certain you'll understand."

Her head turned toward his, eyes still closed. It might have been his imagination, though he swore she muttered something beneath her breath.

"I'm leaving, Sara. You want to accompany me, but that is not a road you wish to travel. I'll only bring you pain. That's all I've ever brought the ones I cared about."

Footsteps approached in the hallway, signaling that Wolf's two minutes were up. He leaned over the bed and kissed her forehead, pressing his lips against her skin until the heat between them neutralized.

"Don't follow me. I couldn't live with myself if I caused you harm."

Outside the recovery room, the doctor waited with Bell. He gave Bell a confused glance, no doubt wondering why only Wolf had visited the patient.

The doctor cleared his throat. "I just got off the phone with the sheriff's department. A deputy named Beckley is on his way to the hospital. He wishes to speak to you, Agent Bell."

"Of course."

"There's a meeting room on the second floor, if you prefer privacy. I can show you where it is after I check on Ms. Brennan."

"Thank you." When the doctor entered Sara's room, Bell turned to Wolf. "You'd better disappear, Logan."

"I'm one step ahead of you."

"I wish you'd take my advice to heart."

"You may not believe me, but I always do."

"Does that mean you'll stop?"

"Would it make you happy if I did?"

"Yes, it very much would."

"Then I'll take it under advisement. I don't wish to disappoint you, dear Scarlett."

He passed the elevators, making a beeline for the stairs. Behind him, Bell urged Wolf to seek a doctor.

If he'd cared about living, he would have.

43

L ogan Wolf lurched awake with a yell.

He blinked and swung his head around in confusion, taking in the front range of the Rockies and the picturesque city of Golden below. The Jeep Wrangler rested between two delivery vans in a shopping center parking lot off the highway. The sun had risen, its flaxen rays painting the slopes and adding to his dreamlike trance.

While he slept, a vision had come to him. Renee splayed on the kitchen floor, her throat sliced open and a sack covering her head. But when Wolf removed the sack, it was Sara's face staring up at him.

Wolf rubbed the sleep from his eyes and coughed into his hand, swallowing the acid surging into his throat. An inferno raged inside his stomach, the pain pulsing and making his head spin. He popped an indigestion pill from the bottle he'd purchased in the Panhandle. After driving all night, he'd discovered the shopping center and laid low, assuming the authorities were searching for the stolen vehicle now. There was only so much Scarlett Bell could do to keep the hunting dogs off his scent. In time, someone at the sheriff's department would recognize his face and ask questions.

The time had come to rid himself of the Jeep and steal a different vehicle. He also needed to hide out until the commotion over the Devil's Rock killer and the mysterious figure known as Don Weber died out. During times like these, he located vacant countryside homes. With Harold's aid at the BAU, he could track the homeowner's credit card statements and figure out who was on vacation and when he might return. Colorado offered countless possibilities, places to disappear to until the public stopped searching for him.

Except the FBI would forever follow his trail. Wolf wouldn't stop running until his time ended. And that time was coming soon.

He studied the GPS and identified a handful of upscale neighborhoods. After nightfall, he'd locate another vehicle and stash the Jeep nearby.

As he reached for the ignition, a phone rang inside his bag. He withdrew his hand and hesitated. That didn't sound like his prepaid phone.

Wolf tilted the bag, and a black phone he didn't recognize toppled onto the passenger seat. Looking over his shoulder, he grabbed the phone and rolled it in his hand. A child's sticker of a golden bell adorned the battery case. Wolf grinned.

"Scarlett," he said, setting the bag upright. "How did you slip a phone into my bag without me noticing? You're a devious one. I dare say you aren't fit for government work."

"Where are you?"

A Volvo pulled into the parking lot, and a man wearing a white shirt and black tie hurried to a men's clothing shop and unlocked the doors.

"It's better to keep a few secrets from you, my friend. You understand, I'm sure."

"It's not like I can't figure it out. You're within a 600-mile radius of Dusk Corners."

"How did you make that determination?"

"Well, I last spoke to you nine hours ago. Assuming you rested an hour or two—and you better have. Don't make me play angry parent with you, Logan—you wouldn't have gotten much further, even if you drove eighty miles per hour."

"I might have driven faster."

"You wouldn't."

"Why wouldn't I?"

"Because you don't wish to attract attention."

Wolf assessed himself in the mirror. He needed a shave, and his breath reeked of a man who hadn't brushed since he left the Irvin Hotel the night before last.

"That hardly narrows my location down. Six-hundred miles might place me most anywhere in the southwest."

"You wouldn't drive to Mexico. Too risky dealing with border patrols."

"Louisiana."

"Gumbo? Not your style. I'm guessing Colorado."

Wolf gritted his teeth. "You see much, Scarlett. Perhaps you'll make a viable profiler one day."

"One day, yes. I have good news, if you're interested."

"Good news is quite rare these days. Give me your report."

"Sara is awake and talking."

Wolf leaned forward. "Is she well?"

"She asked about you, Logan. I can't believe you told Sara your first name."

"A judgment error."

"You risked a great deal by telling her the truth."

"That's all she knows about me, Scarlett. She doesn't know who I am or what I do. Sara believes I'm FBI, or perhaps a bounty hunter or private investigator. The truth would cripple her, I'm afraid. It's better this way."

"So, you'll disappear and go on killing."

"What I choose is none of your concern."

"There's a better way, Logan," Bell said, softening her voice. "The Pronghorn County Sheriff's Department isn't searching for Don Weber anymore. They assume he's my partner, and that's a good thing. I'm a hero for ending the reign of terror."

"Bravo."

"That hair follicle Sheriff Rosario collected . . . It vanished. Imagine that. Along with the license plate number he kept in his cruiser. Nobody is searching for a Jeep Wrangler with stolen plates."

Wolf snickered. "You put yourself on the line when you removed that evidence, Agent Bell. For that, I thank you."

"Come back, Logan. Nobody will ask questions. There's a beautiful girl here who cares about you, and she'll want your company when she leaves the hospital."

"I'm afraid that's impossible. Give Sara my love, dear Scarlett."

"You can do that, yourself."

"She doesn't need Logan Wolf in her life, and there's work to do."

"What work?"

"As you said, they multiply like roaches. Farewell, my friend."

Wolf ended the call before Bell could argue. He removed the battery and tossed the phone beneath the seat. Too much heartbreak existed in the world. Too many loved ones lost to the devils that stalked the shadows.

From his jacket pocket, he removed a list of five serial killers and their locations. The murderers ranged from New England to Michigan and California. A world of possibilities awaited.

He snatched a pen from the glove box and circled the second name from the top. Then he shifted the Jeep into DRIVE.

His name was Logan Wolf, and death was his soul mate.

LOGAN WOLF RETURNS in The Stolen, book two in the Logan and Scarlett Thriller Series. Start reading on Amazon today.

GET A FREE BOOK!

I'm a pretty nice guy once you look past the grisly images in my head. Most of all, I love connecting with awesome readers like you.

Join my VIP Reader Group and get a FREE serial killer thriller for your Kindle.

Get My Free Book

www.danpadavona.com/thriller-readers-vip-group/

SUPPORT INDIE AUTHORS

Did you enjoy this book? If so, please let other thriller fans know by leaving a short review. Positive reviews help spread the word about independent authors and their novels. Thank you.

ACKNOWLEDGMENTS

No writer journeys alone. Special thanks are in order to my editor, Kimberly Broderick, for providing invaluable feedback, catching errors, and making my story shine. I also wish to thank my brilliant cover designer, Caroline Teagle Johnson. Your artwork never ceases to amaze me. I owe so much of my success to your hard work. Shout outs to my advance readers Donna Puschek, Marcia Campbell, Mary Arnold, and Teresa Padavona for catching those final pesky typos and plot holes. Most of all, thank you to my readers for your loyalty and support. You changed my life, and I am forever grateful.

ABOUT THE AUTHOR

Dan Padavona is the author of The Darkwater Cove series, The Scarlett Bell thriller series, *Her Shallow Grave*, The Logan and Scarlett series, The Dark Vanishings series, *Camp Slasher, Quilt, Crawlspace, The Face of Midnight, Storberry, Shadow Witch*, and the horror anthology, *The Island*. He lives in upstate New York with his beautiful wife, Terri, and their children, Joe, and Julia. Dan is a meteorologist with NOAA's National Weather Service. Besides writing, he enjoys visiting amusement parks, beach vacations, Renaissance fairs, gardening, playing with the family dogs, and eating too much ice cream.

Visit Dan at: www.danpadavona.com